CAJUN ODYSSEY

From Nova Scotia to Louisiana
....With Love

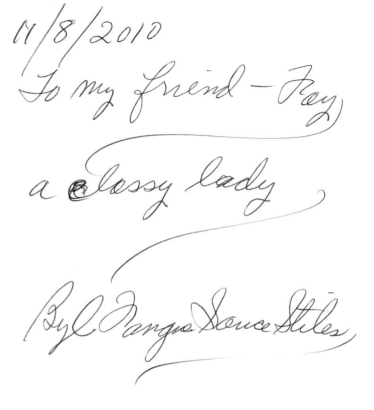

11/8/2010

To my friend – Ray

a classy lady

By Beryl Fangue Sauce Stiles

ISBN: 1451577044
ISBN-13: 9781451577044

Contact Author at
Ber1932@att.net

Contact Cover Artist at
Brett.Sauce@Gmail.com

CAJUN ODYSSEY

From Nova Scotia to Louisiana
....With Love

Beryl Fangue Sauce Stiles

Cover Art by Brett M. Sauce

Photos by the Author

DEDICATED TO ...

My Paternal Grandmother
OCIENIA THERIOT FANGUE
Originally of Theriot, Louisiana (She is a descendant of the line, from
which the Josef Theriot character in this novel was drawn.)
And
UNCLE JOHNNY FANGUE
(One of Grandma Ocienia's sons, who always encouraged me
to write about family history.)
And
My Maternal Grandmother
AZELIE HULIN LANDRY
Originally of St. Martinville, Louisiana
(And to all the industrious French people, who settled South Louisiana)
And
To **LEAH LEBLANC THERIAULT**
Originally of Saulnierville, Nova Scotia On the "French Coast"
(She and her children are descended from the line which the Charles
Theriot character personifies in this novel.)

Special Thanks to...
My daughter & son-in-law Robin & Chris Griffin
For their much appreciated help.

AND...to my talented artist son—Brett M. Sauce,
who recreated the cover—only better.

FOREWORD

"Unfortunately, they left no diaries!"

This is a statement often expressed when speaking about the journey of the Acadian people, who were forcibly expelled by English authority back in 1755. For history has been silent about this happening; only Longfellow's epic poem—EVANGELINE—commemorated this event. But such a significantly tragic historical story deserves more....much more!

Because of an overwhelming desire to tell their story, this seventh generation descendant of Acadians has spent the last five years compiling considerable researched data, as well as traveling to Nova Scotia and across the probable route a certain group of Acadians took onto the Atlantic Ocean, then over the mountains and rivers, in order to put it all together.

As a result, the story of this branch of the Theriot family of Acadians, depicted herein, is based on historical and geographical fact and many of the characters are fashioned after actual people, who lived through that ordeal. However, some names have been altered and other characters created in order to round out the story, since there were no personal accounts to draw from—only cold historical fact.

The reader will notice varied spellings of proper names and places. This is due to the fact that certain variations have transpired over 227 years, in regard to the spelling of names and places. As a result, this author has sometimes used the original French spelling, sometimes the spelling used by the English authorities in 1755 Acadia, and sometimes the present day usage.

However, this novel has been written with extreme love and admiration for those courageous Acadian people—telling their story with as much authenticity as possible, in regard to historical & geographical fact. The human emotions and motivations presented herein were surmised through impressions and intuitive feelings absorbed while living so closely to this Acadian story through research and travel, during these many recent years. But above all, the story has been written particularly so that present day and future descendants of these Acadian people may be proud of their heritage—and rightfully so!

———

"There have been instances in the annals of the past,"
remarked a very wise Mr. Philip H. Smith many years ago,
"in which a country has been desolated in times of actual
war, and where inhabitants were found in arms. But we
defy all past history to produce a parallel case, in which
an unarmed and peaceful people have suffered to such an
extent as did the French Neutrals of Acadia."

———

What follows is their story........

CONTENTS

INTRODUCTION XIII

CHAPTER - 1
"The Mediators" 1

CHAPTER - 2
"Ladies of Grand Pre". 15

CHAPTER - 3
"His Majesty's Soldiers". 25

CHAPTER - 4
"Dawning Of An Infamous Day". 35

CHAPTER - 5
"Return From The Hunt". 51

CHAPTER - 6
"A Place Of Temporary Refuge". 65

CHAPTER - 7
"Departure" 81

CHAPTER - 8
"Weighing Anchor". 93

CHAPTER - 9
"The Ship and The Tempest". 109

CHAPTER - 10
"Arrival On A Foreign Shore" 125

CHAPTER - 11
"To Have and To Hold" 139

CHAPTER - 12
"The Journey Continues West" 157

CHAPTER - 13
"Northward Toward Acadie". 173

CHAPTER - 14
"The Other Side Of The Mountain" 183

CHAPTER - 15
"Harshness In The Wild". 193

CHAPTER - 16
"Westward On The River". 201

CHAPTER - 17
"Cold Homecoming" 213

CHAPTER - 18
"Destination Realized" 223

EPILOGUE **235**

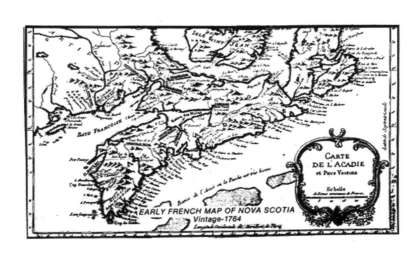

EARLY FRENCH MAP OF NOVA SCOTIA
Vintage-1764

INTRODUCTION

The title, "CAJUN ODYSSEY—From Nova Scotia To Louisiana…
With Love", is indeed an apropos name for this literary effort.
"Cajun" is a designation used for a descendant of French Acadian
people, who came from a land known as Acadie or Acadia—now
Nova Scotia—a peninsular on the eastern coast of Canada. The word
"Odyssey" simply means "extended wandering or journey", and the
remainder of the title is meant to denote the place of departure
and the destination of some of the Acadians. This is the story of
the journey of one group of these people, who were so wrongfully
expelled from their homes so long ago.   Short of Longfellow's
emotional poem, no account in novel form, that is known to
this author, has ever been written to tell the personal trials and
tribulations of these people, until now.

Today, there are descendants of Acadian people in many areas
of the United States, along the north Atlantic coast and the Gulf of
Mexico, in particular. However, by far the largest concentration of
Cajuns (descendants of Acadians) is to be found in south Louisiana.
This book relates the probable manner in which one particular
Acadian family—a branch of the Theriot family line—ultimately came
to south Louisiana. But to better understand the story, the following
background information should be considered before reading on.

ACADIA-A UNIQUE LAND

The area of Acadia, in modern times, usually refers to certain sections of Nova Scotia, New Brunswick and Prince Edward Island, which are inhabited by many French speaking Canadians. These families have lived for numerous generations in that section of the Maritime Provinces of Canada. However, in the past, Acadia referred to another—smaller— sector. This was specifically along the shores of the Bay of Fundy, as well as along the rivers and inlets where the French colonists in the 17th and 18th centuries settled to farm the land.

Thus, this isolated corner of North America nurtured a community of people, who were unique in the new world. While the other settlers in North America, for the most part, cleared the forests or the prairies to plant, the Acadian people chose to dike in the rich red soil of the tidal marshlands along the Bay of Fundy. In this way, they drained the land for agriculture, and the diked land proved to be agriculturally bountiful. For the Acadians grazed large herds of cattle and grew crops of hay and grain, as well as bountiful orchards and vegetable gardens.

While furs and fishing were the most important products in the French colonies along the St. Lawrence River and in Newfoundland, the Acadians were an agricultural people. Of course, game and fish were plentiful in their area, as well. But these commodities generally only supplemented the Acadian economy.

ACADIANS VALUED THEIR INDIAN FRIENDS

The Acadian people, unlike many other settlers of those times, enjoyed a congenial and most cooperative relationship with their neighbors, the Micmac Indian tribe, and there were even some intermarriages between the two peoples. Eventually, the Micmac Indians were, for the most part, converted to Christianity, and the Acadians discovered that these Indians were their true friends, while their real enemies came to be comprised of other European people.

ACADIANS WERE PAWNS OF
ENGLAND AND FRANCE

Frequent attacks from the English colonies in New England, on the North American continent to the south, were endured in the land of Acadia. A number of such attacks were perpetrated by men, who hoped to seize Acadia, because they believed it to have a treasury of furs for the taking. Other attacks came from pirates, who knew the Acadian people to be easy marks for plunder.

However, their most serious threat resulted from the clashing interests between the French and English empires. So, the Acadians found themselves much like pawns, to be shuffled back and forth by these two mighty European nations. The Acadians were considered to be people, who resided on the border of a crucial zone, which these two powers coveted. Acadia was sought by these two powers for it's strategic position, being located between New England and Canada.

As a result, the Acadian people suffered much whenever hostile clashes between these two powers took place. Repercussions were such, that whenever England and France would go to war, this resulted in the officials in Acadia promoting raids with ships and Micmac war parties against the English colonies. Although the Acadian people were seldom ever involved in such efforts, they were the ones to suffer when the New Englanders would strike back.

ACADIANS DISPLAYED INDEPENDENT SPIRIT

The Acadians were French-speaking people, it is true, but usually they looked upon both the French and the English as outsiders. They well knew how different they were from the settlers in other French colonies. Being isolated somewhat, they developed a spirit of considerable independence. In fact, it seems that the Acadians had as much commerce with the English as with the French merchants. Traders from New England brought iron goods, textiles, sugar and rum to Acadia. And this was traded for Acadian livestock and grain. The French government looked upon trade with the English as acts of treason, but this apparently did not bother the independent minded Acadian farmers.

ACADIANS LOOKED UPON AS HOSTILE
But all was not continually well with the English, for relations were often times quite hostile. Since New England was part of the British empire, there were several attempts by men in ships to capture Acadia over the years. Ten times was Acadia attacked by the English colonies, during the first hundred years. Beginning in 1613, Port Royal (which was founded by Champlain in 1605) was destroyed after being looted.

Happenings in Europe were usually felt in Acadia, particularly when in 1621, the English king granted Acadia to one of his Scottish subjects, who renamed it Nova Scotia when the Scots founded a little settlement at Port Royal. However, in 1632, by means of a peace treaty, England lost Nova Scotia to France again. Subsequently, the French persevered to develop the Acadian colony by bringing in new settlers, who farmed the land after diking the red salt marshes in the Port Royal area.

However, in subsequent times, England once again regained Acadia for sixteen years. During those years, the French lodged frequent attacks on the colony, that was expanding out from Port Royal and into the Annapolis Valley and then to the marshes of the Minas Basin, Chignecto Bay and Shepody Bay. Finally, through the Treaty of 1713, the French relinquished claim to Acadia.

ACADIANS WERE BRITISH SUBJECTS AGAIN
Following this turn of events, the French relocated to develop colonies in what is today known as New Brunswick and Prince

Edward Island and on Cape Breton Island, where the fortress of Louisberg was established.

The Treaty of 1713 allowed the Acadians to leave with all of their possessions, if they chose to. But very few of them accepted the offer of French land on Cape Breton Island. Most of the Acadians wished rather to remain on their ancestral lands, even though under English masters. However, the French Acadians, who remained, established trading with the new colony of Louisberg, which was discouraged by the English, but encouraged by the French. The French Governor at Louisberg continued contact with the Acadians, who were former subjects of France, in the hope that should another war with England comes to be, perhaps the Acadians would take the side of France in such a confrontation.

However, the Treaty of 1713 did allow the Acadians to practice their Catholic religion, and allowed them possession of their lands, provided they swear allegiance to the English Crown. The Acadians did agree to swear allegiance, with the provision that in the event of a future war, they could remain neutral, and never have to take up arms against their former nation–France.

ACADIANS - "FRENCH NEUTRALS"

Numerous English governors endeavored to get the entire allegiance of the Acadians. But they would not give in to this stipulation, and subsequently became known as "neutral French of Nova Scotia".

However, this neutrality was put to a test in the 1740s, when war once again broke out between France and England, and French troops waged warfare on Nova Scotia soil. Some Acadians assisted the French troops, usually with shelter and food. But they claimed the French forced them to assist those troops. But during these times, the Acadians in Nova Scotia continued to look upon that war, which was being fought on their homeland, to be the operation of outside powers. Thus they endeavored to avoid reprisals from both sides. In 1747, the English again drove the French out of Nova Scotia.

After this, most of the Acadians believed that they had proved their expressed neutrality to be valid, by not taking sides. However, this was not the opinion of the entire English governing body. For they decided then to send out Protestant English settlers to found a new town in 1749. It became Halifax, which would boast of a large garrison.

The French, in the meantime, planned and built a fortification in the early 1750s called Beausejour, which was located on the northwest shore of the Missaguash River. For it was their contention that this river, which was the isthmus of Chignecto, served as the limits of the English territorial claim. Of course, the English did not agree. So, they erected their own fortification, named Fort Lawrence, on the southeast shore of the same river. After this, French missionaries persuaded numerous Acadian people to leave their farms and relocate on the rivers, which were controlled by the French.

But in the year 1755, the Governor of Nova Scotia, Charles Lawrence, with the assistance of those from the Massachusetts colony, captured Fort Beausejour. As it turned out, amid the surrendered garrison of the French fort, Lawrence discovered about 200 Acadians, who all claimed that they had been forced to fight with the French.

Unfortunately, this discovery served to convince Governor Lawrence that he should immediately set about to acquire from all of the Acadians an unqualified oath of allegiance to England, or be deported from the colony for all time.

History has shown, that the Acadians remained adamant in their continued determination to be looked upon as "French Neutrals". As a result, the expulsion of Acadian men, women and children became a reality, continuing until 1763. Subsequently, it was estimated that this expulsion involved approximately 14,000 people. In some cases, husbands were separated from wives, and children from their parents—never to meet again in their lifetime.

SO IT CAME TO PASS......

But history has remained silent, recording few details and leaving many gaps in the tragic epic story of this re-location of an entire nation—the Acadians of Nova Scotia. Therefore, in an effort to fill in many blank spots as to the ultimate destination for many of their number, and in an effort to relate the truly poignant, human side of this massive exodus....this book has been written.

————

CHAPTER - 1

THE MEDIATORS

September 1, 1755 — Halifax, Nova Scotia

The sounds of their wooden shoes, scraping against the rough floor boards, echoed resoundingly throughout the room, as they were ushered toward the far end of the chamber. Involuntarily, their eyes were attracted to a brilliant glow from a small window, which allowed beams of sunlight to enter into the dark portal, where they were marched.

They were tired. The trip from Grand Pre had been a rigorous one. But surprisingly there had been no waiting at the Halifax Ministry Building when they arrived. For the guards had immediately shuffled them inside, even though it was in a manner much akin to herding cattle into an enclosure.

Lighting up the end of the chamber where they were abruptly halted by the two armed guards, who flanked them on each side, the streaming sunlight cast rays upon each man—much as a dozen spotlights would do. But with a far more concentrated golden hue than any candle power could provide. The bright sunlight did, however, make the dark rough hewn timbers along the walls of the large room seem a bit less foreboding. However, the discomfort felt by this sudden brilliant light, as the golden streams from the window glanced off of the strained faces of those in the group, seem to blind them for a moment. Thus they all blinked repetitiously at the sunlight, as they tried to step back out of it's reach. Each man in his own way was trying to focus on the desk before them, whereat sat the figure of a man.

The guard, who was obviously in charge, addressed the man seated at the desk. For all the while the group had been ushered in, his back had been to them. He appeared as if gazing intently out of the window throughout all of the shuffling sounds, during the noisy entrance into the chamber. Indeed, he appeared to be oblivious to his very surroundings.

"Excellency, Governor Lawrence, the delegation from Grand Pre is here to seek an audience with your Lordship."

"Yes...yes...what is it that you men want?" Questioned an obviously annoyed Charles Lawrence, as he turned abruptly in his chair, and now faced the group before him.

Lawrence, a medium size man with a gaunt, pinched expression around the eyes, had only just recently occupied the position of Acting Governor for His Royal Majesty's Lands in Nova Scotia. And he was beginning to settle comfortably into this new role, which he felt was well worthy of his talents. Of course, he realized that this appointment was only to fill the post in the absence of Governor Hopson, who was back in England on sick leave. But he hoped that with the help of friends in England, Hopson might never return. And then he would be in full control, as he believed this is as it should be. After all, he was convinced that Hopson was not suited for such a position of power.

This Governor has the look of a hard man, thought Father Pierre, as he stepped forward from the group of eight men, with whom he had journeyed from Grand Pre for an audience with this new Acting Governor.

The priest suddenly felt extreme fatigue as he mentally endeavored to sort out the best words to use, in addressing this man, who had such power over so many of his people. Indeed, the journey overland to Halifax had been demanding and he noted that it's fatiguing effects were apparent on the faces of his companions, as well. But he had to effectively appeal to this Governor, for he well knew how much his parishioners in the Minas Basin area had to fear at the hands of such a man of power.

"Bonjour...Mon Excellency", father Pierre began. "We have come in a body, representing the people of Grand Pre, Minas, River Canard and Pigiguit. We have journeyed here in an effort to come to some understanding on behalf of our people, the Acadians of that region.

Father Pierre's companions nodded in silent agreement, all the while staring intently at the face of Lawrence. They were searching for some glimmer of understanding, to be reflected in his expression.

Instead, Lawrence returned their gazes with an expression of sheer disdain from this most powerful position, which he now occupied. His face mirrored these inner feelings, and he made no effort to hide the revulsion that he felt for these Acadians. For they were proving to be a thorn in his side. If not for them, he believed that his power in this realm of his Majesty's holdings in the new world would be complete. For there was nothing he could not deal with. Only they caused him no end of dilemma, and his voice was filled with this disdain as he addressed them.

"By what right do you Acadians seek my indulgence? Certainly you have not shown proper cooperation and respect for his Majesty's authority. So, why then should you seek understanding of any kind?"

"We beseech you Excellency, to look upon our people in a more favorable light," pleaded Father Pierre. "Have our people not proven their willingness to cooperate as much as conscience will allow? Did they not willingly give up their arms in a show of sincerity?"

Lawrence well remembered their petition, which was submitted when they turned in their arms, some two thousand and nine hundred pieces in all, if he remembered correctly. True, they had given in to this demand with little or no grumbling, but this was far from enough. For he believed, these people to be intolerable and should be made an example of. So, his feelings were not veiled as he replied.

"It is not the giving up of arms that impresses his Majesty's government, it is the taking up of arms to defend his Majesty's holdings that truly has merit, and this you will not do!"

"But Excellency, my papa and grand papa took oaths under Governor Phillips, that exempted our people from carrying arms during times of war. We wish not to fight our fellow Frenchmen, nor do we wish to take up arms against the Indians or the English, any more now than when our papas agreed to remain out of the fighting. We wish only to continue being known as French Neutrals, as we have been known these many years now," exclaimed Jacques Saulnier, with no little amount of emotion, as he unexpectedly stepped from the group to address the Governor.

Lawrence peered at the man through squinted eyes, that did not mask the disgust that he felt within, as he replied. "Yes....but when Cornwallis took over, he tried to induce your people to take the unqualified oath to his Majesty's government, and they refused. What of that?"

"Excellency....our papas had already taken the oath of fidelity that Governor Phillips had approved," pleaded Jacques.

"Certainly you know what Cornwallis said about that, do you not? Governor Phillips had not the right to obtain any oath from your people, with any provision which went against bearing arms," replied Lawrence.

"Yes, but Excellency, their papas refused to take such an oath, where they would have to bear arms, so instead asked permission to leave the country," exclaimed Father Pierre, who went on to implore. "And Excellency, you know what happened then. As the people made preparations to leave their homes, rather than submit, their papas and mamas were persuaded to go on and plant the fields while he, Cornwallis, deliberated the problem. He told them that his answer would come after they had sowed the fields. Perhaps you remember hearing that some of the people had already began to get their cattle and belongings together to leave by land, to Bay Verte. Because the governor would not allow them to seek provisioned ships to take them away. So, how can these that you see here before you today, and those they represent, submit to such an oath when it was impossible for their papas and grand papas to do so back then?"

Lawrence was silent for a moment, as he pondered these things. Yes, he remembered learning about the turn of events that the Priest outlined for him. Cornwallis had gotten off his letter to England, whereupon it was answered with instructions by the Secretary of State not to exact the oath for the present. In fact, Cornwallis was directed to do all he could to keep those Acadians from leaving the country.

Deep in thought, Lawrence marveled at the British Ministry's decision in this matter. For apparently they believed these people to be too productive an asset to the French, so did not wish to lose them to a probable enemy, who could make use of their toil. So, instead, Cornwallis was forced to make a change in his approach to them, and indeed this must have been difficult for him to accomplish. For always before this time, Cornwallis had handled the Acadians in a forceful dictatorial manner. After this directive from the Ministry, Cornwallis had to treat the Acadians with passivity, in order to keep them from leaving.

What a pity, thought Lawrence, that the Ministry was so misguided in their dealings with these people. For his thoughts were with Cornwallis on this matter. These Acadians needed a lesson!

As Lawrence returned the delegation's intent gaze, he continued to dwell on these many thoughts that led up to this time, as Father Pierre continued his plea.

"Excellency—did not Governor Hopson, before you, say in his own words to his commanders that the Acadian people were to be looked upon the same way as the rest of his Majesty's subjects? In his very own words did he not command that nothing would be taken by force from our people, and that the law was to equally apply as to protection and punishment, as well?"

"Ah, but Hopson has gone back to England, and it is my word that is law here now. So...forget all that has come to pass before. It is only here and now that is of importance," demanded Lawrence, as he defiantly stood up from his chair.

As he bent over his desk and glared at the small delegation of men, he felt his fists clinch as he recalled his experience after first arriving near Beaubassin, to found Fort Lawrence. He recalled the stubbornness of these Acadian people, who refused then to take up arms even for the French side against the English, preferring rather to take flight into the woods, at the expense of having their houses and barns set on fire. Only then would they seek food and shelter with the French. Difficult to understand the stubbornness of such as these, thought Lawrence. Obviously, the time for talking and pacifying was long past. Something had to be done! After all because these Acadians are Papists and Frenchmen, his Majesty's Protestant government can never be safe from any impending insurrection, as long as these people are tolerated here.

Lawrence settled back into his chair, and thought about how long and hard he had pondered on Hopson's weak handling of these bothersome people. He also remembered how he had to revoke Governor Hopson's earlier decree, in order to put these French troublesome people in their place.

Ah yes, Lawrence recalled his orders to Captain Murray at Fort Edward. "You are not to bargain with the Acadians for their payments; but as they bring in what is wanted, you will furnish them with certificates, which will entitle them to such payments at Halifax as shall be thought reasonable. If they should immediately fail to comply, you will assure them that the next courier will bring an order for military execution upon the delinquents."

However, Lawrence had discovered that it was increasingly more difficult to convince his Majesty's Lords of Trade, back in England, about these indolent and neglectful Acadians, especially after the glowing reports previously rendered by Hopson and others, who reported so favorably. "These Acadians produce grain and nourish sufficient cattle for the whole colony. His Majesty's government should be well aware of their industry and their temperance, and that they are not addicted to any vice or debauchery."

Then, there was Winslow's report that further swayed the Lords of Trade greatly. "I found a fine country and full of inhabitants, a beautiful church, abundance of goods of this world, and provisions of all kinds in great plenty."

Lawrence dwelled on these many things, all the while observing the beseeching group of men before him, who were continuing to press their case. Watching them intently, as they endeavored to get his attention in this matter, by bringing all of these things to light, he scrutinized each face as they implored his indulgence. But he heard little of what they were saying, since his mind was filled with so many other things.

Settling back into his chair, a momentary grin of self-satisfaction crossed his face, as he dwelled on secret thoughts. For unbeknown to these Acadians before him, this Acting Governor relished in other realities. He delighted in the actual secret plans that were well underway, toward a final solution to the Acadian disposition once and for all. These were plans that Lawrence, himself, had instigated with the aid of certain fellow conspirators.

Indeed, with the help of Governor Shirley of Massachusetts and the transports, from the Boston ship owners, the plan was well underway to make short work of these Acadians. Yes, along with Provincial Surveyor Morris, Governor Shirley and his Council, five of whom are from New England, the stage was set.

Lawrence chuckled to himself, as he thought of his command to Morris, who had been ordered only recently to make a detailed report of the terrain where every Acadian village was situated. He was to take note of the number of inhabitants, houses, etc., and the methods to be used to get the unsuspecting inhabitants in their power. Morris did his work expeditiously and all was in readiness. The troops and transports from Boston were waiting, and a time was set for the coup.

Thinking about the intricacies of his scheme still further, Lawrence recalled the orders that had only just been issued to Colonel Winslow. "You must proceed by the most rigorous measures possible, not only in compelling them to embark, but in depriving those who shall escape of all means of shelter or support, by burning their houses and destroying everything that may afford them the means of subsistence in the country."

Also, to Captain Murray, Lawrence remembered that his orders left nothing to chance. "If these people behave amiss, they should be punished at your discretion; and if there is any attempt to molest the troops, you should take an eye for an eye, a tooth for a tooth, and in short, a life for a life, from the nearest neighbor where the mischief should be performed."

Charles Lawrence further pondered on the sequence of events that had come to pass in recent months. Even far prior to his dispatch to the Lords of Trade, dated June 28, he had announced that Beausejour had capitulated, and also informed them of his orders to Colonel Monckton to expel the Acadians found there out of the country.

He recalled to himself that particular communique, which only this morning had been handed him, from Sir Thomas Robinson–the Secretary of State, no less. Apparently, the Lords of Trade in England believed this to be too important a matter for them to handle alone. Thus, this dictate from so high a personage in his Majesty's service was deemed appropriate in this instance.

How eloquent had the Secretary of State sounded in this dictate from England, recalled Lawrence with a snicker, in terms of such far reaching consequence too, which he vividly remembered, almost word for word......

> *"From the Secretary of State - Sir Thomas Robinson - "His Britannic Majesty was pleased to order an answer to be given, which I now wend for your particular information in the following words in regard to the Acadians of the Peninsula— it would be depriving Great Britain of a very considerable number of useful subjects, if such transmigration should extend to those who were inhabitants there at the time of the treaty and to their descendants."*

But what did they know of his problems with these troublesome people, thought Lawrence. Besides, it was too late for them to say. The dye was already cast, and the plan was well underway. Now, it was left only for him to pretend that the dispatch failed to arrive in time to prevent these expulsion plans from being implemented. After all, noted Lawrence, so what if the Lords of Trade, back in England, continue to drag their feet in this matter. They have constantly put off any affirmative action, in regard to the disposition of these irritating Acadian people. So, he—Charles Lawrence—would take the initiative and rid his Majesty's lands in Nova Scotia of this unwanted French presence. Then, after this deed is done, the Lords of Trade, and probably even his Majesty himself, will see the merit of such a disposition, by this Acting Governor. Then his position in the king's service will be secure for all time and it could mean a promotion as well.

How Lawrence relished in this last thought, as he day-dreamed about his scheme that was in readiness. But now, here was this assembled group, continuing to beseech him, but his thoughts dwelled elsewhere. As their voices droned on unheeded, he paid little or no attention to them. Then, all at once his attention was suddenly jarred, as one voice was loudly raised, penetrating Lawrence's complacent reverie.

It was Claude Comeaux, who was suddenly heard above the droning, beseeching tone of Father Pierre and Jacques Saulnier. This outburst succeeded in causing Lawrence to come to abrupt attention.

"Do you not hear our pleas Governor? We have not come these many miles only to be ignored."

Claude had remained quiet up until this moment, while his companions beseeching attempts apparently fell on the seemingly deaf ears of this Governor, who was not even listening to them. But he could contain himself no more.

"By what right do you raise your voice to his Majesty's representative?" shouted Lawrence angrily, rising again from his chair with clinched fists, which he pounded on the desks top.

Father Pierre hastily stepped forward in front of Claude Comeaux, gently nudging him back into the group, as he attempted to plead with the Governor. How well Father Pierre knew of Claude Comeaux's temper. True, Claude was a good family man and usually gentle, except when pushed too far. And Father Pierre knew from all of the signs that this was such a time. But maybe it wasn't too late—maybe he could prevent any further confrontation with so important a man as this Governor. If only Claude will remain silent, thought the priest, as he stepped closer to Lawrence's desk, gesticulating with his arms and hands toward the Governor in a pleading manner.

"Excellency, please forgive my companion, as he is upset and worried about his family and what is to become of them. He is as good a man and as good a farmer as ever dwelled in the land of Grand Pre, as are all of my companions. We want only your good word that we can take back to our people—your word that they will be treated just as others of his Majesty's subjects. May we have your permission to take this dictate from your Excellency back with us?"

"You may have nothing of the kind!" Shouted Lawrence, as his face literally turned red with a fury, that raged within him. "You will not even be allowed to return to your people. You will pay for such insolence. Guard, hear me well! Take these would-be insurrectionists and put them behind bars. Maybe some time spent in a Halifax prison chamber will afford them the opportunity to repent the disrespect they have shown toward the king's government."

As Lawrence shouted out these orders, he waved his arms wildly toward the guards, in a gesture of finality. It was then, that the priest tried to ask for mercy.

"You cannot mean this Excellency! We have come in a delegation in good faith to beg your indulgence. How can you jail us for only wishing to mediate?"

"Spare our priest, Excellency. He came only to speak for us!" Beseeched Jacques. "Allow him to return home with word of us for our families!"

A spontaneous clamor was immediately heard from the group of Acadian men, with each one trying to be heard above the other. In their excitement, they appeared to edge closer to Lawrence's desk, only to be halted by the two guards, who brandished their weapons in front of them, causing the group to halt together in a body.

"Oh no.....your priest shall also be jailed for attempting to help such as you, instead of taking the government's side in this matter. He will have much time to say his beads in penance for his lack of good judgment. Take them away!" Lawrence shouted, as he turned his back to the disheveled, emotionally clamoring group of men in his midst. As before, he stood once again, peering intently out of the window—now more than ever completely deaf to the pleas of the men, who were being herded out by armed guards.

"Father Pierre!" Exclaimed Etienne Gaudet, as he reached out to grasp the priest's arm. "What will become of us?"

"Have faith, Etienne. We must put our trust in the Lord. Only He can deliver us from this time of peril," murmured the priest as he patted the hand of Etienne, whose grasp had become more intense, with a force that was almost painful to the priest.

The guards, clutched their long weapons before them with both hands so as to nudge the backs of the men. They did so gently at first to get them moving, but then more forcefully when they did not immediately respond to this pressure. Thus they were guided out of the door.

In their dulled emotional state, the Acadian men had to be thus guided out of the ministry building and into the dusty courtyard, for all at once they had become silent, to a man. It was as though the magnitude of their present plight had suddenly struck them physically, rendering them mute and disoriented in their dismay.

As the two guards herded the Acadian men across the compound, the area all around them was alive with the usual activity of the day—the hustle of other uniformed guards, servants and assorted people on ministry business—all milling about, each going on their separate appointed tasks and destinations. But the small group of men, being pushed by two guards toward the jail across the way, were oblivious to all of this activity around them.

The priest was well aware of the stark magnitude of their position. For under the circumstances there was no way to know how long they would be kept in the Halifax prison. He knew that this had been the plight of other Acadians before, and that many were still thought to be languishing perhaps behind these very same bars, that awaited within for this group.

"Father....what can we do? What will become of our families, who await word of our delegation?" Jacques Saulnier implored, as he was half pushed along by the guards, all the while trying desperately to keep his place alongside the priest.

"Jacques, we have no way to get word back to them....we can only pray that their fate will be better than ours," answered the priest in a whisper, as he hurriedly shuffled along, trying to avoid being forcibly pushed by the guards.

"Quiet.....no talking will be tolerated!" Shouted a guard suddenly, abruptly silencing the priest's words. It was then, that a guard pounded on the massive, dark door of the building they had reached. Instinctively, each condemned man in the group knew that this foreboding door would soon close behind them for an undetermined length of time. For some of them, perhaps never to open again.

They were pushed through the massive door of the Halifax prison one at a time, with Father Pierre being the last of the group to cross the threshold. But just before taking the last stride into the darkness of the portal before him, the priest gave way to a final urge to glance back toward the sun drenched courtyard, over which they had just come. He looked back toward the ministry building, within which their fate had been sealed at the hands of a man with no apparent human compassion.

Father Pierre's glance took in the scene behind him in an instant, leaving no detail out. For he knew this sight would have to sustain him for possibly a long, long time, as a last glance of freedom. But he found this last glimpse to be marred when he caught fleeting sight of the distant figure of Lawrence across the way, behind the confines of the window panes where he was still standing, peering through the window of the Ministry Building.

There Lawrence still stood, staring intently across the way toward the jail, and the group of men being led inside. He stood there, grinning all the while, as he gazed in their direction.

Then, the door slammed shut, blotting out the distant, fearful sight of Governor Lawrence's insipidly grinning face—blotting out this incredulous sight with an instant penetrating blackness. This was a sudden blackness that these newly incarcerated men tried to immediately blink away. But shortly after, the dark manifested itself in varying shades of gray within the prison chamber.

Rubbing his eyes in an effort to become accustomed to the dark, dank atmosphere within, where these shades of dull gray were made visible only by the emergence of the few rays of outside light, that were permitted to seep through between the heavy bars of the high windows in the cells. Father Pierre crossed himself and shuddered outwardly at the thought of his last glimpse across the compound.

But even at it's worse, the priest thought to himself, by comparison, this depressing scene within the prison chamber was by far a better sight than the remembered, fearsome, grotesque expression on Lawrence's face, as seen from across the compound only a moment before the massive black door was slammed shut behind him.

———

CHAPTER - 2

LADIES OF GRAND PRE

The apples shimmered in the noonday sunshine, and the boughs of the tree bent low with the weight of the fruit. It had been a better than average year for the apple crop, thought Madeleine Bourgeois, as she reached up and plucked a particularly ripe apple from a low bough. Biting into the red skin of the fruit, held cupped with both hands to her mouth, she felt a trickle of clear, sweet juice stream down the side of her face. So, she hurriedly grabbed the hem of her apron, to dab the sweet moisture away.

Continuing to vigorously chew the bite of apple that filled her rather small, young mouth, Madeleine marveled at the sensation of delicious pleasure that she derived from the taste of this fruit, picked with one's own hands. She then sat herself down on the soft green grass beneath the tree. Then, she arranged her petticoat, skirt and apron so as to rumple the homespun cloth of her attire as little as possible. With a feeling of well being, Madeleine stretched her legs out straight on the soft cool grass, until her wooden shoes peeked out from beneath the folds of her skirt.

Leaning back against the rough bark of the apple tree, she took another big bite of apple and thrust her head back until her white bonnet cap rested against the tree trunk. It was such a beautiful morning, she thought. In fact, it was as beautiful a day as Madeleine had ever seen in all of her fifteen years. And it was good to be alive and living in Grand Pre.

It was especially wonderful, because of Josef Theriot, and she thought how she could hardly wait to wed him someday—maybe even next year, if things went well. Josef always made her feel so good, and being with him evoked such feelings of delicious uneasiness, but in the most exciting way. Madeleine stretched out her arms as far as she could reach, as she thought of Josef, who always looked at her with such a piercing intensity, that it made her shyly look away from his gaze every time. But it was with no small amount of embarrassment for her.

She reflected on how they had known each other ever since his Papa and her Papa built their dikes together, and how Josef had started to properly court her last month. So, in time they would be together and make a good life. Perhaps, they would even acquire a nice farm, like their parents had along the dikes.

Josef already had a small piece of land along the Minas Basin, and he planned to dike in more land after they were married. So, the future looked good to Madeleine at this point in time. As she thought about these things, she hugged her shoulders in delight.

Continuing to relish in the beautiful day, her gaze was drawn to the golden and white blooms that brightened up the church yard across the way. As she took in the beauty of the flowers, along the sides of the church, she remembered how those had been lovingly tended by the ladies of the Parish.

She continued to sit there, while she waited for her Mama and Aunt Jeanne to come out of the church of St. Charles. As usual, they had been busy, cleaning and arranging flowers inside, before the next Mass. Madeleine remembered that they had been among the ladies, who tilled the beds and planted the flower seeds each year, as soon as the breezes of summer warmed the land. According to her Mama, helping to grow colorful flowers along the walls of the church was one of her ways to bring beauty to the Lord.

But suddenly, in the midst of her reverie, Madeleine was jolted back to reality. "Madeleine.... Madeleine....we are ready to start back." It was her Mama, who was calling to her. Her Mama, a slightly stout older woman, could be seen carefully treading her way down the front steps of the church, a short distance away.

Upon hearing her Mama's call, Madeleine picked herself up from the cool grass and hurriedly straightened her bodice, brushing the creases from her apron and the grass from the back of her skirt. Then, half running, half walking, she had to stop momentarily to slip securely back into her wooden shoes, which she had just nudged off a moment before. As she skipped toward the church, Madeleine spied her Aunt Jeanne, coming out of the door and preparing to follow down the steps. She was taking every step carefully, as was her manner, because she was getting on in years.

Madeleine hurried over to her Mama, because she had been instructed to wait for them until they finished the cleaning chores in the church. This was so she could help carry the baskets back home. She also knew, that she would have her work cut out for her when she got home. For one basket held the fine linens used on the altar for the Mass. And these would have to be laundered and ironed, then returned to the church before next Sunday's service.

As she ran up to her Mama, who had just sat down momentarily on the bottom church step to rest herself, Marie Bourgeois, Madeleine's Mama was muttering to herself.

"What is it Mama? Why are you fretting so?" Inquired Madeleine, to which her Mama replied.

"Why were you sitting so far from the church? Did I not tell you to wait at the front door for us? You know they can't let us be, camping near the churchyard like that! It is not safe for young girls like you to wander about with all those soldiers nearby. Why won't they let us be?"

Madeleine was all too well aware of his Majesty's English soldiers, who had made camp near the church yard in Grand

Pre. Since last month they had been there, for what purpose the people knew not. But her Papa had admonished her, too, against wandering about unescorted. Because there were so many English soldiers around that camp. But happily, thought Madeleine, these men seemed to tend to their own business, and were usually polite to the ladies whenever encountered. But she well knew how hard it was for her Mama to control herself every time she saw them in the proximity of the church.

This had been the topic of conversation between all the men of Grand Pre recently, when the soldiers first camped there. In fact, in an effort to find out more about the English intentions, everyone knew about the delegation of men from the village, who were even now in Halifax, conferring about this state of affairs.

"Do not distress yourself so, Mama," pleaded Madeleine, taking her mother's arm in a gesture of understanding. "I am sorry I wandered further from the church than you would like. But we will soon be rid of the soldiers. After all, did not Father Pierre lead the delegation to Halifax to plead our case....and you know how grand our Father Pierre can be when he speaks from his heart."

"Perhaps you are right, my dear. All we can do now is to wait for word from Halifax. Perhaps your Papa will have news when we get home," Marie said, as she picked up her basket in preparation for the walk toward the cart that awaited them. "But the proclamation that they have posted about all of the men having to attend that three o'clock meeting at the church tomorrow worries me..... whatever can the English be up to this time?"

Aunt Jeanne had paused part way down the few steps of the church, where she put down one of the baskets she was carrying. So, Madeleine, not wanting to dwell on her Mama's questioning words, hurried over to help her Aunt with the baskets. Madeleine could see that the older woman was out of breathe from her exertions. And she noted her beloved Aunt's strained face. Indeed Madeleine felt a pang of remorse for Aunt Jeanne in her moment of pain. It was then, that she was reminded about how her Aunt had come to live with them.

Aunt Jeanne was her Mama's maiden sister. But then she wasn't really her true sister, for she had been taken into the family by Grandma & Grandpa Cormier, back when they lived in Beaubassin. The story that was told relates, that Aunt Jeanne's Mama died while giving birth to her. And her Papa could not take her either, because he had drowned while fishing off of the Grand Banks in that very same year. So since Grandma Cormier had assisted the midwife at her birth, she agreed to take baby Jeanne into her family and rear her like one of their own. This was in spite of the fact, that she had two little ones at home, and was expecting a baby, herself.

Madeleine reminisced over this tale that she had been told so many times. For as it turned out, Aunt Jeanne never married. When Grandma Cormier died, Jeanne came to live with them. But now, she was getting on up in age, and if memory served correctly, Madeleine believed her Aunt to be over sixty-five now, and it was beginning to tell on her. Indeed, with the coming of each new winter, Aunt Jeanne was plagued by more and more aches, pains, and miseries than before. But she rarely complained. Instead, she busied herself in chores around the house, although she could no longer milk the cows. Because whenever she tried, her back ached too much. But her fine needlework was well known in the Minas area, and quite in demand. For even the very altar linens, they were carrying in the baskets, were embellished with her talent.

As the three women walked toward the ox cart, which was tied to a maple tree at the edge of the church yard, Madeleine skipped ahead, but not quite as lightly as before, because she was carrying the basket of altar linens.

How vibrant she felt, skipping along. And in one concentrated effort, she thrust the basket onto the floor boards with a jolt, which caused the cart to jerk slightly—startling the harnessed ox momentarily. But Madeleine hastily ran around and stroked the neck of the old ox, to calm it back into the reverie from whence it was disturbed. Looking back, Madeleine could see that her Mama and Aunt Jeanne had still not caught up to the cart, as yet. They were treading the path ever so determinedly, but much too slowly to suit her.

While awaiting their approach, she busied herself with day dreams, as the cool midday early Fall breeze caressed her face, and gently stirred the folds of her skirt and apron. This caused her petticoat to hug her legs with a gentle force, and it felt good to her. How good it was to dwell on the sights, sounds and sensations of this cooler breeze, that swayed the wild flowers along the roadside. Oh, if it could only stay this way all year, she thought. But she well knew that these cooler breezes were only the forerunners of another bitter winter to come. Her thoughts were suddenly propelled into the winter world of white, that she remembered from last year. It was then that she and other kids from neighboring farmhouses frolicked in the snow. Winter, she decided, was fun sometimes, but much too long for her taste. However, it has to be, she thought. For we have to get through the winter in order to enjoy the spring, which was her favorite time of year. That is when the dikes became alive with the gentle fragile greens and golds of new vegetation.

Just then a thought struck her and a grand idea took hold, as to how she could dress up the family's usually drab supper table that night. Yes...maybe on the way home, Madeleine reasoned, I can gather some sea heather and red maple leaves to set on the supper table tonight. Papa would like that, she thought, for he enjoyed colorful things. She remembered seeing some maple and heather along the way this morning, and she suddenly recalled seeing some wild cranberries in that same area, too. Maybe, Mama might let her stop and pick some, to eat tonight. My, how grand berries were when mixed with fresh cream from her Papa's golden cows. I must be sure and ask her when the time comes along the way, she decided, just as her Mama and Aunt finally reached the cart.

Madeleine helped them settle themselves in the cart, then she hopped on the back, dangling her legs out over the dusty road. Then, her Mama took the reins and gently enticed the old ox to pull the cart. In this manner, they set off back toward their farm, three miles down the road.

After they were slowly on their way down the road, Madeleine gazed off into the distance, noting the bright early afternoon sun. It really lit up the high bluff of Cape Blomidon, far across the wide water of the Basin. Then, immediately she was distracted again on another train of thought. She found herself pondering how strange it was that their friends, the Micmac Indians, believed their god Glooscap lived on the Cape—only coming out of the sky with the rising sun each day. They even believed that Glooscap made all of the Micmac Indians out of the trees, and made the birds and animals out of the falling leaves. She continued to think about how the Micmacs thought that every river, rock and tree held a good or evil spirit.

But then, who could say if this is true or not, she thought. For Losmic their best Indian friend of all the Micmacs had told the Acadian children this story over and over again. He would do so on occasion when he stopped at their farm house over the years. Each time, the kids were entranced by his stories. And it had them thinking as to whether the Indian god Glooscap was the same God, that is worshipped during the Mass at their church.

"I will have to ask Father Pierre when next he visits our Parish church, or Father Francois, who is older, but not as easy to speak with." Murmured Madeleine to herself.

"Speak up....Madeleine...I cannot understand what you are saying if you mumble." Admonished Mama Marie, as she held onto the board of the cart where she was seated, just as the wheel jerked roughly when the ox pulled it over a rut in the road.

"Oh, it is nothing, Mama," Madeleine answered. "I was just wondering if I should ask Father Pierre if they believe the Micmac god to be the same as our God."

"My dear girl, why do you bother yourself with such things, when there is so much more to think about?" Exclaimed Madeleine's Mama. "Have you forgotten that your sister's third banns of marriage for her wedding will be announced at this Sunday's Mass....and that guests will be stopping by the house after Mass, to celebrate the betrothal? You know, the wedding day is but a week away....and still I have not finished the skirt of her dress."

"Nor have I completed the crochet lace on the bodice," added Aunt Jeanne, who had been silent until that moment, but had been taking in all that was being said.

Oh yes, thought Madeleine. Genevieve was soon to be married to Albert Bertrand. But then Genevieve was already eighteen years old, so it was about time she decided to wed Albert. After all, had not he been courting her for two years? But then sister Genevieve had a way about her, as Madeleine well knew. For she was stubborn beyond reason some times—making Albert wait around all the time, when there were so many other eligible girls in Grand Pre, who had eyes for Albert. Why it was only last Sunday after Mass, that Madeleine remembered seeing Anastasie Melancon try to catch Albert's eye—right there on the steps of the church. Genevieve was just lucky, that Albert could see no one else when she was around.

Well, next week Genevieve will finally become Albert's wife and go to live in that small cottage that she insisted he build for her, near his Papa's house.

Albert had promised to be back in plenty of time for the announcement, but had not as yet returned. Madeleine had overheard her Papa and some of the men from the village, discussing the delegation that went to Halifax. They were talking about the need to become informed as to why the necessity for those soldiers, camped so near the church yard. She heard them talking about other problems, that escaped her comprehension. But she did hear, that Albert volunteered to be part of that delegation. Of course, they had departed, gone now for more than two weeks already. So, surely any day now, they would be coming back into the village. It was their hope it would be in time for the betrothal celebration on Sunday after Mass.

That would be nice, mused Madeleine, since it was beginning to get a bit difficult living in the same house with her sister, what with all her fretting about Albert not getting back in time. Yes, Madeleine decided silently to herself, life at home will be considerably more tolerable, once Genevieve is married off to Albert and out of the house.

———

CHAPTER - 3

HIS MAJESTY'S SOLDIER'S

L t. Colonel John Winslow sat in the shade of one of the willow trees of the Presbytery, where he had made his quarters, on the grounds near the Church of St. Charles. It was from this vantage point, that he peered over in the direction of the church, some yards away.

He had busied himself most of the morning, going over the packet of communiqués that he now had in his possession, in regard to Governor Lawrence's secret plan for the disposition of the Acadian people. The number of dispatches in his possession had become bulky, so numerous were these messages in recent months.

Winslow well knew that no slip-up in this scheme to rid Nova Scotia of these so-called French Neutrals would be tolerated by Lawrence. Thus it was extremely important that all instructions be thoroughly digested in order to insure the complete success of the operation.

Thoughts of the event, scheduled to take place tomorrow, continued to weigh heavy on Winslow's mind. And as he looked up from the sheaf of papers that had commanded his attention a moment before, his gaze focused on the three distant figures, standing near the church steps across the yard.

What a delightful young girl...so full of life, Winslow murmured to himself, as his eyes settled on the young Acadian girl in his line of vision. She had been seated under an apple tree minutes before and his gaze continued to take in the slimness of her emerging young figure, that apparently was just beginning to blossom. He also took note of the curves of her small breasts and her tiny waist that was cinched in by a bodice, which was the fashion among Acadian women.

No doubt about it, he surmised. What a temptation this must be for my men, encamped hereabouts, having to view the wives and daughters of the Acadian men, as they go about their everyday business. He continued to dwell on the view that he be held across the way, contemplating further on the subject. He knew that being far from home in New England for some months now had been a strain for many of his men. But it was to their credit that they have acted with honor, for the most part. For they caused no incident to disrupt the complacency of these unsuspecting Acadians.

Colonel Winslow reflected on the order from Governor Shirley, which caused this First Battalion to be in Grand Pre at the present time, in the first place. He then diverted his attention back to the sheaf of papers on his lap, particularly the top one, which he re-read again.

> "Instructions to John Winslow from Governor Shirley——- With this you will receive orders from me to enlist men into his Majesties Service to be employed in the removal of the Frenchmen on his Majesties Territories in North America, to the Eastward and Northward to Pennsylvania. You are to enlist none but able bodied men not under the ages of seventeen years nor above forty-five. You are to give each man at the time of his enlistment two dollars in part of ten pounds as bounty money. You are to enlist each man for one year from the date of his enlistment and to advise them that they shall in every

respect be treated as others in his Majesties forces serving with them. You are to direct, and order them that they be in Boston, without fail the twenty fifth day of March next."

Looking up again and over in the direction of the three women some distance away near the church, his eyes caught sight of a flash of white petticoat, as the older woman walked toward the ox cart, that apparently awaited them. True, she was obviously older than the girl, thought Winslow, but not too old for his tastes. Rather, she was seasoned like a fine wine. He pondered these things, as his eyes rested on her well rounded figure, that strained at the fabric of her blouse. And her full hips did not escape his view, with her figure swaying provocatively in spite of herself, as she walked toward the cart. Ah...what a fine figure of a woman, thought Winslow.

Oh...I have been away from home for far too long, he thought, and it is beginning to tell on me. He forced his eyes once again to rest on another of the dispatches. This time, it was a copy of one of his own communiqués, written on June 14, 1755, which he re-read again.

"Near Cape Chignecto Bay of Fundy—From on board his Majesty's Ship—from John Winslow— Sir: I take this opportunity to send you a copy of my instructions received from his Excellency Governor Shirley and to acquaint you that agreeable thereto I am now under the command of Colonel Monckton, Commander in Chief of the Expedition and that two Battalions consist of about 1,950 men and officers. Included now on board the transports, the men in general are in good health and spirits and all wish to be on land. Expect tomorrow will be the day. Expect our first landing will be a time of action, which should it happen, hope all commands will do their duty as becomes their station, and behave in a like manner...."

Shuffling through the papers, forcing his attention to remain on the subject before him, Winslow continued to read from another of his dispatch copies, which was more recent,

> *"From my camp at Grand Pre Minas - August, 1755 - From Colonel Winslow: Have encamped here having the church on my right of which I have made a plan of arms. The churchyard is on my left and have 313 men, officers included, and expect to be soon reinforced....."*

Meditating on the substance of the dispatches in his hands, Winslow once again marveled at the local Acadian population and their reaction to the military presence. Ever since he and his soldiers first set up camp in the middle of the Grand Pre community, and in such close proximity to their church, which seems to be the focal point of their society, no undue heed had been paid to them. At first the Acadian men inquired as to why they were there. But they seemed satisfied when told that this was a temporary duty for his Majesty's soldiers. Strangely enough, they seemed to accept this explanation and the population went about their business as usual. These people seem to suspect nothing about the real reasons for this encampment, nor could they even imagine the magnitude of what was outlined in the secret dispatch from Governor Lawrence, which Winslow now held.

> *"Halifax - August 11, 1755 — Instructions for Lieutenant Colonel Winslow, Commanding his Majesties Troops at Minas, or in his absence, for Captain Alex Murray, Commanding his Majesties Troops at Piquid, in regard to the transportation of the inhabitants of the District of Minas, Piquid, Canard, Cobequid out of the Province of Nova Scotia—Having in my letter of the 31th of July last acquainted Captain Murray with the reasons which induced his Majesty's Council to come*

to the solution of sending away the French inhabitants and clearing the whole country of such bad subjects (which letter he will communicate to you, together with the instructions I have since sent him) it only remains for me to give you the necessary orders and instructions for putting in practice what has been so determined.

'That the inhabitants may not have it in their power to return to this province, nor to aid in strengthening the French of Canada or Louisburg, it is resolved that they shall be dispersed among his Majesty's colonies upon the continent of America.

'Upon the arrival of the vessels from Boston and Chignecto in the Basin of Minas, as many of the inhabitants of the District of Minas, Piquid, Coliquid, the River of Canard as can be collected by means, particularly the heads of families and young men, are to be shipped on board.

'And to give you all the ease possible respecting the victualling of these transports, I have appointed an agent and given him particular instructions to that effect.Which he has directions to communicate to you and to furnish you with a copy upon his arrival from Chignecto with provisions ordered for victualling the whole transports.

'Destination of the vessels appointed to French in the Basin of Minas—To be sent to North Carolina such a number as well transport five hundred persons or thereabouts.

'To be sent to Virginia such a number as will transport one thousand persons.

'To Maryland such a number as will transport five hundred persons, or in proportions of the number of those to be shipped off should exceed two thousand persons.

'When the people are embarked you will please to give the Master of each vessel one of the letters, of which you will receive a number signed by me, which you will address to the Governor of the Province or Commander in Charge for the time being where they are to be put on shore and enclose therein the printed form of the Certificate to be granted to the masters of the vessels, as agreed upon by charter party. With each of these you will give the Master their sailing orders in writing to proceed to the above destination, and upon their arrival immediately to wait upon the Governor or Commander in Chief of the Province to which they are bound with the said letters and to make all possible dispatch in debarking their passengers and obtaining certificates thereto agreeable to the form aforesaid, and you will in the orders make it a particular injunction to the Masters to be careful and watchful as possible during the whole course of the voyage to prevent the passengers from making any attempt to seize upon the vessel by allowing only a small number to be upon the decks at a time and using all other necessary precautions to prevent the bad consequences of such attempt and that they be particularly careful that the inhabitants have carried no arms or other offensive weapons on board with them at their time of embarkment.

'As Captain Murray is well acquainted with the plight of the country, I would have you consult with him upon all such things, and particularly with regard to the means used for collecting the people together so as to get them on board and if you find that fair means will not do with them, you must proceed by the most vigorous measures possible not only in compelling them to embark, but in demanding them to do so.

'If it is not very inconvenient I would have you send the Sloop Dove to Annapolis to take on board part of the inhabitants, their destination for Connecticut, to which place that vessel belongs.

'As soon as the transports have received their people on board, and are ready to sail, you are to acquaint the

commander of his Majesty's Ship therewith that he may take
them under convoy and not out to sea without loss of time.

'When you have executed the business of shipping off
all that can be collected of the inhabitants in the District
above Minas Basin, you will march yourself or send a strong
detachment to Annapolis Royal to assist Major Hanofieled in
shipping off those of that area, and you will order it as all the
stragglers that may be netted by the way may be taken up and
carried to Annapolis in order to their being shipped with the
rest. Signed-Charles Lawrence."

Winslow suddenly felt terribly fatigued. The magnitude of what
lay ahead for him and his men consumed his very being, as so many
controversial thoughts continued to fill his mind. True, thought he,
throughout his career he had always done his duty in his Majesty's
service. But this time, somehow his duty did not seem so clear cut
and reasonable. For it was not in his nature to condone making war
on women and children. This time, the merit of this plan of action
from his Majesty's representative escaped all civilized reason.

Since encamping at Grand Pre, Winslow had come to observe
close hand the very people, who were the subject of the many
dispatches of recent months, and his conscience was troubled as a
result. He continued to dwell on this, as his mind recalled another
order from Fort Cumberland Camp only last month. This time, it
was a dictate that all horses, oxen, cows, sheep and cattle, heretofore
the property of these French people, had become forfeited to the
Crown. Therefore, no soldier or officer in his Majesty's service
should try to purchase or butcher any of this livestock, since it all
now belonged to the Crown.

Another dispatch, from Halifax on August 11, was recalled by
Winslow, as he continued to be lost in thought, dwelling on the
many dictates that he would have to implement in regard to these
Acadian people. It read as the following:

*"Though the inhabitants by your instruction are allowed
to carry with them their household furniture, yet they must
not put on board quantities of such to encumber the vessel...if
after there is room for other articles, suffer them to carry what
they conveniently can."*

Winslow repeated these words to himself— "suffer them to carry what they conveniently can". This dictate seemed somehow incongruous to his sense of reason. For how indeed, he thought, could anyone carry conveniently the fruits that represented generations of living for these people of Nova Scotia?

But it was not for him to say in this matter, for the overall picture must be considered in this instance, as in any military operation, he reasoned, as he recalled vividly his words after the fall of Beausejour.

"We are," said he at the time, "now hatching the noble and great project of banishing the French Neutrals from the Province. If we accomplish this expulsion, it will have been one of the greatest deeds the English in America have ever achieved, for among other considerations, the part of the country which they occupy is one of the best soils in the world, and, in that event, we might place some good farmers on their homesteads."

Once again Winslow found himself gazing over in the direction of the three women, who had by now climbed into the ox cart in obvious preparation to be on their way. He observed the older woman, as she lightly prodded the ox, which in turn began to pull the cart. Soon, they would be out of sight of his vantage point.

How strange, he marveled to himself, that these women can go about their everyday duties when tomorrow will usher in the end of the life they have always known. But then they know nothing of what is to come about. And for their sake it is best. Let them relish for a few more hours in what they have come to know, for tomorrow who knows what paths lay ahead for them.

Winslow's observations seemed to concur with a dispatch that he had only just received from Murray at Fort Edward that very morning. And he mentally recalled the short communique.

"September 4, 1755— I was out yesterday at the villages. All the people were quiet and very busy at their harvest. If the day keeps fair all will be here in their barns. I hope tomorrow will crown all of our hopes....."

DIKED FARMLAND, from the Minas Basin, produced thousands of acres of rich marine alluvium soil, where cattle grazed and bountiful grain fields prevailed, nurtured by Acadian farmers before the expulsion of 1755.

CHAPTER - 4

DAWNING OF AN INFAMOUS DAY

The day dawned bright and crisp on Friday, September 5, 1755, with a chill in the air that only hinted at the winter soon to come.

Distant Cape Blomidon, across the wide water of the Minas Basin, seemed to loom bigger than life, so brightly illuminated was it by the morning sunshine.

Jean Theriot treaded his way along the path on the dikes, much like he had done almost every morning at this time of year, after seeing the cattle to pasture. This morning seemed no different to him, as he made his way toward the house just a few yards away from the dikes where he trod.

Leaving the path along the dike, he cut across and down through a patch of Golden Rod, which was blooming, intermingled with delicate Queen Anne's Lace and other Fall wild flowers, that brightened the dikes with colorful hues at this harvest time of year. On the other side of the dike, the sea grass waved in the September breeze, just as it did during other months of the year, except in winter when it became weighted down with the ice of winter.

How fortunate, Jean Theriot pondered as he walked, that the people of Minas Basin were so blessed with such rich soil that had been reclaimed from the sea by so many Papas and Grandpas, in years before. He dwelled on these things, with every stride that was bringing him closer to his home. It seemed to him, that there was no end to the richness of the red mud flats that rimmed the great Minas Basin. But then, had not he too, and others of his generation, also diked up more land from the sea, adding additional good farm land for the next generation. The young ones would soon be taking over his chores in a few years, when he was too old to carry on. Why, already Josef, his oldest, had plans for diking that small section of marsh just a few yards to the east of the very place where he now walked.

Yes, thought Jean, it was indeed a fortunate turn of events that motivated his forefathers to claim the rich land from the sea, for it had paid off handsomely. Even into his generation, he thought, each harvest season seems richer than the one before. It was his belief, that this would not have been so had they chose to cut down the trees on the eastern slopes of the hills and plowed that soil. Because life would have been much harder. True, substantial work was needed to dike the rich red marsh mud, but the resulting farm yield is considerably more bountiful, compared to those distant people, who farm the slopes.

Yes, Jean decided, nodding to himself as he neared the back door of his house. The Lord has been kind to we people in this land of Acadie!

Magdelene Theriot busied herself in the kitchen, rolling out the dough on the floured board. Glancing momentarily out of the window, she caught sight of her husband, Jean, who was approaching the house. Hurriedly, she wiped her hands on her apron and went over to the hearth, to pull the kettle of water from over the fire. Grasping the hot handle of the kettle with a doubled up cloth, so as not to burn her hand, she proceeded to brew a cup of tea for her husband. Thus was she employed when Jean opened the door and walked into the kitchen.

"Good morning, my dear," Jean remarked, as he pulled a chair out and sat down at the table.

"It is a good morning, Jean. You were out early today," his wife said, as she set the cup down.

"Where is Charles?" Jean questioned. To which his wife answered. "He is bringing some wood from the pile out back for the fire place. I am running low."

"I will need him to bring the cattle in from the field later, as I have to go over to the church for that meeting." Jean remarked as he bit into a chunk of hot bread.

"Oh yes, he knows....and he will take care of the chores this evening. We can be proud of him.... after all, he is still only a boy. But he has stepped into his brother Josef's shoes well these last few days," she said breathlessly, as she busied herself setting the table. "Ah...but I am beginning to miss Josef, since he went to the hills to hunt with the Indian Losmic. He promised to be home on Saturday, did he not....so we could all attend the Sunday betrothal celebration at the Bourgeois house?"

Just as she finished speaking, their younger son Charles came through the door, straining under the weight of a load of firewood, that he carried. Then, he attempted to answer his Mama's question. "Oh, he will be here....no doubt about that. After all....since he started courting Madeleine Bourgeois, it isn't likely that he would miss an event at her house!"

"Charles....you should not tease Josef about Madeleine," his Papa admonished. "After all, he is old enough to be thinking of taking a wife. He is 23 years now, and I was a year younger when I took your Mama as a bride." As he looked over at his wife, he asked. "Where are our little ones?"

"Francoise has gone over to the Pierre LeBlanc house. You know....every day I notice how our Francoise is fast becoming a young lady. So, she wants to get out more. Since she seems to get on so well with Pierre and Elise's girl, Marie, I let her go. It is only one farm over and Charles can fetch her if need be." His wife replied. "As for our youngster Ednee, she is out in the barn, getting eggs. Since she promised not to break even one, I trusted her to do this chore. After all...she is big enough now to take on more chores."

Just then, a young girl of about age eight opened the back door to the kitchen and walked in. Slamming the door behind her, she ran over to the table, and exclaimed. "Papa....Papa...you are back!" To which, Jean chastised her.

"Careful, Ednee....put the basket of eggs down on the table before you drop and break them." But immediately, he reached out for the child with both arms and took her up to sit on his lap. He hugged his little daughter warmly and kissed her on the cheek, as she continued to chatter on in her young female manner.

"Papa...how is Golden Mademoiselle this morning? Is she eating enough grass with the other cows in the pasture?"

"Oh yes, my little one...your Golden Mademoiselle is fast growing into a fine cow, which will soon be giving us rich cream to put on your cranberries," answered Jean, as he well knew how much she loved that young cow. He recalled how attached Ednee had become to that particular calf, ever since it was born out in the barn. And he remembered how he had promised to teach her to milk the cow, just as soon as her Golden Mademoiselle was old enough, which would not be very long from now.

"Oh Papa....I can hardly wait to milk her! She will be my very own cow...won't she, Papa.... just as you promised?" Implored Ednee, as she looked up at Jean with her big dark brown eyes.

"Yes...my little one...she will be just for you, as I promised." Jean assured her, at the same time hugging her warmly again. How could he deny Ednee anything? She continued to hug him around his neck, nuzzling his cheek with the shiny long dark brown hair on her little head.

"You must hurry and finish your breakfast, Jean," his wife interrupted. "Or you will be late for the meeting at the church.

You told me last evening, that you wanted to get there early, so you could confer with the other men before the English Colonel begins."

"Papa....let me go with you," implored Charles, who abruptly pulled a chair up to the table near Jean. "I am almost a man...do I not do a man's chores these days?"

"Charles....the order posted by the English called for a meeting of all the men of Grand Pre, and you are not yet a man," explained Jean. "Do not be impatient, my son, your time will come soon. Besides, you will have to attend to my chores while I am away today."

"Oh Papa....let me just go with you to the church. I will come back home and attend to the cattle....just like you say. I want to see what is going on," implored Charles. "What do they want with the men of the village, Papa....I want to know?"

"I have no idea of what they want, Charles...but the order demanded that we men attend, on pain of forfeiting our goods if we do not," answered Jean. "That is why I have to go, since the Colonel had posted not just a request, but a demand! It was an order for all of the men to be there...even from Perreau, des Habitants, Canard and Gaspereau. Josef would have to be there also, if he were here. But the order was posted after he had already left with Losmic to go on the hunt. So, that just cannot be helped....I only hope that I can justify his absence to the English."

"Jean....let Charles go with you," pleaded his wife. "He can come back and bring word to us of what the meeting is about, for you will no doubt be late in returning. I know how you men are, when you get together...you lose all track time....and I want to know what new restrictions the English plan to impose on us this time!"

"Oh, my dear....you women are so curious," admonished Jean. But at the same time he realized full well, that this was little enough concession for him to make in order to keep his wife from fretting about what is to transpire at the church. So, he conceded.

"Yes, Charles...you may accompany me to the church. But you can only stay long enough to find out what is to happen. With these words, he put his hand on his son's shoulders and noted the delight in Charles' eyes, as he comprehended his Papa's words. "Now go....and get the cart ready. We will ride to the church this day, as befits a prominent farmer of Grand Pre and his son, who will soon be a man."

With this, Charles sprang out of the door, almost toppling over the chair in which he had been seated in a moment before.

"He is a good boy, Jean," said Madelene, looking after Charles, who was already out of the door, which in his haste he had left slightly ajar. "Thank you, my husband, for taking him with you.... you have made us both happier this morning."

She spoke these last words, as she walked over to Jean, who still held the child on his lap. Filled with appreciation for his gesture on her behalf, Madelene bent down and enwrapped them both in her arms, pressing Jean's head against her bosom tenderly. At the same time, she closed her eyes momentarily, and let her entire being feel the warmth of his closeness, fully realizing how very fortunate she was to have a man such as Jean Theriot for her husband all of these years.

But a moment more and she had regained her composure, and was once again at the hearth, stirring the big black pot, filled with the broth that simmered over the fireplace fire, as she remarked. "I will let the soup cook slowly for a few hours, so that the chunks of meat will be tender to the taste, as you like it. It will be a fine meal for you upon your return. For there will be more hot bread baked by that time, and a new batch of fresh butter ready from the churn."

"You are a good wife, my dear," Jean said, as he stood up from the chair, gently setting his little daughter down, as he did so. "We will be on our way now, my dears....for Charles must have the cart hitched by now. Madelene....do not fret....I will be home as soon as I can."

With these words, Jean walked through the back door and across to the barn, where the harnessed cart stood ready, with Charles seated, holding the reins. Magdelene stood at the door, with Ednee. Then, they waved, as Jean mounted the cart and Charles prodded the animal, for them to be on their way. Abruptly, they drove onto the road, raising a small cloud of dust behind them.

Magdelene stood there at the door for a while, until they were out of sight, behind a grove of willow trees in the bend where the road took a sharp turn along the dike, and she could see them no more. Many thoughts filled her mind, as she watched her husband and son in the cart, on their way to the Church of St. Charles.

My, how proud her Papa Michel Bourg would be today if he could see these fine grandchildren of his, she thought. And how Mama Elizabeth would take such delight in the girls. But the Lord had taken them both some years after the family came to Grand Pre from Beaubassin. So, they never had the opportunity to see the babies.

She continued to remember well how her Mama would tell her about her parents, the Melancons', who lived their entire lives in Beaubassin. And also, she recalled hearing what a sad tale it was. For after marrying Papa Bourg and coming to Grand Pre, her Mama never again saw her parents.

The thought saddened Magdelene, for her Mama's sake. But she felt elated about the fact, that her Papa and Mama Bourg had chosen to come to Grand Pre. For if they had not, thought she, never would she have met and wed so fine a man as Jean.

Oh, such deep thoughts, she murmured to herself, as a tear came into her eye. Shooing Ednee into the house, she dismissed her reverie abruptly. "There is not time enough to dwell on such things....I have chores to do." Then, she sighed, and closed the door behind her.

———

Pierre Hebert handed the dipper to Claude Boudreaux, who stood by the well in the church yard, waiting for a drink of water. Ah, how good the cool well water tastes, thought Pierre, for it had been a long walk from his fields to the church.

"I hope they do not keep us here too long, Claude," Pierre remarked. "For I have only just yesterday started to harvest my fields and there is much work left to be done."

"Yes....Pierre, I know what you mean." Claude replied, after he had swallowed some water from the dipper. "It is the same with me....for even now my two young sons are toiling in the fields until I can return to help them."

"I suppose it is at such times that having six sons comes in handy," remarked Charles Granger, who had only just then joined the group at the well."

Jean Landry walked up to the group of men, and reached over for the dipper that now rested in the bucket on the rim of the well. He then added his share to the harvest lament. "At least all of you have more than one son to help with the harvest. I have just the one and he is yet too young to do a man's share of the work. So my four almost grown daughters were working right along side of me in the hay field this day."

As the men stood near the well and related their tales of harvest woe, the cart carrying Jean Theriot and his son Charles pulled up nearby. Whereupon the boy, Charles, jumped down and busied himself hobbling the animal, so it would not wander away while they attended to the business at the church.

Oliver Aucoin, who was standing nearby among the large crowd of Acadian men in the church yard, had observed their arrival and walked over to Jean Theriot and began to converse. "Good day to you," Monsieur Jean," as he extended his hand. "I trust Madame Theriot is well, and that Josef has returned from the hunt."

"Yes, Madame is well," answered Jean, taking Oliver's hand in greeting. "But Josef has not yet returned...so you will not be seeing him here today."

Oliver was about the same age as Jean's son, Josef, and they had been friends since boyhood. Like Josef, Oliver was still a single young man, and a resourceful one. For everyone knew that he was farming a section of his Papa's diked land, and had already accumulated several head of stock on his place.

"What do you suppose they want of us here today, Monsieur Jean?" Inquired Oliver, as he turned slightly from Jean to survey the church yard, which was by now fast filling with a large crowd of men, from the surrounding villages. They were all milling about, conversing with friends and acquaintances.

"No one seems to know what it is all about, Oliver. But let us hope that it is not another scheme by the English to levy more taxes or restrictions on us, or on our harvest," speculated Jean, as he suddenly noted a large group of soldiers being marched into their midst.

All at once a vocal directive from an officer, who had halted the soldiers, was shouted. After which, they broke ranks and went immediately among the Acadian men, all the while displaying their bayonets before them. Then the officer, who had led them, bolted halfway up the church steps and began to shout at the large crowd of men in the yard.

"You will all come into the church at once," shouted the officer. "Anyone, who fails to do so in an orderly manner, will be dealt with harshly!"

This announcement was accompanied by his gestures to the armed soldiers in their midst, who by now had fully infiltrated among the large crowd of men outside the church—all of whom were suddenly jarred to attention by the harsh words, which had been shouted at them.

Jean suddenly felt a sharp pressure on his back and with a shock realized that an armed soldier was prodding him to move toward the church.

"Move on now," shouted the soldier behind him. And before Jean could tell him to allow his son Charles, whom he had pulled toward him, to leave, because he was just a boy, more soldiers surrounded them. Charles, Jean and Oliver were then pushed toward the church, and forcibly directed up the steps and into the portals of the church of St. Charles.

Once inside the church, the crowd of some four hundred Acadian men hardly had time to cross themselves and hastily genuflect, as was their custom upon entering their place of worship. For they were all crowded inward, where some sat on the pews and others were pushed together, to stand wherever they found a space. Because the interior of the church was not large enough to accommodate such a large crowd all at one time.

As soon as they were inside, at about the hour of 3:PM, an officer in full regimentals entered and the soldiers made way for him. This allowed him space to walk to the middle of the church, where a table had been previously set up for this occasion.

"What is happening, Papa," whispered Charles, who stood crowded between his Papa and against the wall of the church. He was holding onto Jean's arm in an effort to keep from being separated from him in this melee of confusion.

"I do not know, my son," replied Jean. But I recognize the officer who just came in as a Colonel Winslow. He is in command of the English soldiers, who are encamped in the church yard. I have seen him several times."

"Everyone will be quiet," was the shouted dictate that came from another officer, who also had positioned himself at the table, alongside of Colonel Winslow. "The Colonel has a communique from his Brittanic Majesty, which he will read to you. I will endeavor to translate his English words into French, so that you will all understand, and that there will be no question as to the words he will speak. Now, everyone will be silent so that Colonel Winslow can begin!"

The Colonel had taken a seat by the small table at the head of the middle aisle of the church, but he now rose to his feet, unfolding a paper as he did so. Focusing his eyes on the communique before him, he began to read slowly in English, as the officer, who was doing the interpreting, repeated each line in French for all in the church to hear. The dictate read as follows:

"Gentlemen– I have received from his Excellency Governor Lawrence, the Kings Commission which I have in my hand, and by which order you are convened together to manifest to you his Majesty's final solution to the French inhabitants of his Province of Nova Scotia, who for almost half a century have had more indulgence granted them than any of his subjects in any parts of his dominion, what use you have made of this, you yourself know.

'The part of duty I am now upon is very disagreeable to my natural makeup and temper as I know it must be grievous to you, who are of the same species. But it is not my duty to decide, but to obey such orders as I receive and therefore without hesitation I have delivered you his Majesty's orders and instructions, that your land and cattle of all kinds be forfeited and not molested in conveyance and that whole families shall go in the same vessel. This dictate which I have brought forth must give you a great deal of trouble as we in his Majesty's service will admit and hope that in whichever part of the world you may travel you may be faithful subjects and a peaceable and happy people. I must also inform you that it is his Majesty's command that you remain in security under the inspection of the troops that I have under my command."

As his last words died away, shocked silence permeated the atmosphere in the church. It was as if the Acadian men present within those portals could not comprehend the magnitude of the words this man had just spoken. But before they could collect their wits, Colonel Winslow continued reading from another dispatch that he held in his hands.

"To all officers, soldiers and seamen employed in his Majesty's Service as well as all his subjects are hereby notified that all cattle, horses, sheep, goats, hogs, and poultry of every kind that was this day belonged to the French inhabitants are this day forfeited to his

Majesty whose property they now are. And every person is not to kill destroy anything of any kind, nor to rob orchards, or gardens or to make waste of anything dead or alive in the districts, without special order given at my camp this day."

With those last words, Colonel Winslow folded the papers from which he had read, and marched out of the church, followed by some of his staff.

Then the melee began, as the voices of numerous Acadian men in the church were suddenly raised in protest, as each man seemed to grasp the meaning of what had just come to pass. For all at once each man appeared to be shaken from the shock that had only just registered in their mentality. Thus this terrible realization literally made many of them feel the need to shout out some objection to the dictate just handed them—no matter how futile.

"No...no!" Shouted Pierre Hebert, whose voice was abruptly heard above the others. "How can this be...how can they make us go and leave our land?"

"Yes," shouted Jean Landry, who was crowded in near Jean Theriot. "What so terrible a thing have we done, to warrant such action?"

The objections of the men were silenced one by one, as the soldiers went among them with threatening weapons, in some cases right in the very faces of those uttering objections.

One man, Etienne Boudreaux, was struck from behind by a soldier, as he bolted toward the closed door of the church, in an apparent attempt to escape. He fell to the floor unconscious as a result of the glancing blow to his head. Whereupon two men nearest him, Michelle Trahan and Germain Richard, stooped down and sat him up, in an effort to revive the fallen man.

Amid all of this clamor, Jean Theriot had remained silent, still dumfounded as he mulled over the words of the dictate that his ears had just heard. All at once, he became aware of an increased pressure on his arm. When he looked down, he realized that his son Charles was clinging to his arm, all the while staring up beseechingly at his

Papa, silently, but with a pleading expression in his terrified eyes. Then it suddenly struck him.

"Oh my God.... son...I almost forgot! We must get you out of here at once! You are but a boy and should not be here." As he whispered these words to his son, he grasped the boy's shoulders and tried to make way, guiding him through the crowd of despairing men, some of whom were moaning to themselves. Some were even crying quietly, as evidenced by their trembling shoulders. In this manner, keeping Charles close to him, they made their way slowly through the crowd toward the officer in charge, who was surrounded by soldiers stationed at the door. Jean wanted to get close enough to get the officer's attention, among the chorus of imploring voices that prevailed there. For each was trying to get the attention of that same officer.

"Capitan...Captain!" Cried out Jean as loud as he could, as he reached his arm high into the air above the men, who were still in front of him, blocking his view of the officer. "Let my son return home....he is but a boy and should not have been made to come into this gathering!" It was necessary for Jean to repeat his plea several times, before his voice caught the officer's attention above the clamoring shouts.

"Let that man through....you there.... make way for the man behind you," ordered the officer to those in front of Jean. You....yes you! Do you have a boy in here....do I understand you correctly?" A disheveled Jean nodded, as he and Charles were pushed on through a last line of shouting & beseeching Acadian men, as he continued to be heard.

"Yes, Captain......this is my son, who should not be here," Jean shouted at the officer, as he pushed Charles in front of him. The officer, who seemed to comprehend his words, shouted out, imploring the boy to come forward.

"Yes....I see! Guard....see that this boy is taken out of the church and sent home at once! The order only called for men this day at the church!"

Charles' arm was immediately grasped by a soldier, who proceeded to urge him away from Jean, and through the crowd that was stationed around the front door.

"Charles.....hurry home and bring word to your Mama about what has happened," shouted Jean, as his son was being hurriedly pushed away from him and on toward the church door. "Tell her I am alright....and not to worry!"

"Bring word to my family too, Charles," another voice implored after him. "You know me....Joseph Gautreaux...my farm is down the way from you!" Then other voices started to shout at Charles. "Yes....let my wife know too what has happened this day. Tell my young son Phillipe of this matter!"

Jean recognized the last voice coming from the crowd of men as that of Charles Thibodeaux, another neighboring farmer. Then, before Charles was finally pushed out of the door, he heard two more voices imploring after him, to bring news for their families, too. Jean recognized both men. One was Batiste Babin and the other was Joseph Benois, who were old friends of his.

But then, a moment more and the door was slammed shut, after Charles and his escort soldier excited the church. At that moment, there was a sudden silence, followed by a low hum of voices, as the men became somewhat more subdued, choosing to consider their present plight in a calmer manner.

A very depressed Jean Theriot found his way back toward the far wall of the crowded church, and there near the altar, he sank down to a sitting position, leaning against the wall. He rested his head on his knees, all the while mulling over the stark reality of what had just come to pass. It was at that very moment, that he fully realized the futility of his position, and that there was nothing he could do now......except pray and wait.

AN ACADIAN MAIDEN MODEL, attired in the fashion of 1755 Nova Scotia/Acadia, is featured here at St. Charles Church Museum in Grand Pre.

CHAPTER - 5

RETURN FROM THE HUNT

The smoke from the Indian's pipe floated away from his face, as he exhaled slowly. In his half sitting, half reclining position on the ground, he leaned against the trunk of a large birch tree. Losmic was in close proximity to the small camp fire's brilliant flames, and he reached over to pass the pipe to Josef, who was sitting on the ground just a few feet from him.

Josef popped his last handful of wild berries into his mouth, as he reached out to take the pipe, that was being handed to him. Then, he commented. "It has been a good hunt, Losmic."

"Yes....we did not bring down the great moose at the top of the mountain. But the time spent tracking was good," the Indian agreed. "Our god Goosclap is kind, to allow us the time to spend as brothers."

After taking a puff, Josef gazed over at his Indian friend, as the smoke from the pipe encircled around his head. How grand it is, he thought, to have such a Micmac brother as Losmic. Glancing over at his friend, Josef took note of the chiseled features of the Indian's face. He noticed the beads on Losmic's headband, which kept the two feathers in place. The beads seem to sparkle faintly in the morning sunlight, that filtered down between the overhead branches of spruce, birch and maple trees, that towered far above their heads.

As his eyes drifted over to where a butterfly lit on a stalk of Queen Anne's Lace flower, which was growing just across the little clearing where they sat, Josef was lost in thought for a moment. He marveled at the fact that he, Josef Theriot, a simple young man, had the remarkable good fortune to have been befriended by so high a personage in the Micmac tribe as Losmic. For this Indian was no ordinary Micmac. He was a Shaman, a highly revered individual, who from time to time chose to share some hours, hunting with a French brother, like himself.

Josef well knew how much power a Shaman could wield within the tribe. For the Micmac Indians believed that a Shaman was a most powerful individual. And that he is special, because he has it in his power to understand the supernatural, the physical and the psychological. Also, it was well known that Shamans possess curing abilities.

Years ago, Losmic had explained it all to him. It seems that some Shamans come to be, by inheriting the position from a long line of Shamans in a family. But Losmic had acquired his status through a "power quest", when he had gone into the forest to live by himself. During this time, he had to fast until a megumawesoo, or spirit helper, appeared to bestow the Shamanistic powers on him.

Every Shaman in the Micmac tribe carried a sacred "sack", which contained all manner of mysterious objects. Once, Losmic had shown him some of the items that he carried in that sack. Josef recalled it well, for there was a nut-size stone, bits of bark with figures carved thereon, a small bow with a card interlaced with porcupine quills, a foot long stick decorated with red and white quills and a number of straps attached to the end on which claws hung, and a little wooden bird figure.

But Losmic, and the other Shamans of the tribe, were not the only individuals, who could treat those when they lay stricken by some unknown, or particularly severe, illness, even though they were held in the highest esteem of all by fellow tribesmen. Others in the tribe, although not held in such reverence as the Shamans, could also treat those who were sick.

As he recalled, it was an old Indian woman who had come to the house of his Papa, when summoned on one occasion some years back. He recalled the event, because it was a time during his boyhood when he had an extremely painful boil on his shoulder, which resisted all of his Mama's medication. It was an old Micmac Indian woman, who had told his Mama to steep the leaves and twigs of the Sweet Fern as a remedy and to give the boy a tablespoon of it before each meal and before going to bed. He would never forget how expedient this remedy had been. For it cured him of that pesky boil. As a result, his Mama continued to use this method when such future treatments were called for. So satisfied with the result of this cure on her boy, his Mama shared the remedy with other neighbor ladies, who dwelled near their farm.

Yes, the Micmacs had indeed shared much of the good things in their culture with the people of the dikes, Josef reflected. Indeed, life without the aid of their Indian friends would certainly be difficult to imagine. As he dwelled on the good things he had learned from Losmic and others in that tribe, he suddenly became a bit saddened. Because this latest hunt was now coming to an end. And this morning, they would be covering the remaining distance down the mountain to Grand Pre and home. But he would be happy to be back with his family, and also to see Madeleine.

At the very thought of Madeleine, an exciting warmth encompassed his very being. But then, thoughts of her always had that effect on him. Someday soon, he thought, she would become his wife, if everything went well. Then they would be together always. This could not happen soon enough to suit him.

Abruptly, Josef was jolted from his revere, as a small cloud of gray, dusty smoke drifted toward him from the fire, which Losmic had just smothered, with a dash of water that made the coals sizzle audibly. It was a sound of finality, which seemed to proclaim within the small shaded forest clearing wherein they sat, that it was time to depart. So without a word, Josef immediately began to gather the few articles of camping gear that had made sleeping outside in the wild tolerable the night before. Then, they were off, down the narrow tree shaded path that Losmic seemed to know quite well.

The early September morning air was a bit nippy, Josef noticed, as he endeavored to keep pace with his friend, whose strides covered substantial ground amid the bushy underbrush along the ill defined path. He clasped his deer skin bag to him countless times, each time the thorns and tendrils of a blackberry bush scratched at him—one time mauling the back of his hand when he passed too close.

But he kept up with Losmic's swift pace, close on the Indian's moccasin heels. Josef could see glances of blue sky overhead through breaks in the spruce and birch canopy. A slight shower had fallen the night before around the area where they traveled. The vivid green ferns on the forest floor were still covered with beads of water that sparkled as an occasional ray of sunshine reached in through the boughs above, causing brief manifestations of brilliant highlights along the ground.

Other than the sounds of the two men's hurried passage through the unmarred dark green forest, only the blue jays and squirrels could be heard from above. But as they rounded a rather large spruce tree that stood in their path, the men came across a surprised red fox, which upon seeing them, sprinted out of sight into some thick underbrush.

Thus their journey down the mountain toward Grand Pre, was uneventful, except for such occasioned encounters with forest wildlife and flora. Finally, in early afternoon the dark canopy of overhead forest began to thin out a bit at a time, until it gave way completely to a wide expanse of blue sky and sunshine, which beamed down brightly on the little Grand Pre community, off in the distance.

But it was such a clear day, Josef noticed, from their vantage point up on the side of the mountain as they burst through the dark forest, that off in the distance Cape Blomidon could be seen clearly. It appeared even more vivid than usual, way across the Minas Basin. It was at that moment in which they each took in the view. And they both appeared to each catch their breathe in awe, upon beholding those distant familiar cliffs, gleaming distinctly in the distance. The two friends grinned at each other in a silent, complacent acknowledgement that they were almost home again. Views of the Cape always seemed to affect them that way, no matter how many times they viewed it's beauty from afar.

As they proceeded on the downward path, it was becoming steeper. But it mattered not to Josef, because after viewing the Cape and Grand Pre in the distance, he felt rejuvenated. Thus he had little difficulty, keeping up with his Indian friend, as they set a quick pace—sometimes stumbling only now and then on loose pebbles and fallen stones.

Soon, they reached the bottom of the last hill, which leveled out into the flat terrain. It was there that the outlying golden fields of Grand Pre farms were seen— dotted only with grazing cattle here and there. It was a view, spread out before them, as far as the dikes in the distance.

"Let us take the path along the dikes and by-pass the village," Josef suggested to Losmic, "For I am anxious to get home." His friend looked over at him in agreement.

"It is as you say, my brother...I had planned the same. For I am weary of the trail."

They then took a turn on the path that led in the direction of the Theriot farm, a short distance away. As they hurried upon the soft grassy carpet that covered the dikes, Josef was seized with a feeling of uneasiness, especially when he peered over at the fields, farm houses and barns they were passing along the way. But before he could comment on this to Losmic, the Indian spoke first.

"All is not well here....my brother!"

"I know," agreed Josef. "Look over there at the Gautreaux fields...they are only partially harvested and no one is about.... yet, there are still hours of light left in this day. It is not like Joseph Gautreaux to waste day light like that!"

"Oh yes....some evil spell is here in this land," exclaimed Losmic. "But I cannot tell what it is."

"Look at that!" Exclaimed Josef, as he came to an abrupt halt along the path, and pointed toward another nearby field. "Our neighbor Charles Thibodeaux has left his barn door ajar and his pitch forks are strewn about the hay field...and yet no one is to be seen! Look....the door to the house is closed tight and no smoke is coming from the chimney....even thought it will soon be supper time!"

"Let us hurry.....my brother!" Losmic exclaimed. "We are almost to your Mama and Papa's house.....we will soon learn what strange evil spell has been cast over this land."

No sooner had these last words been spoken, when the two men picked up their pace and set off, half running down the dike. They cut across the nearest field toward the grove of willow trees, some yards away, which shaded the familiar farm house that Josef knew so well.

———

The abrupt loud pounding on the door startled Magdelene Theriot, causing her to almost spill the kettle of hot water, which she was pouring into a tea pot on the table.

"Charles," she shouted over her shoulder. "See who is at the door!"

Thus disturbed from his reverie, by his Mama's command, Charles groggily rose up from the chair at the table where he had been sitting. He hurried the few paces to the door, from which the forceful pounding was heard. Handily pushing back the bolt on the door, he opened it ever so slightly and cautiously peered through to the outside.

"It is me, Charles....your brother back from the hunt. Let us in!"

"Oh...my dear Lord!" Exclaimed Magdelene, when she heard Josef's voice. Excitedly, she shouted out. "Come here, children.... your brother is back!"

As the door sprung open, revealing the figure of Josef and the Indian Losmic behind him, Magdelene's outstretched arms reached out and enveloped Josef, as she hugged him to her forcefully, sobbing and murmuring unintelligently all the while.

"Mama....Mama...what has happened...why are you crying?" Josef questioned, as he held his Mama against him, returning her emotional embrace.

His Mama, who was about a foot shorter than her son, rested her head—at chest level—against the deerskin jacket he wore, as her shoulders began to shudder in jerks. It was then that her tears spilled fourth profusely.

As his Mama cried audibly in Josef's arms, Charles stepped forward and grasped his brother's shoulder, and at the same time extended his other hand in greeting toward Losmic. Since they were both still standing in the doorway, he motioned them both to come in and close the door behind them. At that moment, Magdelene had stifled her tears long enough to speak.

"Oh Josef....what will we do...they have taken your Papa and we can do nothing!"

In confusion, Josef stared over at his brother. "Charles....will you tell us what has come to pass here? What is going on?"

"The English are holding all of the men of Grand Pre, and some from other villages too....and the Lord only knows how many others are captive in other places," Charles answered. "They say we are all to be put on ships and sent away from here...and they will not say where they are sending us. After they heard of this... our neighbors, the Gautreauxs', left their farm and headed for the hills....we saw them pass on the road, carrying whatever they could on one cart. They were going in the direction away from the ships at anchor in the Basin."

"How can this be....when did it happen?" Questioned Josef.

"They seized the men from the village two days ago," Charles endeavored to explain. "When they went to attend that meeting at the church. I was there...I heard and saw everything! Most of the men are still being held at the church....but since it was too crowded for all of them, the English transferred some to be held as prisoners on the ships....and our Papa was one of them!"

"Yes my son.....and your Papa is still on that ship," Magdelene added, as she sat herself on a chair and dabbed her eyes with her handkerchief. "Since then, Charles, along with some other families too, have been bringing your Papa's and their Papa's meals to the shore, where the English soldiers take the food into the rowboats, to be rowed to the ships. They will not let us see him...but they have said that we must be ready soon to embark on the ship...all of us together!"

"Josef....you are back!" Exclaimed a young voice, as Ednee came running into the kitchen toward her big brother. Josef reached out for his young sister and hugged her to him. The little girl was followed closely by her sister, a girl of about twelve, who reached out to Josef in an effort to hug him, too.

"Oh Josef....those mean English soldiers will not give Papa back....and Mama says I will not be permitted to take my Golden Mademoiselle when we have to leave. Please, let me take her Josef....Papa gave her to me to be my very own cow. How can I leave her....who will take care of her?" Pleaded Ednee, as her little arms entwined around Josef's neck, and tears fell from her big brown eyes.

Just then, Josef's attention was diverted from his little sisters, as he looked up to see a familiar form enter the room.

"Josef....I hope you are well. We are so happy to see you and Losmic safely back from your hunt." Greeted Madeleine Bourgeois, as she walked into the kitchen and held her hands out to him.

"Madeleine...how wonderful that you are here!" Josef exclaimed, as he hurried over to her and grasped both of her outstretched hands. Oh, how he wanted to envelope his beloved Madeleine in his arms, but he refrained from displaying too much emotion, as they were not yet formerly betrothed. So, such excessive behavior on his part might embarrass her in front of his family. Instead, he squeezed her hands and for a moment gazed longingly into her dark eyes, becoming somewhat anesthetized by her nearness. But suddenly, he was brought back to earth by his Mama.

"My son...in all of the excitement, I forgot to tell you that Madeleine is here with us, waiting for you to return." She then looked over at Losmic, who had been silent during these emotional greetings in Josef's behalf. The Indian was still standing just inside of the doorway, surveying all that had just transpired in the room. It was then that she spoke to him.

"Oh... Losmic....you must be hungry after the long trail. Sit here and I will pour you a cup of cool milk...and soon some bread will be ready from the oven."

Losmic pulled a chair out and sat at the table. Magdelene set a freshly poured cup of milk before him on the table. Losmic looked up at her and spoke.

"It is good, Madame Theriot....the milk is cool!" Losmic never did speak much in all the years they had known him, but everyone knew that when he did speak it was purposeful and pointed—usually expressing much wisdom. So, the lack of conversation from Losmic was common place and all were used to his quiet manner. However, his presence was always welcomed, because of the valued friend that he had always been to the family.

Josef forced himself to get back to the reality of the moment, for he had momentarily become lost in Madeleine's presence, and this was reflected as he spoke.

"How come you are here, Madeleine....I never expected to see you welcoming me and Losmic this day?"

Madeleine looked away from Josef for a moment, as she sat herself down in a chair next to where Charles was sitting at the table. She touched her handkerchief to her eyes, as glistening tears emerged from her lashes.

"Josef, Madeleine came to us last evening," his Mama interjected. "Her Papa is imprisoned on board one of the ships too....and her family has been told that they will be taken soon also. Madeleine wanted to wait here for your return."

Shocked, but elated by these words, Josef looked from his Mama, and back to Madeleine, as he spoke. "I am so glad that you waited here for me.....to think, that I might have missed seeing you at such a time!"

""Oh, it was terrible, Josef!" Madeleine began. "Mama and my brothers and sisters were told to be ready to leave soon to join Papa, on one of the ships where he is being held. They told us that some English soldiers would come for all of us soon, and that we should take only what we can carry in a cart. Genevieve was in a state over this....you know, she and Albert Bertrand are betrothed, and he has not returned from Halifax. You know....he went in that delegation weeks ago, to plead with the Governor. Genevieve blamed Albert for leaving her at a time like this....it was all we could do to subdue her tirade, and calm her down!"

Madeleine's words were intermingled with sporadic sobs, and she paused to dab the tears that had spilled onto her cheeks before she continued.

"I begged my Mama to let me wait over here with your family for your return. Poor Mama..... she did not want me to leave the house, but she had her hands full with the rest of the family. My Aunt Jeanne

took to her bed, when she heard the news that we all had to leave....
and she just seemed to give up. She told all of us, that she was not going
to leave....she wanted to die in her own bed...and not on some foreign
ship or in some strange land. Oh.....it was awful....and it looks like
they will have to carry Aunt Jeanne and put her on the cart when the
soldiers come! I told Mama, that I wanted to wait over here for you....
and what with all the disruption, she finally gave her permission."

"Oh Josef....you might be in danger," his Mama exclaimed.
"The English...they will be looking for you. It is not safe for you
here!" Somewhat in alarm, Charles also agreed.

"It is true, Josef....the English took prisoners of all the adult
men in Grand Pre and surrounding villages. But you were still on
the hunt, so you were spared. But they are out everyday....rounding
up other men, who tried to escape. And they will no doubt come to
take you prisoner, too......once they hear that you are back!"

"Good Lord....Josef....what can you do?" Madeleine Bourgeois
cried out, rising from her chair, as her face mirrored the concern
that she felt for her beloved.

"They will not take me!" Josef proclaimed, pounding his fist on
the table so hard that it made the bowl of freshly churned butter,
that his Mama had just placed there, vibrate resoundingly.

"But Josef....it is said that the English have put a bounty on the
heads of all we Acadians caught, trying to escape from here," Charles
exclaimed, "and that is not all. There is also to be a bounty on the
head of any Micmac, who helps us to escape! Some say that scalps of
our people and the Micmac people will be evidence enough for the
soldiers to collect the bounties. It is also being said, that they will
track down all who try to escape....then they will take the scalps
and turn these in to collect the bounty money! It is all so terrible...
but people say it is true."

"Can this really be so?" Josef questioned incredulously, as
he looked from one member of his family to the other. "Did the
Gautreaux family know of this before they left this day?"

"No, my son....we saw them leave soon after we heard the news of your Papa being taken on the ship," his Mama answered, with a sigh of resignation. "So the word about the bounty had not reached us yet."

"Well....I still will not turn myself in....I would be of no help to anyone here, as a prisoner like Papa on an English vessel," proclaimed Josef. "There must be something else we can do!"

"There is...my brother!" Spoke up Losmic, as he set his cup down on the table, having just downed the last of the milk he was drinking. "There is a place....deep in the forest at the top of the mountain, that overlooks the land of the dikes. It was the place of my Shaman quest long ago....where the megumawesoo appeared to me in my youth. No one knows of it...perhaps you would be safe there. If you wish it....I will take you there."

"Losmic....you cannot risk such a thing," Josef exclaimed, as he looked into the dark, wise eyes of his Indian friend. "You heard what Charles said about the bounty on Micmacs! I cannot ask such a thing of you!"

"You are my brother, Josef," Losmic said, rising from his chair and placing his hand on Josef's shoulder. "I will not see the English take you prisoner!"

"Go with Losmic, Josef," his Mama said suddenly. "He is wise in the ways of the forest....if anyone can protect you...it is Losmic."

"But Mama....how will you manage?" Josef asked, as he walked over to her at the fireplace.

"Charles is here....and the girls will help me until the soldiers come to take us to your Papa," Magdelene reasoned. "Maybe when that day comes to pass, things will be better and then you can come back to us!"

Charles nodded in agreement. "Mama is right, Josef! I can bring you food every few days to a meeting place that Losmic thinks is safe....none of us wants you to be taken prisoner!"

Josef looked from one to the other, pondering their remarks, lastly settling his imploring gaze on the face of Madeleine, as she spoke to him.

"They are all correct...dear Josef. I will remain here, if it is all right with your Mama, and help her too. Together, we will send food to you and Losmic; as Charles has said...it is the only way."

"Then it is settled!" Mama Theriot proclaimed, as she gathered a basket from the side of the fireplace, and put the butter from the table into it. After which, she continued to collect items around the kitchen that her son and Losmic would need. They then put all of these things into the basket, as she directed her young daughters thusly. "Hurry girls....go get some fresh eggs from the barn."

Thus the departure preparations were made, under the direction of Madame Theriot, as everyone in the room scurried about gathering items that she ordered brought to her. When all was ready, the sun had set and early darkness was enveloping the land.

"The god Glooscap is good!" Proclaimed Losmic, as he peered through a small opening in the door to the outside. "He has given us a cover of darkness for our departure....and the English eyes do not see so well in the dark. Make haste, my brother...we must be on our way!"

———

CHAPTER - 6

A PLACE OF TEMPORARY REFUGE

It was just as Losmic had described, during the hurried nocturnal march to his Shaman place. Far up the mountain, located more remotely than any place that Josef had ever traveled, and there it was. An outcropping of rock, which formed a sort of shallow cave; this was Losmic's Shaman place of refuge.

It was hidden by several dense evergreen trees, with low hanging branches that dragged onto the ground, making it necessary for one to lift several of the limbs in order to gain access to the cave, which was always concealed beyond. If one did not know to look beyond this curtain of profuse dark green branches, the cave would certainly never be discovered.

As usual, Losmic was right, Josef decided. It was a perfect hiding place, offering adequate shelter and protection, too. Since arriving at their secret place, many days had passed, while they waited. Just as promised, Charles met them every three days, bringing provisions at an appointed place that Losmic had informed him of before they departed. It was a spot, further down the mountain on a bluff, which overlooked a panorama of the dike country, which was laid out below on the flat lands that ended on the shores of the Minas Basin, far off in the distance. As usual, the always familiar vision of Cape Blomidon, loaming far off on the horizon, could be viewed, too.

There was another advantage to this particular vantage point, for activity in the distant dike country below could also be seen. But of course, everything appeared so tiny and extremely far removed. Nevertheless, certain activity below could be observed from time to time, and these observations, along with Charles' reports, whenever he would briefly rendezvous with Josef and Losmic kept them informed. In this way, they were in touch with activity around Grand Pre. So, on this day, once again there they were—at the appointed place of rendezvous on the bluff, waiting for Charles' arrival.

Josef sat on the ground, with his back leaning against a small embankment, from which the trunks of large birch and spruce trees towered overhead. The thick foliage of these trees shaded him from the vivid sun, the brightness of which marred his vision somewhat. However, the warmth of the sunshine did feel good, for the days were getting increasingly colder, since winter would soon be with them. He shivered slightly as he positioned himself, so that he could peer through some short underbrush that framed his view of the panorama spread out far below, much like the patchwork quilt his Mama used to cover him with on cold nights when he was a boy.

Losmic, who had been standing guard just a few yards from where Josef sat, now hurried back to him. Because his Indian friend seemed in such haste, Josef questioned why. "Is it Charles, Losmic.....is he coming....did you see him?"

The Indian motioned to him to be quiet, and together they waited, crouched on their knees behind the thick underbrush, through which they strained to see the path, from which Charles usually emerged each time. Soon, the snapping of twigs heralded the emergence of two individuals from the dark forest path, as they hurried into the sunshine that enveloped the small clearing. All at once, Josef whispered emotionally to his Indian friend. "Losmic.... do you see? Can it be true that she is here?"

The Indian nodded slowly, apparently surprised at what he saw. "Yes...it is true...it is your Madeleine, who has accompanied your brother up the trail. But be cautious....for all may not be well!"

As if on cue, Josef sprang to his feet, and hurried in the direction of the figures, who were still approaching across the clearing. He spanned the few yards of distance that lay between himself and the approaching pair in record time. With open arms, Josef enveloped both Charles and Madeleine to him forcefully. All three of them were silent for a moment, seemingly struck speechless with emotion, as they remained briefly in this three way embrace. It was Losmic, who spoke first, for he had been close on Josef's heels.

"Come...it is not safe out in this open clearing....make haste back here to the safety of the trees, in case any English eyes are seeking!"

Knowing full well that Losmic spoke the truth, as was always his manner, the small group complied. And soon all were back under the protection of the towering trees that provided the shaded darkness they were seeking. At this point three voices erupted in greeting, albeit in subdued tones—with Josef questioning the pair, and both Charles and Madeleine volunteering explanations in unison. Again, it was Losmic's words that seemed to bring some semblance of order to the exuberant reunion.

"What has come to pass, Charles....why have you brought Mademoisle Madeleine...it is not safe for her here."

"What you say is true, Losmic," Charles began, looking from the Indian over to Josef, as he continued. "But it is not safe for her below here, in the land of the dikes either....the soldiers came for Mama and our sisters this morning!"

"What.....you left them at such a time, Charles?" Josef exclaimed, grabbing his brother roughly by the shoulder, as if in reprimand.

"Josef! Do not be angry with him," Madeleine pleaded, grasping his arm. "Charles made arrangements with Madame Landry and her two sons yesterday to look after your Mama, Ednee and Francoise until they joined your Papa on the ship. You know....it is the family of Germain Landry, down the road from your farm...he is a prisoner on the same ship as your Papa! We were informed that the soldiers were to come for both families today, so we all spoke at length of this thing, and what to do last night."

"Like you, I did not want to be taken, Josef," Charles exclaimed, looking up at his brother entreatingly. "I told Mama that I would leave before the soldiers came....and join you and Losmic here on the mountain."

"Yes.....and then I decided to come to you also, Josef....so do not be angry with me. I could not bear to be parted from you, perhaps never to see you again! I saw how anguished my sister Genevieve is, being parted from her intended! It is too late for her...but not for me! Together, we will all hide from the English until this terrible thing is ended," Madeleine added, looking down at her hands that rested in her lap, where she sat on the ground. With a sigh, she leaned her back against a tree trunk and choked back a sob, as her dark eyes stared back at Josef, seeking some glimmer of understanding from him.

"Do not worry, Josef," Charles added. "We asked Mama and the girls to spread the word to everyone they meet on the journey as to where they are bound.....always relating your name and mine. This is so word can somehow get back to us....reaching our ears in times to come. This way, we can learn where the English have sent our family...so we can join them again, when this is all over, or at least send for them when it is safe to return. We could think of no other way...is it not a good plan?"

Josef heaved a heavy labored sigh, upon hearing the explanation that Charles and Madeleine offered. Seemingly drained of all energy for the moment, he put his hand to his forehead and leaned against a nearby tree. His eyes reflected the remorse and frustration that filled his being, and he was obviously fighting back tears of sadness, as the magnitude of the situation struck him all at once. At that moment, he was filled with a sudden weakness that caused him to drop to his knees. Giving way to his emotion, Josef slid to the ground in a sitting position. Looking up at Losmic with his pained eyes, he spoke imploringly to the Indian. "What are we to do, Losmic? You are so wise...can you not give us direction in this time of trouble? You are my brother and I will heed your advice....only tell us what we should do!"

Losmic was silent for what seemed like interminable moments to the three young Acadians, who awaited his counsel. Their eyes were directly fixed imploringly on the countenance of their Indian friend, as he stood warily, peering back toward the clearing from whence they had just come. His bronzed facial expression did not betray the turmoil that existed within him, as he returned their pleading gazes and spoke.

"Let us be gone from this place....the English may be close on our heels. Did you not hear sounds of pursuit along the trail to the rendezvous, Charles? Were you followed?"

"I cannot say, Losmic.....we made such haste to get away. It was all we could do to keep our footing along the path, so hurried were we," Charles replied, looking over at Madeleine for confirmation of his words.

Madeleine, who was still resting on the ground, looked up at Losmic as she spoke, pulling her black shawl tightly around her shoulders. She shivered slightly as a sudden chilled gust of wind rustled the leaves on the ground around her, and disturbed wisps of her dark hair, which were tucked beneath the head covering she wore. She hugged her arms to herself, in an effort to maintain some warmth against the chill of the cold gusts. Then she spoke. "It is as Charles has said....we were making such haste to get here, that we paid little heed to anything else. But we saw no one along the trail. Do you believe we were followed, Losmic?"

Suddenly, the quiet of the shaded glade, where they deliberated their plight, was disturbed ever so slightly by the faintly audible sounds of snapping twigs back in the direction from where they came. Almost at the very moment that this sound was heard, Losmic's head jerked back toward the direction of the clearing, and at the same time an obvious expression of alarm took hold of him. Then, his body seemed tensed for action, as he urgently whispered words of alarm to his companions.

"We must go....now! It is not the sound of the great moose that we hear. Someone follows...let us make haste! This way....come!"

Hastily, Charles grabbed the bag of provisions that he had brought with him that morning and slung it over his shoulders. Josef hurriedly pulled Madeleine up on her feet. At the same time, he grabbed hold of the rather large bundle of clothes and bedding, which she had also carried up the trail with her that day. In the haste of the moment, Josef's eyes caught sight of some colorful cloth that showed through the edge of Madeleine's bundle. And while slinging the bundle over his shoulder, his mind was instantaneously reminded of what that item of bedding represented. For he had recognized it immediately as the old patchwork quilt, which was always kept at the foot of his bed. His Mama must have packed it for Madeleine before she left, he thought. As he recollected thoughts of his beloved Mama, tears instantly welled up and partially marred his sight. But he roughly brushed his shirt sleeve across his face in a hasty effort to clear up his vision.

No time for such things now, Josef reminded himself, for he well knew how much each of them needed all of their wits about them, as they hurriedly fled after Losmic. It took all their energy to keep up with the Indian, who led their way deeper into the dark forest ahead of them. Even though the tentacles of dried brambles scratched at his leggings, and low growing tree branches whipped back into his face from time to time, Charles kept pace immediately behind Losmic.

Josef, with a firm grasp on her arm, half pulled, half lifted Madeleine along the trail, close on their heels in an effort to keep up. But Madeleine was a young healthy girl and although obviously winded, kept up with the others in remarkably good form. Although breathless, she never complained once about the pace Losmic was setting— this pace which continued for what seemed to the three young people as interminable. But in reality it was only a matter of about a half hour. Then, they were stopped abruptly at the base of a large out-cropping of rock, which marred their way ahead. Regrettably, it became obvious to them, that they would have to climb over it in order to continue their flight on the other side.

Losmic quickly bid them to remain there while he went ahead and climbed upon the outcropping, trying for a series of footholds in the rock. At that moment, his three exhausted companions took the opportunity to slump down onto the thick knee high, dried weeds that grew at the base of this formidable obstacle—each trying to take advantage of the short interlude that this interruption of their flight allowed. In their half sitting, half lying position, they watched as Losmic hurriedly climbed up the outcropping, shortly disappearing over the rim.

"Get ready....for Losmic will soon reappear to help us over to the other side," Josef instructed his exhausted companions. They all strained to catch sight of the Indian high on the rim, at the same time gathering up their bundles, as they prepared to climb.

It was then, that they suddenly heard a strange voice, booming at them from behind the thick stand of trees. "Stand as you are.... our weapons are aimed at you!"

Struck numb by the sound of this strange, foreign, commanding voice, Josef stood as if frozen, except for his hand, which he motioned ever so slightly to Madeleine and Charles in an effort to bid them remain motionless.

There was a rustle of leaves and twigs, from the direction of where the voice had emanated. All three of them turned their heads slowly to peer in that direction, all the while standing tensely.... waiting. Three men could be seen carefully moving toward them, each pointing a fire arm in their direction, as once again the booming foreign voice could be heard, filling them with dread. "Thought you could escape his Majesty's justice, did ya? Well....we have you now.......and you shall pay!"

The captors just stood there for some moments, each man aiming his long gun in their direction, only a few feet from where the three Acadians waited.

In an instant, Josef sized up the three burly men, dressed in worn deerskin attire, who stood menacingly in their midst. He assumed them to be English Rangers, or at worse—bounty hunters. At that moment, he mentally recalled the warnings about the bounties to be put on any Acadians, who tried to escape, and also the bounties that were put on the heads of any Micmac Indians, who attempted to lend them aid. Immediately, thoughts of Losmic assaulted his mentality. If only Losmic will not show himself, Josef hoped, almost out loud. His eyes mirrored this alarm as he gazed over at Madeleine and Charles, who returned his terrified stare with their own.

But it was not to be, for a moment more and a frighteningly shrill cry filled the clearing where they all stood. Then, the Ranger, who had been standing nearest to the outcropping, over which the Indian had previously disappeared, dropped to the ground under the weight of Losmic. The Indian had pounced on him from above, and now frantically the two rolled over and over in the dry grass, as Losmic endeavored to bring his knife down onto the throat of the man. But the Ranger was grasping Losmic's wrist with all his might, in an effort to stop the sharp blade, which was only an inch or so from his skin.

Taking advantage of the momentary diversion, created by the life and death struggle occurring in their midst, Josef leaped for the gun held by another of the Rangers nearest to him, when the man's attention was diverted for an instant by the melee on the ground. Josef's grip on the long barrel of the gun succeeded in wrenching the weapon from him, and for a moment he felt triumphant, as he pushed his adversary to the ground and aimed the barrel at the man's head.

But his triumph was short lived, for suddenly Josef experienced a sharp pain on the back of his head, and almost immediately a dulling, foggy haziness descended over his eyes, followed by an oblivious blackness, that blotted out all consciousness, as he fell to the ground.

It seemed only a moment to Josef, but it was in reality quite a few minutes before his eyes opened and a sort of semi-consciousness was restored to him. Taking his hand away from the back of his throbbing head, where it had involuntarily rested for a moment as he regained his senses, Josef noticed that there was blood on his fingers. It was his own blood, that had apparently resulted from the glancing blow to the head, that he had sustained only minutes before. As he raised his upper body from the ground, where he had fallen, he braced himself on his elbows and endeavored to focus on the figures around him. He especially peered over in the direction of where he last remembered Madeleine to be. But what he beheld jolted his senses exceedingly, and a fierce inner rage manifested itself within his entire being, as his eyes fixed upon his beloved.

What he saw was Madeleine being pinned on the ground. Her long dark hair was strewn about her shoulders in total disarray. The front of the bodice of her dress had been torn, so that her shoulders were now exposed, and she was struggling with one hand to keep the torn cloth together in an obvious attempt to prevent further exposure. At the same time, she was trying to fight off one of the deer skin clad men, who had her on the ground, with his body kneeling over her.

She cried out in vain, as the rough hand of the man found it's way under her skirt and began to tear away at the cloth of her petticoat, that lay bunched up between her legs. She screamed as his hand pierced through the cloth and began rubbing the skin between her thighs. Then, he forcibly maneuvered his body between her now exposed legs. As he struggled to hold the girl down with one hand, his other hand was frantically engaged in loosening the belt of his trousers. Then, he roughly yanked his deer skin pants down over his loins, exposing the now unrestrained, throbbing erection that protruded from him.

As he hastily prepared to make the initial thrust between the legs of the kicking, screaming girl, who lay pinned beneath him, a sudden blow hit him from behind. Immediately, his body went limp, and he instantly laid still, half pinning Madeleine beneath him, with the full weight of his heavy unconscious form. The blow to the man's head had obviously been delivered by one of his companions, who now stood over him. He then leaned over and roughly rolled the unconscious form of the prostrate man off of the girl, muttering angrily out loud all the while.

"There will be none of that! We are here on the King's business....to do a job. There will be no raping as long as I am in charge!"

Madeleine lay for a few moments, gasping for breath, as the heavy body of her assailant was rolled off of her. And she cringed when the two massive hands of the man, who now stood over her, reached down toward her. But the words he spoke comforted her. "Fear not....Mademoiselle...no one will hurt you now!"

"Merci Monsieur....merci!" Madeleine managed to utter breathlessly, as she found herself being helped to a sitting position by the Ranger, who had just saved her from sexual attack.

Breathing heavily as a result of the exertion from the struggle, she felt that all of her strength had been sapped from her. Brushing the strands of dark hair from her face, and with head bowed, Madeleine pulled her torn clothing over her partially exposed body. She fastened her bodice together tightly, securing it as best she could to cover herself, and began struggling with what was left of the heavy homespun cloth of her petticoat and skirt, now dusty and grass stained. She hastily pulled down the ripped fabric over her torn stockings. She attempted to gather up the other items of underclothing, which lay around her in disarray, into a bundle. Then she grasped the soiled bundle to her chest, as she held her head down in humiliation.

Her shoulders began to tremble. Then, a torrent of tears made trickles down her flushed cheeks, causing tiny trails to become evident, amid the dust and scratches that now marred the beauty of her usually lovely countenance. As she sat there and sobbed unabashedly, the degradation she was feeling at that moment was permeating throughout every fiber of her body. Emotionally, she was experiencing a multitude of feelings in that instant—physical pain, hatred and rage—all of which had welled up within her. And the audible sobbing moans and groans, that she was now muttering, as a result, found release that was difficult for those around her to hear.

Josef lay there in a stunned state of mind, having beheld the hatefully violent attack on his beloved. But being physically unable to come to her aid, because of the blow he had sustained, the pain he felt was even more multiplied, leaving him dizzy and weak. However, he managed to lift his arm and weakly call to her across the clearing, where she sat sobbing.

She looked up and upon hearing him call her name, immediately she began to crawl over to where he lay on the ground. When she reached him, Josef pulled her into his arms warmly and began to stroke and kiss the disarrayed dark hair on her head, all the while murmuring words of compassion—meant only for her ears to hear—until her sobbing subsided.

Sitting there, holding his beloved, the dizziness he had been experiencing moments before appeared to subside considerably, and Josef seemed better able to focus on the activities transpiring among their captors in the clearing. Finally, his searching eyes beheld Charles, only a few feet away. He was sitting there, with his back to him. His wrists were tied together in front of him, and one of the Rangers stood over him with the barrel of the gun aimed at Charles' head. But he stared over his shoulder at Josef, with painfully dulled eyes, that were obviously filled with tears. All at once, there was an exchange of angry voices over on the other side of the clearing where Madeleine had been attacked. For the would-be rapist had regained consciousness and was angrily denouncing the leader, who had struck him, with all manner of vile language. However, the leader, who had come to Madeleine's rescue, could be heard to say.

"I told you we would have none of that, Samuel! Our job is to take them in....that is all!"

But the offending man was still defiant, as he rubbed his head and remarked. "Aye, but so what if we have some sport with the women first? That one is a virgin too, I will wager....and ripe for the pickin'. You can have her first if that is what you want....I will take her after you finish! What say ye, William? After all....I agreed not to scalp them, did I not? You know, we could probably get a handy bounty reward for that one over there....maybe as much as thirty pounds sterling even...maybe twenty-five each for the boy and the girl!"

"No Samuel," was the answer from the leader. "We will turn them in with the others we caught....and that is all I will say on the matter. Be content with the Indian's scalp...it will bring a good return!"

Upon hearing these words, Josef's eyes frantically darted all around the clearing in search of his Indian friend. "Where is he?" Josef whispered to Madeleine. But almost before the words had left his lips, he caught sight of something familiar hanging from a Ranger's belt. Almost instantly, a groan left his lips, as he recognized the beaded head band that was always worn by his friend. Then, he also noticed, secured to the belt, a clump of long black braided hair, matted on one end and attached to the head band. "No...no....it cannot be!" Josef cried out in dismay.

"Be still Josef," Madeleine whispered in his ear, as she held him close to her. "It is true....they killed and scalped Losmic, during the time you were unconscious. Charles tried to stop them...but he is but a boy and no match for them. They overpowered him and then the mean one came at me, like an animal! Be grateful Josef that you were unconscious and did not see it all happen!"

"Oh Madeleine...he could have saved himself...he did not have to die!" Josef lamented, with a voice that quivered and eyes that reflected the pain of his loss.

"Losmic looked upon you as his brother, Josef....how could he have done less, than try to save you?" Madeleine replied, whispering close to Josef's ear, so as not to be overheard by their Ranger captors, who were still standing over there, arguing with each other. "Now, you must pull yourself together, dear one. Losmic would have wanted you to go on. Charles and I need your strength more than ever. For what will become of us at the hands of such men?"

Josef pondered her words that seemed to penetrate into the depths of his great despair. But his mentality was so wounded, over the traumatic loss of Losmic, that it was difficult to search his pained consciousness for the words with which to answer her. However, it was to no avail, for the shock of all that had just transpired was far too fresh for him to render any rational plan of action. He needed time to sort out his feelings and pull himself together. But such a healing lapse of time was not to be his for the moment, as the words of the man, called William, who was apparently the leader of that motley group of captors, spoke out authoritatively, commanding the attention of all within earshot.

"Let us depart from here now! Samuel...untie that one over there so he and the girl can help the injured one to walk. But mind you, guard them well, and no funny business, Samuel! We have much distance to cover if we expect to get to the transports before they set sail on tomorrow's tide. If we make haste, we can rendezvous with Bradford's group further down the mountain. No doubt, his men will have collected a few more of these Acadians to turn in.... so, we can travel together to the ships. Campbell....take the rear and see to it that no one lags behind. Now....let us be on our way!"

The last words pronounced by this Ranger leader had scarce left his mouth, before those in his party began hurriedly rushing about, making preparations to depart as commanded. Two of them roughly assisted Josef to his feet and directed Madeleine and Charles to support him on either side, so that they could all be on their way. One of the Rangers was appointed to help carry some of their bundles—all that remained of their worldly goods—on his back, so that the pair could better direct all of their energies to helping still groggy Josef, to keep to the path they now traveled.

Thus this shabby group of armed men began the rugged trek, down the mountainside, forcibly escorting their unwilling Acadian prisoners downward, toward the low dike country......and to the waiting ships.

REPLICAS of Acadian wagons and carts, of the type used at the time of the 1755 expulsion, are pictured here on the grounds of the Church of St. Charles at Grand Pre, Nova Scotia--as seen in September 1979.

CHAPTER - 7

DEPARTURE

He dreaded another of these days! Even though his military training dictated that this was a necessary operation, somewhere deep down in the depths of his being the nagging dilemma still persisted. No matter how hard he tried to discipline his mental thinking and dismiss such thoughts, Lt. Colonel John Winslow's conscience burdened him. Because it manifested feelings of injustice in regard to this entire Acadian Expulsion operation.

But the operation was necessary, he repeatedly reminded himself mentally, for someday everyone would look back on this entire thing and realize that it was all for the best. At that moment, Winslow was reminded of his very own words, in regard to banishing the French Neutrals from the province. For these were written in his own hand within his journal not long before– "If we accomplish this expulsion, it will have been one of the greatest deeds the English in America have ever achieved".

His mind was filled with all of this and more, as he stood on the grassy dike that rimmed the shore of the Minas Basin near Grand Pre. He was some distance from where the large group of Acadians and their scanty belongings waited on the shore. As Winslow peered over at the current crowd of despondent men, women and children, who had been congregated to await the next long boats from the ships anchored out in the basin, his thoughts wandered.

This scene, that he now beheld, had become a familiar one during the countless hours that had transpired in recent days. It seemed to him, that this unsavory task would never end. For daily, countless long boats made the trips to one ship or another, out in the basin, loaded with groups of Acadian people and their belongings. And then return empty to the shore, in order to take on more people to be transported. But there were always more, with the end not yet in sight!

John Winslow was supervising the entire operation from the temporary camp, set up in a rye field only a few yards within the last dike. He was happy to note, that everything was going smoothly so far. Of course, there was the ever present emotional outbursts from an occasional man, woman or child, who inadvertently became separated and was placed on a long boat, bound for a ship other than the one his kin had been embarked on. Also, there was no closing one's ears to the sobbing and wailing of so many of these people, who were so loathed to leave the only land they had ever known. But this was to be expected, Winslow thought, and had to be endured.

He realized that this was unfortunate, but unavoidable, considering the hundreds of people being expelled upon each sailing tide. But this did not make their pleas and beseeching sobs any easier to dismiss from his—or his soldier's—mentality each time a separated Acadian had to be restrained at bayonet point in a particular long boat. This had happened several times, whenever one Acadian was ordered on a different long boat, than that which held the rest of his family. Of course, these problems were to be expected, during such a large embarkation as this. He and his men quite simply had to become hardened to such things and consider the overall picture, while dismissing these individual situations.

Making a mental note of the latest long boats being filled, Winslow hurried over to his command tent, which was located about a yard from the dike where he had been standing. For it was almost time to deliver the latest sealed dispatch from Governor Lawrence to the Captain of the next transport, now being loaded and presently scheduled to depart on the tide.

It was Lawrence's instruction that this sealed notification was to be handed to the various Masters of the vessels, who would thereby be informed as to their destinations. These sailing orders also included a letter, addressed to the Governor of the Province or Commander in Charge where each shipload of these Acadians would be put on shore. Winslow, being a thorough man, felt a particular obligation, to see that these important papers were personally and properly conveyed to the various Masters of the transports, whenever the ships became filled to capacity with their unwilling human cargo.

Once within his tent, he shuffled through the stack of sealed communiqués, still remaining to be delivered to ship's Masters. Winslow fingered the one on top thoughtfully, recalling from his previous instructions that this particular directive would order this next ship's commander to the Colony of Maryland. Of course, the ship's Captain would not know of this destination until he was ready to sail. It would be at this time that the sealed order would be opened by him. It was the same procedure as followed on the other ships that had already set sail, destined for Massachusetts and Virginia, if he remembered correctly. But this one now loading would be the first ship, so far, directed to Maryland. All at once, Winslow smiled, for he could not help but marvel at the efficiency of this operation, and of the shrewdness of Governor Lawrence's expulsion plan, that was going along just as planned.

However, some distance away at the base of the same dike upon which Winslow had just stood, surveying the mass of Acadian humanity that was gathered there, things were less than efficient.

For huddled close to the red mud shore and the marsh grass that lined the narrow inlets, upon which the long boats had repeatedly transported their human cargo at each high tide, dismay reigned supreme.

As Seaman Cobb helped maneuver the long boat into one of the narrow inlets, steering it in the direction of the assembled group of Acadians on the shore, he heaved a sigh of resignation. For it was proving to be a very long, taxing day. Indeed, this would make the fourth trip that day, to and from the ship whereupon he served. With each trip, it continued to be an emotionally draining experience. But not because of the work involved for him and others, who manned this boat. More specifically, it was because of the emotional outbursts of despair from so many of the men, women and children, who were being delivered to the waiting ship. Their pleas and entreaties were taking a great toll on all of the young seamen, who worked the long boats that day. This continual stress was increasing their nervous uneasiness, in regard to each group of Acadians they ferried to the vessel. He became lost in deep thought, as he remembered the sweet motherly Acadian lady, who was in the group that they had only just delivered to the ship. He was amazed that this woman, who was being forcibly expelled from the only land she had ever known, could be compassionate in his regard. For he remembered her words exactly, as she sat next to him in the crowded long boat, having resigned herself to this plight.

"How are you holding up, my son?"

"I can only do my duty…as ordered. But thank you for asking." He replied, as he marveled at her compassion for the discomfort of his splitting headache that must have been obvious to her.

Then there was the young Acadian woman, with a tiny baby, who could not have been more than a week old. An older woman—obviously the girl's mother—sat at her side, with an arm around the young mother's shoulders, as the baby cried softly. He overheard her remark to her daughter.

"Poor little babe....she must be hungry. Don't worry, my dear, we will soon be on the ship. Perhaps it will be the same vessel that your husband and Papa were imprisoned on for so long. God grant that it will be so....and we can all be together again."

"But Mama, what if it is not the same ship?" Cobb could not help but overhear the young woman cry out loudly to her Mama. "Then we will be alone....and this poor child will never know his own Papa in this world!" To which her Mama replied.

"We can only pray, my dear, that God will be merciful to us...." her Mama murmured, as she strained her eyes in the direction of the ship that lay over the water still some yards away. As she spoke, she fingered her obviously well-worn rosary beads, all the while uttering non-distinguishable words of prayer under her breath.

Seaman Cobb remembered being overcome with compassion, and he turned away from the two women and stared down into the water that with every pull on his oar lapped at the hull of the long boat foaming each time it rippled off of the port side.

Perhaps only two or three more trips and the ship will be ready to sail, he thought. There were already enough people on board two trips ago, he had observed. But still they had been instructed to bring more and more. Such a number will far exceed the amount of passengers for which that transport was designed. He pondered this fact, as he shuddered when thinking about what would lay ahead on the voyage yet to come, and the deprivations which would certainly lay in store for those on so crowded a vessel. True, the provisioning of the transports, with supplies for the coming voyage, had been done days before beginning the task of forcibly taking on board these people. But that ship's store would certainly not be sufficient for the large number of people, who—as it turns out—will be sailing on the ship. He well recalled that the provisions loaded on board were meant for a far smaller number than even those, who were already on board.

Of course, Seaman Cobb speculated that when it came right down to how the provisions would be distributed during the trip, the ship's crew would no doubt not be the ones who would be deprived. Rather, this plight of deprivation would befall the Acadian passengers, who were there against their will, and consequently would be considered to be expendable. These thoughts were distasteful to Cobb, for he realized only too well that his conscience would be heavily taxed to it's limitations, when it came time to daily observe the suffering of women and children on board throughout the voyage to come.

Perhaps the voyage will be a short one, Cobb hoped. After all, not even the Captain yet knows where this ship is bound, so maybe the distance will not be too great. For it was his belief that the mental well being of the entire crew would be at stake, especially if this voyage turned out to be a long one.

With a jolt, the long boat knifed into the red mud of the marsh inlet, instantly interrupting Cobb from his thoughts. The long boat's bow had hit shore, only a few feet from the outer perimeter of the crowd of Acadians on shore, where some sat on the grass of the dikes. Others stood along the red mud shore, amid the meager bundles and provisions that represented all that they were allowed to take on board. Some paced up and down on the mud bank, while others sat dejectedly amid their bundles. A number—both men and women—cried softly with heaving shoulders that shuddered with each sob, while some prayed audibly, interjecting an occasional outburst shouted upwards at the gray, foreboding sky, presumably aimed at their God in particular. At best, the scene was one of emotional chaos, but order was maintained by the bayonet-wielding soldiers, who stood guard over the disheveled group on the shore.

Antoine Gautreaux stepped back hastily in an effort to make room for the seamen, who had jumped out of the long boat that had only a moment before stuck fast in the red mud of the shore. Antoine had been standing there, a few feet apart from the group of Acadians who waited on the slope of the dike. His wooden shoes were coated with the red mud of the shore. Because he had paced along the bank, closer to the tidal stream over which he had been observing this same long boat making numerous trips back and forth to a particular ship, out in the deep water. Now, he hurriedly climbed back a few feet up the grassy dike to where the rest of what remained of his family waited.

He covered the short distance to the spot where his wife and young son sat huddled together, at the edge of the larger group of people, who waited there. At that moment, he was startled upon hearing his name being called, loudly amid the noise of the assembled crowd. Turning at once in the direction from whence the greeting came, Gautreaux's eyes scanned the faces of the numerous individuals that made up the group in his midst. He searched the crowd of Acadians, in an effort to see a familiar face. Then suddenly, his face took on an expression of recognition and a broad smile instantly brightened his features. Shouting out loudly, he directed his acknowledgement in reply, as he strived to be heard above the din of voices, all the while pushing his way through the crowd.

"Bonjour...my friend, Josef!"

"Antoine....Antoine...we never expected to see you again," was the reply from Josef Theriot, who struggled up from the spot where he had been sitting, in order to grasp the approaching Antoine's shoulders in greeting. "Mama told us that you had all left before the English could take you! What happened to you?"

"What you say is true, Josef," replied Antoine, somewhat out of breath as he also greeted Charles and Madeleine, whose faces both became illuminated with broad smiles upon seeing such a familiar acquaintance. "We did leave before the soldiers could even detain the men in our family....all of us....Mama, Papa, my two brothers and little sister, Marie, as well as my wife and son. We wanted to stay together as a family and have no one separate us. But it all went wrong."

"Go on, Antoine," Josef urged, as he noted the sudden sadness that came over his friend's face. "What happened to everyone?" Antoine blinked back tears, as he answered.

"My wife, Therese, and baby son, are over there....but they are all that remains of my family. The others became separated from us in the dark woods of the mountain, while we were being chased by the English. They had come across our hiding place unexpectedly, and all of us fled as fast as we could, but in opposite directions. The soldiers caught we three....and brought us here to be put on the ship.....but I do not know what became of the rest of my family."

"Oh Antoine...I am so sorry, but thank God you still have your wife and child," Madeleine implored, looking over at his saddened face, as she patted his arm. "We too have been separated from the rest of our family, but we still have each other...and for that I thank God! Come...let us go over and sit with Therese and the baby."

Gathering up their bundles, they made way over to the edge of the crowd of people, where Antoine's wife and son waited. Together, they all sat and talked softly, each relating the tale of woe, that had befallen them since they had last met. However, their reunion was to be short lived, for only minutes more and the soldiers directed the crowd, at the points of fixed bayonets, to make ready to board the next long boat that waited against the shore.

Everyone moved as best they could, but the boarding went slowly, as women, children and old people had to be helped into the boat. When it came time for Madeleine, Charles and Josef to board, they stepped in, seated themselves and pushed close together with their bundles, in order to make room for the Gautreauxs', who were behind them in line.

Antoine had just stepped into the boat and was reaching out to Therese and the baby, to help them into the vessel. At that moment, a soldier, who had been keeping count of those boarding, approached and grabbed Antoine's wife by the arm in a forceful manner, ordering her in no uncertain terms.

- 88 -

"This boat is full....you will have to wait for the next one!"

"NO! No....she is my wife....there is room! Here...she and the baby can sit on my lap....they will not take up much room," Antoine screamed out in alarm, as he clutched at the sleeve of her dress. But two soldiers were pulling Therese back on shore, away from the boat, while almost at the same moment another soldier struck Antoine across the side of his head with his fist, causing him to fall back onto the laps of Josef and Charles, both of whom had also been endeavoring to reason with the soldiers, as were most of the people, who were already on board.

At that moment, an elderly man, who had been seated at the rear of the vessel, stood up and raised his fist at the soldiers, shouting aloud above the countless alarmed voices that had been raised in answer to the tragic separation that was taking place in their midst.

"Take me.....let me go on the next boat! Put the woman and child aboard....they can sit in my place!" But the man's entreaties were to no avail. For the soldier in command of the shore party gave the order, and the long boat pulled away from the marsh grass rimmed shore, as the oars dug into the muddy water of the tidal stream.

"Oh God!" Screamed Madeleine, raising her arms to the sky. "Do not let this happen...Jesus, my dear Jesus...help them!"

Josef reached out and drew Madeleine to him. Her sobs, muffled against his sleeve could scarcely be heard among the loud din and wailing of those in the boat. Charles sat silently amid the melee, stroking the unconscious head of Antoine, as the paddles plied the vessel out toward the bay. But somehow, Charles could not look away from the shore, for his eyes remained as if glued in the direction of the figure of Therese on the bank. She was still screaming and clutching the baby to her with one arm, while the other arm was reaching out toward the boat beseechingly. By now, the long boat was some yards from the shore, and it was obvious that the soldiers no longer held her back, since the boat was out of reach. However, as soon as they released her, she could be seen wadding knee deep out into the muddy water, all the while her cries and screams were aimed out toward the long boat, which was now entering the bay waters.

Nevertheless, she could still be heard above the moans and sobs, coming from those in the long boat. It seemed like an eternity to Charles, until finally—mercifully—her entreaties were out of earshot, and she could be heard no more. But still she was seen on the shore, wadding up and down in the water, now appearing to be no more than a tiny figure off in the distance.

Charles swallowed deliberately in an attempt to stifle the emotion that had welled up inside of him. His throat felt constricted as he choked uncontrollably, allowing the stifled tears to rush down his cheeks. But his tears went unnoticed amid the emotional voices on board, as he struggled to tear his attention away from that last glimpse of the smoke shrouded shore of his homeland, where the almost unrecognizable figure of Therese, way off on that distant shore, could still be seen.

He forced his eyes away from that distant pathetic figure and stared down in defeat at Antoine, who still lay unconscious across their laps, as he remarked to Josef . "How fortunate.... that Antoine was spared this final pathetic sight of Therese and the child!"

Josef considered his brother's words for a moment, silently nodding his head in sad agreement. He could feel the continuing trembling of Madeleine, who was still crying softly against his shoulder. Pulling the heavy homespun shawl up around her shoulders he made an effort to ward off the chilling effect of the autumn air. Then, he turned to look back toward the shore, and the dike country that had always been his home.

Everything looked so different to him. Indeed, it was difficult for him to comprehend the meaning of it all. For only weeks before, those same dikes he now beheld had been decorated with the lacy whites, golden yellows and delicate lilac hues of blooming Fall wild flowers, that had swayed in the pleasant breezes from the Minas Basin. Now, a hazy fog was drifting in from the direction of distant Cape Blomidon across the bay, adding another dreary shade of gray to the already depressing atmosphere. It seemed to Josef, that the very elements were conspiring to set a distressingly dark backdrop for the tragedy that was taking place in his homeland.

The sky had been overcast for days, with low hanging gray clouds as far as the eye could see. The air hinted of winter weather with a penetrating cold, which added to the misery of those in the long boat, and always there was the ever-present dingy smoke hovering over the land and the sea. This was from the smoldering ruins of buildings that had been put to the torch by the English. Still, there had been more smoke everyday from the countless fires that were being set to the farms beyond the dikes.

He cursed under his breath, recalling the appalling sights that he, Madeleine and Charles had observed as they were forcibly escorted through Grand Pre, by their captors, who were taking them to meet the long boats. His heart sank, as he realized that no longer could the tall spire of the Church of St. Charles be seen by anyone. Only the blackened burned out ruins remained of their beloved edifice. He remembered how he had strained in the direction of the family farm in an effort to perhaps catch sight of the house still standing. But it was too far off on the horizon to tell. Besides, he had reminded himself that it was pointless to be concerned, for if the farm had not been put to the torch, then it would probably be occupied by English farmers in a short time. Besides, deep down he knew that he would never see it again.

All at once, a thought struck him! What of his little sister's young cow, "Mademoiselle"? She had so wanted him to save it for her. All at once, a wave of emotion swept over him, as thoughts of his Mama, Papa and sisters surged forth. He had deliberately tried not to think of them. For the English had come for them some days ago, and there was no way of knowing where they had been taken on the ships.

All of a sudden, the degree of this sadness was too much for him! And he buried his head in his hands and moaned audibly as the emotions that he had been holding back suddenly surged forth in a torrent of tears. It was the tears of so much grief, that had become too much of a burden for him to carry within any longer. Thus, he cried unabashedly until the long boat reached the ship.

TIDAL STREAMS are shown here, separating the Acadian dikes from the waters of the Minas Basin. It was through similar tidal streams at high tide, that the expelled Acadians were taken onto the long boats and rowed to the ships, anchored out in the Basin.

CHAPTER - 8

WEIGHING ANCHOR

The cabin seemed more cramped than ever to Edward Phillips, as he pondered his particular place in time. But then, thought he, these quarters are no smaller than a Master's cabin on any transport this size. And soon this six foot by seven foot space will probably become the most spacious place on board for a long time to come.

Yes, decided Captain Phillips, this same cramped cabin will no doubt be coveted in a short while by the very mass of humanity that is even now milling about on deck. However this vessel was never built for ferrying human cargo in such a manner.

Phillips, a silver haired man of slight build, frowned as he studied the charts laid out before him. In the dim light afforded from the one open porthole, he squinted at the ship's layout that was set forth in lines and designations on the parchment before him. How often, Phillips reflected, had he gone over and over this vessel's diagram, which depicted cargo holds, crew's quarters, galley and every other possible space on the transport, in an effort to take in every inch of the less than 100 foot length of the vessel. This was in an effort to designate quarters for the exorbitant number of Acadian passengers, whom he had been ordered to transport.

However, no matter how often he studied these plans, one fact of life remained clear to him as Master of this vessel. There was just not enough room for the large group of men, women and children now on board!

Indeed, he pondered to himself, it will be a difficult voyage, and at this point no one knew how long a journey it would be. As yet, their destination was still unknown, for the sailing orders had not been delivered on board. But Phillips speculated that these would be shortly forthcoming, since the last long boat had only just delivered the final group of people, designated for this ship.

Well, it could not be too soon for him, thought Phillips. Indeed, this entire campaign was getting tiresome, especially so during the last few days when he had gone ashore. For it seemed to him that the situation was getting more and more distasteful each time he observed the operation. It was bad enough having to see so much misery among these unfortunate people. But there seemed to be no end to the number of Acadians being removed from this province. Each new day brought a different group of old people, babies, children, men and women to the shore. And their faces had all merged into one disdainful countenance in his mind. Most of the time, he had endeavored to look away from them whenever he observed the crowds. After all, this entire expedition was unpleasant enough, without having to look upon all of those expressions of misery, day end and day out.

But apart from the human element, what bothered Edward Phillips the most was the waste he observed everywhere. This made him wonder secretly as to the wisdom of a plan that made no provisions for the care of livestock and perfectly sturdy structures that were being needlessly destroyed. For everyday on shore, there were more barns, farm houses and structures of every kind being put to the torch. Yes, with the dawning of each day, the sky seemed ever darkened with the drifting smoke of some new destructive fire, that just added to the already dreary dark haze from previous days, that hung in the air like a shroud of destruction.

Why, he also remembered seeing the burnt out charred remains of what had been a very substantial looking church building only days before. In his logical mind, this went against all reason. Granted, he agreed that the Acadians should be replaced with English farmers, since they insisted on being so stubborn. But what need was there to destroy those perfectly good structures, that could be put to good use by new tenants.

However, what appalled him the most, Phillips concluded was the abominable manner—or lack of manner—in which the unattended livestock was being treated. There was no question in his mind that the Acadians had been excellent farmers, for one had only to observe their fields, lush with partially harvested grain, their bountiful gardens and the healthy livestock on every farm. The pity of it all is that they would not cooperate with English authority. For they might have spared themselves all of this pain. But those Acadians insisted on bringing all of this upon themselves, and they were probably getting what they deserve. Still, should not the Crown make good use of their produce and animals, rather than allowing such waste?

The answer to this still escaped him. Had he not seen for himself ashore the extent of this neglect? For everywhere fat healthy cows wandered about moaning woefully, as their utters were swelled past capacity. Because there was no one to milk them. Many of the cattle had broken through fences into the fields, and were eating the yet to be harvested wheat. From one farm to another in this diked country, horses could be observed running free in herds amid the fields. There were goats, as well as cows, standing—from habit— each evening at their usual milking places, near burned down farm houses, waiting in vain to be milked. Pigs could be heard, squealing from hunger, still enclosed in pens around blackened ruins of what had been barns. Oxen, still hooked to the yoke, bellowed for someone to set them free. And in frustration, many of these oxen could be seen running into the marsh, in an effort to escape the yokes and carts, which were still attached to their bodies.

Phillips shuddered upon being reminded of several oxen that had overturned their carts and tumbled down the dikes into the red marsh mud, and lay there with broken bodies, at which point only death could free them from their miseries. The entire thing was abominable, he thought to himself. For to see pigs, that had broken through their pens, rooting up vegetable gardens, and laden fruit trees standing amid rotting fruit on the ground, was difficult to view. What's more, to see fields—as far as the eye could see—still remaining lush with partially reaped grain, went against all good reason. He moaned in frustration every time he beheld such waste, and it had become so distasteful to him, that he had ceased to go ashore. Instead, he had kept to his cabin most of the time, during the last couple of days, only going on deck when his supervision was absolutely necessary.

But now, that these same decks were crowded with all of those forlorn Acadians, he dreaded having to look at them most of all. Yes, he decided, those sailing orders could not come soon enough for him, in order to hasten the day when his human cargo would be delivered, and there would be an end to this terrible experience.

Just then, there was an abrupt knock at the cabin door, whereupon Captain Phillips without even looking up from the charts that now held his attention, commanded entry.

The door was promptly opened by a youthful, uniformed man, who stood stiffly at attention with an extended hand that held a packet of obviously important documents. "Captain....the sailing orders have just been delivered to the ship," spoke the young man. "I was requested to bring these to you immediately."

"Thank you," replied Phillips, as he accepted the packet from him. "That will be all." Then, he lost no time, opening the packet, so impatient was he to learn where the vessel was ordered to proceed. There were two documents within. One was addressed to him, as

Master of the vessel, and the other was addressed to the Governor or Commander in Chief of the Colony of Maryland. Immediately, he opened the one meant for him, and read hurriedly.

It was from Halifax, dated August 1755, and it read as follows: "When the people assigned to your vessel are embarked, you will proceed to the Colony of Maryland and see that the passengers be put on shore there. By way of route, your ship will join those from Shepoudie and Cobequid in the Basin des Mines, and proceed together past Cape Blomidon into the Baye Francoise, joining any ships there that have proceeded from Beaubassin. You will sail together to the south and your appointed individual destination, as ordered. After proceeding accordingly to the destination appointed you, and upon your arrival immediately wait upon the Governor or Commander in Chief of the Colony of Maryland, to which you are bound by the enclosed letter. And make all possible dispatch, after debarking your passengers to obtain certificates thereto agreeable. As Master of said vessel, you will be careful and watchful as possible during the whole course of the voyage, to prevent the passengers from making any attempt to seize upon the vessel by allowing only a small number to be upon the decks at a time and by using all other necessary precautions to prevent the bad consequences of such attempt. Be particularly careful, that the passengers have carried no arms or other offensive weapons on board with them at the time of embarkment."

Phillips was thoughtful for a moment, as he absorbed the last words of the communique, that he held in his hands. All at once, a feeling of alarm stirred him to action, as he remembered the crowd of Acadians still on deck, and the warning that he had just read. Hastily, he deposited the packet of sailing orders amid the ship's charts, and hurriedly proceeded out of the cabin door.

Making a mental note, as he gingerly fingered the keys in his pocket, he satisfied himself that the arms chest keys were safely in his possession. But he proceeded below decks anyway, to double check the lock on the arms chest, which was located just below the main hatchway. For it held the ship's store of cutlasses, muskets, ammunition and bayonets. Following this, Phillips emerged on deck, where he was joined by First Mate Thomas. Together, they surveyed the despondent crowd of Acadians milling about on the main deck.

The Captain raised his arms in an effort to get the attention of this noisy mass of people, and to obtain some semblance of order from the crowd. However, his shouts went almost unheard above the noise on deck. And it took some minutes before the armed guards, who surrounded the crowd, could maintain order—albeit while brandishing their bayonets threateningly. With this use of force, finally, all eyes were directed up in the direction of the Captain, who now attempted to address the group.

"My name is Captain Edward Phillips. I am the master of this vessel, and if you will be silent, I will attempt to address you. Your presence on this ship has resulted from your own undoing. As a result, you are to be transported to another land far from here, where you will be put ashore in order that you may make another life for yourselves. Accommodations below decks are not adequate for your large number, so many of you will occupy—as best you can—areas within the hold of this ship. You will be allowed only certain rations each day, and only a small number of you at a time will be permitted on deck during this voyage. There will be armed guards on duty at all times....so any attempt at seizing this vessel will be treated as an unforgivable crime against the Crown. And it will result in the immediate death of the perpetrators. Your cooperation is expected during this voyage.....and anyone caught stealing rations while on board will be put in chains until we reach port. As yet, I am not at liberty to divulge your destination to you. But it is of no consequence, since you are bound for such place as his Majesty's government deems expedient, whether it is to your liking or not. So, I say to you, cooperate and this voyage will be less difficult....make trouble and you will suffer the consequences!"

With this, he turned to his First Officer, and addressed him thusly: "Make sure all of the passengers and their possessions are settled below decks, as this ship is set to sail at once!" Then he turned and went back to his cabin.

———————

Sea birds, setting up their usual constant chatter, soared just above the ship's mast. An occasional curious gull swooped low just over the heads of the Acadians on deck. But for the most part, these people paid no heed to these feathered creatures, being preoccupied as they were with matters of their own.

But Charles Theriot's eyes were fixed on the birds, as he leaned against the ship's starboard rail. For these birds reminded him of the countless times he had whiled away the hours, sitting on the dikes when he was younger. Of course, those times seemed far removed from him now. For it was as though his youth had been abruptly snatched from him prematurely, in light of the many traumatic events he had experienced since then. Only the birds remained constant and unperturbed about it all, Charles observed. As usual, they were going about their daily business, oblivious to the human misery in their midst.

He was reminded of the many flocks of chattering shore birds that he had watched so often, as they fed on small marine creatures left by the receding tide on the mud flats around Grand Pre. Charles recalled vividly how the high tide, or the "marees les plus hautes", as his Papa used to say, would drive the feeding birds, with their long beaks and long legs, to seek the dry sanctuary of the higher beaches. There they could be observed, resting and preening, until the water receded once again. Then, they would fly back out to the salt mud flats and repeat the cycle all over again. He dwelled on these things, and wondered if there would be birds similar to these in the new land, where they were bound. Silently, he decided to himself, that sea birds were probably much the same wherever only salt ocean lapped against any shore.

Shifting position and straightening up as best he could, Charles felt somewhat confined, being crowded as he was against the ship's rail by the mass of people on deck. Now that the Acadians on deck had just heard the words of the transport's Captain, they were trying to understand the orders that were issued—both in French and English—by the ship's officers, who were attempting to direct them to designated quarters below deck. However, Charles was in no hurry to go below, for he wanted to relish in as much time as possible, gazing off toward the Grand Pre shore, which was well off the starboard side of the ship. He knew only too well that this sight would probably be his last glimpse of home.

All at once, thoughts of home flooded his consciousness and remembrances of Mama, Papa and his sisters took hold of him. Poor little Ednee, he thought, who indeed would take care of her very own cow, that is no longer her own.....and what of the family? Where had they been taken? No one seemed to know. Certainly no one in the crowd that had been congregated on shore, from whence they had just come, seemed to have any news of the Jean Theriot family. Charles was particularly aware of this fact, since he had spent hours going from one to another, inquiring about them while he, Madeleine and Josef, had waited on shore to be taken on the ship.

It was true, as Charles reasoned; they had been taken away some time before, and had probably been embarked on board a ship just shortly thereafter. So, if this was the case, it would seem that little hope remained in regard to learning anything about which ship and which destination had been their destiny. He did, however, find comfort in the thought that the family may have possibly had the good fortune of being sent to the same shore for which this ship was destined. So, for him, there was still hope, and he wasn't about to give up. After all, how many destinations can there be for these ships? Charles would keep this in mind each day, and include this request in his prayers every night. For maybe it was the good Lord's plan to allow the family to be reunited in the new land.

Just then, he was disturbed from his day dreaming, as Josef nudged his arm, making sign for him to assist with the bundles. Apparently, they had just been appointed to their quarters, during the time that he had spent obliviously lost in thought.

"Would you carry this for us?" Requested Madeleine, as she leaned over and directed Charles' attention to what appeared to be a cradle at his feet.

Madeleine had struck up a conversation with two women, during the time they had waited on deck to be assigned below and the cradle belonged to the young girl, about Madeleine's age, with whom she had been conversing. The girl's features were delicate, with large brown eyes dominating her lovely young face. She was of small frame, but gave the impression of possessing much inner strength. And she was quite obviously large with child. Her name was Louisa LeBlanc, and she was accompanied by her mother, Madame Anastasie Trahan. When asked where her husband was, Madeleine was saddened to hear that Batiste LeBlanc, her husband, and Albert Trahan, her Papa, had been members of the delegation of mediators, from the River Cannard area, who had gone to Halifax some time before and had never returned. Madeleine could relate to such a sad tale, as her sister's intended had never returned from there, either!

"When the order came for us to proceed to the ships Mama and I did not want to leave without Batiste and Papa, so we packed a cart and ran off into the countryside, where Mama's sister lived," Louisa had related to Madeleine and Josef. "We had hoped to be forgotten in the confusion by the English....and we were too....for a time. But they discovered us, hiding in Aunt Marie's barn, after

they had come to take that family away also. So, now we are here....
and Mama is in poor health. She has been so saddened since being
separated from Papa....that I fear for her!"

Louisa's big brown eyes, which had been so full of sparkle a
moment before, suddenly spilled over with tears that ran down over
her cheeks. But she collected her emotions in short order and began
the business of gathering up what bundles she could carry, and at
the same time, leaned over to help her Mama up from the deck
where Madame Trahan had been sitting since they came on board.

"Oh...do be careful with it," exclaimed Louisa, pointing to the
cradle that Charles had just picked up. "I had not the heart to leave
it. Batiste made it for the baby with his own two hands....and it may
be all that his child will ever know of him!"

"Look Josef," Madeleine cried excitedly, running her hand over
the smooth surface of the wooden object that had stood next to
the cradle. "How wonderful, Madame Trahan....you managed to
bring your small spinning wheel too! I just know it will be most
useful....I had to leave my spinning wheel....and Papa had made it
for me, to be part of my trousseau!"

Madeleine forced herself to put such thoughts out of her head
and to direct her attention to the present—and to the matters at
hand. There was no time for such reminiscing now, thought she.
We must get on with what is to be and make the most of it. Had
not the officer in charge directed them to go below with all haste?
The vessel was putting on full sail, preparing to enter into the vast
ocean, so it would be best if they were settled below decks as soon
as possible.

But the process of movement for the large number of people on
deck was slow, since so many had to climb down the ladder one at
a time, and then be directed to their assigned space below. Madame
Trahan had to be assisted when it came time for her to climb down,
so weak was she. And of course, Louisa needed help also, so large
was she with child.

Josef looked back on deck, in an effort to make sign for Antoine Gautreaux to join them. But since regaining consciousness on board the ship, Antoine had not been himself, and of course it was to be expected. In fact, so despondent was he, since regaining consciousness and suffering the despair that came with the realization that his wife and baby had been left on shore, no one could get through to him. He would just stand there stiffly, clutching the starboard rail, squinting off into the distance searching for some sight of another long boat approaching the ship. But they had been on the last boat to reach this ship; no other was coming. However, Antoine refused to accept this and continued to strain his eyes toward the distant shore unrelentingly. When it came time, Josef had tried to urge him to join their group below, but Antoine would not move from his place against the rail. Indeed, he could not even be forced away, so tight was his grip on the ship's rail. So, Josef had decided that this task would have to be left for the soldiers to accomplish, as he had done all that he could to try and persuade his friend to go below.

This distressed Josef exceedingly, but he had no recourse. He so yearned to help his friend. But in Antoine's despondency, he simply would not cooperate. Apparently, Antoine had become disoriented as a result of the dismay and sorrow that consumed him. Thus, only the use of force would succeed in extricating him from his place at the ship's rail. Of course, this situation weighed heavy in Josef's mind, as he handed down their last bundle of clothing to Charles, who grasped it from his perch on the hatchway ladder, while in the process of transferring their only possessions—one bundle at a time— downward into Madeleine's waiting hands.

Suddenly, there were shouts on deck and Josef instinctively directed his attention to where Antoine had been standing. But he could no longer catch sight of his friend. Instead, he saw two guards leaning over the rail shouting and gesticulating wildly. Everyone, who was still on deck, rushed to peer over the rail, where Antoine had apparently jumped, when the guards came for him.

Josef also ran over and anxiously leaned over the rail as far as he could, in an effort to see his friend in the water. But he could not catch sight of him.

"What has happened here?" Shouted one of the ship's officers, as he pushed his way through the crowd that had gathered against the rail.

"It is an Acadian man, Sir...." replied one of the guards excitedly. "He climbed over the rail and jumped when we tried to make him go below....he came up once and tried to swim...but he went under again!" At this, the ship's officer shrugged his shoulders and remarked.

"Well, it is no matter....he cannot possibly make to any shore.... we are too far out. Disperse these people...and get them below!"

With this last order, the officer pushed his way past the exited Acadians, who were still hugging the rail. Josef lingered there also, among the crowd of others, who were straining to catch sight of Antoine in the water. But the surface ripples, lapping against the ship's side far below, remained undisturbed and gave no sign of the splashing of a life or death struggle. It was as though Antoine had been swallowed up in the depths of the water—never to be seen again in this world.

But who knows, thought Josef, as he allowed himself to be herded below decks with the remaining Acadians, after observing this drama. Perhaps Antoine, who had always been a strong swimmer, will make it to a shore. In his mind, Josef knew the chances were slim to none. But in his heart, he wanted to believe that he would make it!

Two days had past, since they were last up on deck. Two days, that seemed to them more like two months—down there in the deepest bowels of the ship. It was a dreary place, where the sounds and movements of the ship were constantly evident, as it ploughed it's way upon the surface of the sea. They were down there—in the hold, where the cargo was usually carried. It was damp and cold there, and except for the sparse light of a few lanterns, that cast eerie shadows on the crowded human figures, who huddled in the ship's depths, it was dark too!

From the time the ship had gotten underway, the constant rolling and pitching of the hull had taken it's toll in discomfort amid the crowded mass of people, whom it carried. Indeed, almost from the beginning the sporadic retching of many of the men, women and children, who were unused to the movement of a ship, could be heard throughout the long hours. Now, two days later, the stench of vomit permeated the dank atmosphere below, to such an extent that the very act of breathing was becoming more and more difficult.

Madeleine had done what she could to add to the comfort of her small group, who was crowded into a little space against the rough timbers of the hull. She had come to think of them as her family, and felt that she should do what she could to make this dreadful experience as bearable as possible for everyone. After all, Josef, her husband-to-be, and his brother Charles, were the only family she now had. Then, there were the two women, whom she had taken under her wing—Madame Trahan and Louisa. They were in no condition to take care of anyone, for Madame Trahan, who was already in a bad way when they came on board, now lay gravely ill. And Louisa was too large with child to be of much help.

Just then, Madame Trahan began coughing again, much as she had done—but with increasing intensity—ever since boarding the ship. Louisa hurriedly poured some water from their precious rationed portion into a small cup, and as Madeleine held the ill woman's head up from the pallet where she lay, Louisa put the cup to her Mother's lips. But another coughing spell took hold of her, making drinking impossible. The water merely driveled down the sick woman's chin, as a series of hacking coughs continued, and would not be suppressed. Then, as suddenly as it had begun, the coughing subsided and the woman's head went limp against her daughter's arm. Louisa put her hand to her Mama's forehead and gently lowered her back to a reclining position, as Madeleine pulled the blanket up around Madame Trahan's neck.

"Oh Madeleine!" Louisa pleaded. "What can we do for her? Her head is hot with a high fever....and so full is the congestion in her. I fear that Mama cannot hold on much longer....if only we had our priest. If nothing more, he could comfort her and at least she could receive the last rites, and be ready for the end.... if it must come!"

Before Madeleine could answer her, another voice was heard from an old man, who was sitting next to their group. He sat so near to them, that apparently he could not help but overhear what was going on. He leaned over and remarked to Louisa. "There is a priest on board....well, we think of him as our priest, because he was studying for the priesthood. We call him Father Joubert. He was at Riviere aux Canard, where many of us were taken. He chose to come onto the ship with us, for he knew he would be needed. Let me go to find him for you. Remember, he is not yet a priest, but maybe he could bring comfort to your mother. I have not seen him since we were brought on board....so; he must be in another section of the ship. I will try to find him....if you wish me to."

Louisa and Madeleine both nodded anxiously to the old man, as they helped him up from where he had been sitting. Then, carefully, he made his way through the huddled people, who crowded the hold of the ship, stepping over those reclining on the floor, as he went. The two women watched him make his way among the people, until they could see him no more, as the surrounding crowded figures merged together, marring their view.

"Pray that he will find the man, who serves as their priest, Louisa, before it is too late....for at least he could help to put her mind at ease," Madeleine remarked, looking down at the ill woman.

"Dear God.....see how labored her breathing is! Madeleine... she cannot last much longer like this....if only he will come in time! Oh, Mama....you deserve better than this!" Louisa cried. "Mama....Mama....do not leave me, you are all that is left of my family...I need you!"

With these last words Louisa broke down and the tears flowed freely, as her broken hearted sobs echoed through the wretched surroundings, there in the eerie light of that ship's dark hold!

———

CHAPTER - 9

THE SHIP AND THE TEMPEST

She held her face up to the sky, so as to absorb the comforting warmth of the sun's rays. In spite of the considerable nip in the November sea air, Madeleine spread her arms out from her body in an effort to dry her cape, which had felt damp for what seemed like days.

Madeleine was there top side, with Louisa and many other Acadian women, who had brought their bundles up on deck. It was their group's turn to enjoy a brief respite on the ship's deck. The women hoped to take this opportunity to air out their clothes and bedding. The Acadian men were below, for the Captain had granted them another rare opportunity to wash down the floor of the hold with buckets of sea water. This process had become a necessity, since the Acadian's home at sea–the ship's cargo hold–fast became unlivable if not washed down periodically.

Several of the original passengers, who embarked from Grand Pre, had since succumbed to the deplorable conditions on board, especially in recent weeks. The constant pitching and tossing of the ship, along with the below decks stagnant air and stuffy atmosphere that was also permeated somewhat with smoke from the ship's stoves, added to the misery. All of this, intermingled with unwashed bodies and human excrement, as well as the damp clothing and bedding, the cold draftiness of the hold and the inadequate dreary rations that they were forced to subsist on, took an additional toll. All of this contributed greatly to the miseries of the unwilling passengers, who were being forced to endure the voyage on this transport. Then, there were those, who on day one had been separated from their loved ones. Many of them had simply given up, thus the mortality rate soared.

For those who lay ill, the conditions were almost unbearable. Indeed, the close quarters and cold damp conditions below decks had made the plight of those with rheumatism, dehydration, congestion, fever and diarrhea extremely difficult. As a result, many lay seriously ill and seldom did a few days go by without the occurrence of a death among the people. But it was especially sad for everyone whenever a small child had to be buried at sea.

"Thank God for Father Joubert," mumbled Madeleine, as these thoughts and the seriousness of it all coursed through her mind.

"What did you say?" Questioned Louisa, turning to look over at Madeleine, as she went about her task of rinsing out some clothing in a bucket of sea water.

"It is nothing, Louisa.....I was just thinking how fortunate we were to have someone so learned in priestly affairs, as our Father Joubert on board at such a time of need." Madeleine answered. "Hand me that shirt you have just rinsed....I will hang it here on the ship's rail, and maybe the sea air will dry it a bit before we have to go below again."

Louisa nodded in agreement, as she handed the damp cloth to her friend. "Thank the good Lord for him....he made Mama's death more bearable weeks ago, when he came to our aid. Did you notice how she seemed to truly relax toward the end, after he came and prayed at her side? Was there not a slight smile on her lips just as she took that last breath? I did not imagine that, did I, Madeleine?"

"No, Louisa….it is true," Madeleine agreed. "It was a smile…. truly a smile! Your Mama was ready to go then, but it would not have been the same without his comfort."

As the women on deck continued their tasks of rinsing and airing out clothes and blankets, the ship's deck had begun to take on an industrious feminine appearance for a time. But now, it was approaching late afternoon. However, remarkably the sun had shown itself for a number of hours on this November day, during the women's sojourn on deck—much to their delight. So, they continued to hurriedly go about their tasks, for they well knew that their time allotted topside was limited. Soon, the order would be given for them to go below.

Louisa and Madeleine certainly did not relish in the prospect of going below again. For they knew it would be as cold and damp as ever in the cargo hold. It would probably be even damper since the floor was being washed down while they were above decks. So, there would certainly not have been enough time for their quarters to dry out. But then, since the beginning of this voyage, the hold had been continually damp. However, the women accepted the fact, that it would be cleaner down there for a time—even though the damp cold would once again chill them.

There was no doubt that every woman on deck was thankful for the little bit of sunshine they were being treated to on this day. They knew only too well that this weather was indeed a respite for all on board, since it had been common knowledge for two days that the transport had been engulfed in a dense fog for a long period, when visibility had been extremely limited to just a very few feet off the sides of the ship.

But now, visibility had returned and the sea looked like a sheet of glass, with naught but a few ripples to mar it's surface. The sun still shone sporadically, but was becoming increasingly less evident, as an occasional cloud now interfered from time to time. The day was fast approaching sunset, and the sky seemed to take on a soft red hue. A substantially large bank of clouds of a noticeably dark purplish gray color could be observed some distance off the port side—appearing increasingly ominous to every observer on deck.

The ship's course lay directly in the direction of this giant cloud bank, and it was not long before strong gusts of wind began to pepper those on deck. At that point, the sea was fast losing it's placid appearance, for the wind was becoming more turbulent. The mountainous cloud bank still lay in the path of the ship, and as the distance between the two diminished, the ship began rolling from side to side as an increasingly gustier wind made it's presence known.

Madeleine and Louisa, still on deck with the other women, were trying to gather all of the clothing and blankets, which they had been rinsing and drying. But the sudden gusts of strong wind were making the task quite difficult. This was especially so, because of the rolling on the deck, which made good footing impossible. A number of the women had lost their balance in their haste, and had fallen to the deck, for the order had been given for them to go below with all speed.

"Make haste, Louisa….here let me carry that bundle," shouted Madeleine, as she tried to keep her footing and not lose their few meager belongings to the gusty wind, which was becoming increasingly stronger. She reached out for Louisa's hand, in order to help her to the hatchway, and to keep her from falling. But as Louisa reached out to grasp Madeleine's hand, the pregnant woman's foot slid out from under and she hit the rolling deck hard.

Crewmen, dressed in foul weather wear, were scurrying all around the few remaining women on deck, as a couple of officers shouted out orders above the wind, making the ship's crew hop to. In their haste, one seaman, who almost stumbled over Louisa after she had fallen, stopped to help Madeleine get Louisa to her feet and over to the hatchway ladder.

At that moment, a torrent of rain began to pelt them, as they struggled to get Louisa down the ladder of the still open hatch. Then, a particularly hard gust of wind struck the ship. And a ripping sound from above decks was heard, accompanied by a cracking sound which no doubt represented the tearing of canvas and the snapping of sail lashings, as this strong storm was now upon them in ever increasing force.

Josef and Charles were waiting at the cargo hold hatch, and Madeleine caught sight of them amid the crowd of scurrying women, who were all trying to find their way back down below decks. But it was difficult, because the ship was rolling and pitching significantly. So, she shouted out to them. "Josef...Charles.... help me!"

Between the three of them, they succeeded I assisting Louisa, who was quite awkward in her advanced state of pregnancy. And finally, they assisted her back to their allotted space below decks, where they eased her down into a sitting position so she could recline on the pallet if need be. But as soon as she was seated, Louisa cried out loudly.

"Louisa....what is wrong?" Josef questioned, as he reached out to ease her shoulders down on the pallet. But instead of a reply from the pregnant woman, she cried out with another piercing scream, to which Madeleine exclaimed.

"Oh dear God.....Josef....it is her time! The baby is coming. What can we do?"

"Be calm, Madeleine," Josef cautioned. "Do you not remember anything about when your Mama helped birth your cousin's baby? Think back....you told me that she let you help."

"Yes....yes...Josef! But that was last year....and Mama did everything," Madeleine replied excitedly. "If only I could remember more about it!"

Louisa's cries of pain continued at intervals, and a number of women made their way over to where she lay, in an effort to offer their advice. But what with the noise of the wind and the rolling of the ship, which was pitching so from the force of the raging storm, their voiced advice could scarcely be heard above the noise. Meanwhile, it was taking the efforts of both Madeleine and Josef to keep Louisa, who was now in ever more obvious discomfort, from rolling off of the pallet, as the ship pitched and rolled. Charles busied himself by trying to keep the blanket over Louisa, for since the storm, it had become even colder in their small space, in spite of the crowd of bodies that had gathered around them.

Soon, it became almost impossible for them to think of anything else, but to hold on so as not to be tossed about the cargo hold. For the storm had intensified considerably and the jolting movements of the ship had escalated. Then suddenly, there was a new sensation—an even more sinister one! It was a feeling that the entire ship was being lifted upwards, and in fact it was. This was beginning to occur each time the ship was taken up onto the crest of a rolling wave in the raging sea, at which point the vessel would teeter for a moment—it's bow poking out toward the sky—seemingly suspended in mid air for a few moments. Then, abruptly the sensation was followed by a sudden feeling of sliding headlong—downward at a great speed—which was in effect exactly what was happening each time the vessel slid down the side of a monstrous wave. Whenever this occurred, the ship's keel seemed to instantly slam downward as if caught in an avalanche, until the vessel finally leveled off, as it slid into a trough between waves. At that point, the ship was deposited momentarily, only to be picked up again and carried upward onto the next crest, and put through the same avalanche experience— over and over again.

But bad as it was deep in the hold of the ship, where many of the terrified Acadians were becoming exhausted by the constant strain of holding on, in order to keep from being tossed about, it was worse outside. So, it was just as well that they could not observe the full force of the raging tempest above decks. For it had become as dark as pitch out there, with a driving horizontal rain that made visibility impossible, except for the lightning that would brighten the sky for a moment with a flash that served to illuminate the terrifying scene of this tempest at sea. With each bolt of lightning, the bow of the ship could be seen plowing into the waves, splashing sea spray that was constantly being blown over the entire length of the vessel. And then there were the forcefully relentless gale winds. And the decks could be seen constantly awash with heavy waves, that literally exploded onto the deck, depositing angry sea water that foamed up everywhere. Seamen on deck were holding on for dear life, to keep from being swept over the side, as they struggled to keep the ship from floundering.

Time seemed to lose all meaning to the Acadians, who had been bracing themselves as best they could, against the wrath of the great stormy winds and sea. To those down in the cargo hold, it was akin to an interminable, tumultuous, nightmare atmosphere that seemed to never end. But in reality, the interval spent in weathering the worse of the tempest had been no more than three quarters of an hour, before the transport's movements began to take on a more bearable quality.

As soon as a reprieve was felt, from this traumatic experience at sea, some of the passengers began their efforts to retrieve possessions, which had been roughly tossed about during the storm. Others were moaning from injuries and bruises sustained, during the experience, while friends and family members attempted to assist them in seeing to their wounds, as well as helping them to recover their senses. Because, so muddled had many of their minds become from the sheer horror of the experience they needed comfort, in order to regain their senses. Thus, even more noise and confusion filled the cargo hold by those within. Although, the ship was still rolling considerably on the surface of the rough waters, which continued to be somewhat evident from the slowly subsiding remnants of the storm—a storm that seemed to die much too slowly as far as those on board were concerned.

The weak light from the few swaying lanterns, which represented the only illumination down in the hold, cast even more eerie shadows than usual on the crowded scene of chaos below decks. But with the slowly subsiding movement of the ship, some order from the mass of disoriented passengers was becoming apparent. Voices that had been previously raised to a high pitch of terror were now silent, or were manifested only by low moans, as these previously terrified people began to take on a calmer demeanor.

Madeleine felt a twinge of pain from her upper right arm—the result of being thrust against the hard timbers of the inner hull when a particularly harsh wave struck the port side of the ship. But with a subdued whence of discomfort, she pulled herself up to a sitting position, and in a somewhat disoriented manner gazed about her. Looking over at Louisa, she saw that the young woman had managed to stay in a partial reclining position on the pallet, due to Josef and Charles' efforts. She attempted to speak some comforting words to her. "Louisa…we are still with you….you are not alone. Are your pains still coming?"

Upon hearing those words, Josef added his own. "Yes Louisa…. do not despair…we will help you." Turning to Charles, who was kneeling beside him at the edge of Louisa's somewhat disarrayed pallet, he pointed over to the two women, who had previously offered advice, and directed him thusly. "Go over to them and seek their aid for Louisa…ask if they would help us. I will go to inquire about the ship's doctor….there must be one on board…maybe he will help us! It should not take long for me to return….I will hurry!"

With this, Josef made his way through the multitudes in the hold, taking care to reach out for support whenever he could, in order not to lose his footing on the still rolling ship. Meanwhile, Charles crawled over to the two women, not far from where Louisa lay, and where Madeleine was endeavoring to do what she could to make the pregnant girl as comfortable as possible.

It seemed that Charles was only gone for a few minutes, when he returned, accompanied by one of the Acadian women, who appeared to be in the same age bracket as had been his Mama. She was a heavier set woman, though, with plain facial features and dark circles beneath her eyes, a result no doubt of the rigorous voyage she was being made to endure. However, her smile, which was most pleasant, seemed to radiate maternal warmth, and her manner was one of confidence that seemed to put everyone in her presence at ease. As she spoke, her voice fell on anxious ears, as Madeleine, Charles and Louisa listened with anticipation to her words.

"I have come to help you, my dear," she said with a smile, as she kneeled alongside of Louisa and placed her hand on the pregnant girl's brow. "I am Madame Marie Bergeron from Pigiguit....do not despair....I have brought many a tiny babe into this world in my time!"

Upon hearing her words, Madeleine grasped the woman's arm anxiously and implored of her. "Madame...you will help Louisa then? What can Charles and I do to assist you....you have only to ask of us."

The woman did not answer immediately, for she was busy examining Louisa and questioning her in whispers as to the intervals of her labor pains. Then a moment more, after the woman pushed her fluffed sleeves up to her elbows and settled herself into a sitting position alongside of the pallet, she looked over at Madeleine, and with that reassuring smile of hers, replied. "My dear girl....calm yourself....I have delivered babies many times since becoming a woman. First let us hang a blanket up here for some privacy, for her time of delivery will be here soon enough. But perhaps not for a few hours yet. Do you have anything that she could eat right now....she will need strength to get through the hard labor that is to come.... and she is so frail."

"Yes....yes...Madame," Madeleine hastily answered. "I was saving my last ration of cheese...it is small and a bit moldy, but still good. Here Louisa, eat this, and do as Madame says"

Just then, a somewhat out of breath, Josef appeared from behind the blanket that Charles was in the process of hanging. Taking in the situation at a glance, he exclaimed anxiously, reporting on his efforts in Louisa's behalf.

"The ship's surgeon could not come....he was busy tending some of the crew, who were injured during the storm. But he gave me this ration of rum for Louisa to drink during her labor....and this vial of oil to rub on the baby when it comes! Look....he said we could use this basin to bring rain water from the deck, too!"

Madame Bergeron silently considered his words, reaching for the small container of rum, that Josef held toward Louisa. She took it, put the cup to the pregnant girl's lips and coaxed her to drink. Looking up at Josef, she directed him further.

"It is good....we will need these things....so little do we have to work with down here in this miserable place! Go...my son.... and fill the basin with clean water...we will have need of it!"

"What can I do?" Questioned Madeleine excitedly. To which Madame answered.

"You can try to relax. For the night will be a long one. Many is the time I have seen these things last beyond fifteen hours....so you have to rest, as I will have need of your help at the end."

Just then, Louisa moaned slightly, as an exhausted fitful sleep began to overtake her. But Madame stroked her brow and tucked the cover in at her neck in an effort to protect the girl as much as possible, from the penetrating damp cold that had settled within worse than ever.

As it turned out, the night was indeed a long one—just as Madame had predicted. Josef, Madeleine and Charles made themselves as comfortable as possible and fell into a sort of exhausted, nervous slumber, awakening many times as a result of Louisa's moans during the long night hours. Madame had tended to Louisa's needs throughout those long hours, whenever the girl experienced some labor discomfort. By the dawn hours, her pains were coming closer together.

"Will it never end?!" Louisa suddenly shouted out, as she writhed violently on the pallet. And then a piercing scream burst forth from her, as a particularly hard contraction took hold.

"My dears....awaken...the time is near!" Madame called out to Josef, Madeleine and Charles, as she reacted to the increased labor pains Louisa experienced. But she need not have exerted herself, as they had been awakened with a jolt as a result of Louisa's louder than usual scream.

"Bring that other lantern and hang it here," Madame hastily directed Josef and Charles. "Then stay beyond the blanket.... Madeleine, come here....I will need your help!"

"Oh, dear God....my back is paining me so," shouted Louisa. "Make it stop, Madame, please!" In reply, the exhausted older woman tried to comfort her with soothing words.

"I know it is hard, my little one....but have patience...it will be over soon." She then directed Madeleine with a wave of her arm. "Here raise her up from the pallet and massage her back. But keep that cover on. Bundle one of those blankets and stuff it behind, to brace her." Just then, Louisa screamed in pain, amid which Madame attempted to shout instructions to her.

"Push when it comes again, my dear....but if it becomes unbearable try to relax and breathe deeply...it will not be long now!"

Louisa was now in a partial sitting position, as Madeleine endeavored to brace her back in the manner in which Madame had instructed. Just then, a violent spasm made Louisa's arms grasp out with a jerk. Madeleine reached over and instinctively grabbed the girl's hands, which gripped with a relentless pressure. All the while, terrible screams, caused obviously by the severe pain were emanating from Louisa, as tears streamed down her cheeks in torrents.

By this time, Madame Bergeron had pushed Louisa's skirt and petticoat up around her waist, after removing her under garments. Now, she was in the process of trying to keep the pregnant girl's trembling knees apart so as to better observe the progress of the labor. Only Madame's somewhat harried voice betrayed the anxiety she felt as once again she implored Louisa's help.

"It is coming...my dear...push....push harder!"

With another piercing scream, Louisa's strength seemed to fail her and she suddenly slumped back against Madeleine, who had been grasping the girl's hands tightly all the while. Alarmed, she cried out. "Madame....Madame.....Louisa has fainted....what should I do?"

For a moment Madame Bergeron seemed to take no notice of Madeleine's alarm, so intense was her interest directed in the birth process. But suddenly, with a squeal of delight, she shouted out for all to hear. "Merci dear God....it is here. The petite babe's head is coming. Madeleine...come and help me....see one shoulder is already out!"

"But Madame....what of Louisa....she is barely conscious?" Madeleine questioned in alarm. It was then, that Madame swiftly looked up over Louisa's now limp body and face, while she hastened to handle the emerging baby, which was now in the process of being fully born. Her eyes mirrored the depth of wisdom that she possessed in such matters and her voice was filled with confidence as she answered.

"Do not dismay....she is exhausted from her ordeal and her strength is gone. But the babe is here and this new mother has earned her rest....see here is the baby!"

Madeleine's eyes were filled with awe as she beheld the tiny reddish form that Madame held up for her and Louisa to see. Peering up through half closed weary eyelids at the little form,

Louisa managed to smile. But an instant more and the smile had disappeared. Instead a look of deep concern took over as she beheld the new born infant. Then, through trembling lips, she managed to utter an anxious question. "It makes no sound…Madame…why does it not cry?"

"Be patient, my dear…..let me clear it's mouth." Madame answered, as she ran her finger into the infant's mouth hurriedly, in an effort to clear it of any mucus. Suddenly, a muted cry could be heard from the new infant, followed by a series of stronger wails, which caused the broad smile to once again appear on Madame's face.

In that moment, both Louisa and Madeleine heaved simultaneous sighs of relief, as a smiling Madame Bergeron placed the tiny babe on the new mother's stomach. As she did so, she continued to massage the infant's breast to assist it's breathing. When she finally spoke, her grin was evident as she looked piercingly into Louisa's shining eyes, which had suddenly once again taken on some of it's usual sparkle. "It is a little girl….my dear. Here, Madeleine…hold the babe while I attend to Louisa's needs…you may wrap the child in this cloth!"

Madeleine reached out somewhat awkwardly and took the tiny, squirming baby and wrapped it in the cloth that had been handed her. Madame continued to direct them, as she now massaged Louisa's stomach. "Lay the baby in the new Mama's arms….and try to raise Louisa up from the pallet so I can see to the afterbirth. And…oh yes, pass that basin of water here."

Hurriedly complying with Madame's requests, Madeleine watched with fascination as the woman tied the umbilical cord an inch from the baby's navel, and then made another knot in the cord about an inch from the first. Then, she neatly cut the cord with a small knife, midway between the two knots. Finally, heaving a deep sign, which did little to disguise the obvious fatigue, that the older woman was apparently now feeling, Madame spoke once more.

"Ah....it is done, my dears. Now...Louisa you must rest and regain your strength, for your new babe will be in need of your milk. It is her only chance for life down here in this dark hold!"

With these words, Madame got slowly to her feet with much effort. For the ordeal had been an obviously exhausting experience for this woman, who had not been in good health from the onset of this trying ordeal. However, she immediately reached toward the hanging blanket and pulled it aside, to reveal the anxious faces of Josef and Charles, as well as many others, who had for some hours now been gathered closely on the other side of the privacy blanket. Now, their eyes reflected the emotional strain of that listening experience, as they glanced at Madame. Quickly, they all looked over at Louisa, who smiled back at them, as she cuddled her new baby.

It was but a moment more, when Josef and Charles both instinctively reached out and hugged Madame Bergeron warmly, both speaking their words of emotional appreciation for her efforts. However, Josef summed up their feelings of gratitude in a few words, as he spoke. "Madame.... You are surely a Saint to help us in such a time of need. The good Lord must have sent you to assist Louisa, for we knew not how!"

The woman brushed a sleeve across the tear filled eyes of her face, which now showed even more signs of strain and exhaustion, as she made an effort to regain her composure. After extricating herself from the two young men's emotional display of appreciation, Madame grinned broadly at them, and turned back toward Madeleine, Louisa and the baby. As she continued to extend her warm smile in their direction, she spoke one final order. "Now.... take good care of that babe, my dears. And Madeleine make sure you spread the oil all over the little one's skin and see to Louisa's needs. She will need much rest. Now, I must go and lie down...I am so tired."

"May the Lord bless you, my dear Madame...do not fret, we will look after Louisa and the baby," Madeleine replied enthusiastically. "You need not worry!"

The woman stood there for a moment, as she pondered these words of assurance. Then, she turned slowly, as a grimace of discomfort suddenly erased her smile, clouding her expression with pain. Madame immediately turned her face away from the young people, so that they would not see her pained expression. She then made her way back—ever so slowly—to her appointed place on the far side of the cargo hold.

Once there, she hurriedly lay down on the damp floor and covered herself as best she could with her quilt, in an effort to subdue the violent chills that had suddenly taken hold of her. With her entire body quivering periodically from these chills, Madame Marie Bergeron finally fell into an exhausted sleep—a sleep from which she never awoke.

———

"L'embarquement" - courtoisie: College Sainte-Anne.

CHAPTER - 10

ARRIVAL ON A FOREIGN SHORE

Clouds had shrouded the horizon, making the distant strip of land barely discernable. But the white froth of breakers on the shoals, a few yards off the starboard side, had been easy to see

For Captain Edward Phillips, the sighting had been more than welcome. Because this landfall, which marked the entrance to the Bay of Chesapeake, had special meaning for him. One of the sister transports had left the convoy days before, steering west toward Massachusetts Bay and Boston Harbor. And then, later when another of the ships made for a Connecticut port, through Block Island Sound, he had experienced somewhat less apprehension. But now, increasing anxiety was taking hold of him, when he realized that his ship was also nearing it's destination. However, even after entering the Bay of Chesapeake, Phillips knew full well there was yet considerable distance to cover, in order to reach Baltimore City.

It also meant that the transport was now alone, having left, at a point south of Smith's Island, which marked the entrance to the Bay, the remaining three ships that proceeded on their way. The Captain had observed upon departing from the sister ships, that those other transports were apparently steering due south. Probably making for Virginia or the Carolinas, he surmised, or perhaps even to the colony of Georgia, which was considerably further south. Well, he certainly did not envy the Captain of any ship that was destined for a longer voyage, since this journey had already proven to be such a trying experience.

A number of gray winter days had past, since departing from the other transports, and much of the Bay water was behind them. By his calculations, Captain Phillips expected to encounter the mouth of the Patapsco River soon. But it seemed strange to him, that no other vessel had been sighted since leaving the other transports. But then, these were not heavily traveled waters at this time of year, as he well knew. He had noted though, with some distress, that the December weather had turned much colder as they proceeded on their course.

Standing on the deck, with the cold, freezing wind assaulting his face, he hunched his shoulders and stamped his booted feet, in an effort to keep warm. Then a moment more, and his attention was captured by the hazy form of another vessel, far off the port side. As the deck of his own vessel rolled slowly from the slightly choppy surface, while the ship slowly plied the icy waters of this Bay, his attention was still riveted to the far off vessel. It was slowly emerging from a shroud of mist that had previously hidden it from view.

All at once, with a look of disgust and an audible sneer, the Captain cursed softly to himself, as he recognized the other ship. Way off in the distance, he knew it for what it was. "Ugly slaver…. the curse of the seas. Fast sailing on the trade winds, though….have to be bringing all that Negro human cargo in from Africa for the slave market. But then it is what these vessels were designed for…. and their only reason for being.

Scrutinizing the far off ship with a knowing eye, Phillips surmised to himself that it was probably making for Annapolis, which he figured to be due west of their present position, as the vessel was moving swiftly through the water, and veering off in that direction. Must give that one a wide berth, since those ships smell to high heaven when downwind of such as that!

Continuing to stare intently at the distant vessel, he pondered these things silently to himself. Then all at once, Phillips was overwhelmed with the irony of it all. For he realized at that moment that his ship probably did not smell too good either, what with the massive numbers of human cargo on board, in cramped living space.

Once more, feelings of guilt slowly began to surface in his conscience, and he endeavored to reason for himself that he had done his best to cope with conditions on board. Trying to rationalize this, he muttered to himself. "It is certainly not the same situation! Had not he given permission for the people below decks to wash down their quarters a number of times during the voyage? Had he not made available extra rations of rain water after the storm, for those who lay ill below? After all, these Acadians were certainly not being transported in order to be sold into slavery. On the contrary, they were merely being relocated. Besides, it was for their own good, was it not?"

He continued to rationalize his position and mutter to himself, as these thoughts filled his consciousness, gazing all the while as he was—as if hypnotized—in the distance at the slave ship that was now sailing far off the port bow. "Why had not he—as Captain—even said final words time and time again over the Acadians, who had died during the voyage, whenever it was necessary before burial at sea? No slaver Captain would ever do that, I will wager!"

The Captain continued to silently justify his position to himself, as he strained to see the slaver that was slowly being swallowed up in the misty gray of a fog bank in the distance. He watched intently until it was completely out of sight.

But justify as he tried, over and over to himself, his conscience continued to be plagued by the gaunt, hungry expressions on the faces of those people on board. The children particularly got to him. For the sight of their pathetically thin bodies and dark circled eyes caused him to stay in his cabin, whenever they were allowed up for their short periods above decks. However, try as he would, he could not escape these feelings of guilt. For their visions even plagued his dreams whenever sleep would finally overtake him. All of this caused no end of nightmares for this man—whether while asleep or when awake.

Shaking his head abruptly, as if to force such thoughts from his mind, he noted that the cold December wind had let up somewhat—for the moment. But he then noticed numerous flows of ice to be seen, floating on the surface waters. Shivering slightly, the Captain turned and proceeded to his cabin. And it was some hours later before Phillips once again came out on deck and took his place along the port rail. He had not been there long, before a flock of sea birds began chattering and soaring above the masts of the ship. It was as though the feathered creatures were heralding the river entrance that lay on the transport's appointed course. His sharp eye immediately noted the mouth of the river, and he shouted orders to the Mate, who stood steering the ship's wheel.

"There she is...Mr. Tyler! Steer due west into the Patapsco River. Mind you, Mate, steer well clear of Bodkin Point and make for Rock Point off the port side!"

"Aye, aye, Sir!" The Mate shouted in reply, turning the ship's wheel so as to make for the appointed direction.

Edward Phillips' expression seemed to change ever so slightly, as he breathed deeply of the crisp cold air, which was scented with the smell of evergreen trees from the shores of the river. He noted silently how he always delighted in the scent of the thick forests of the land—a scent that was gently wafted over the water by an offshore breeze, which seemed to encompass the ship with this fresh smell of land. Indeed it was a familiar scent for Phillips, and one that was most welcome. Because this was a clear signal that this voyage would soon be over. In this manner, the Captain passed considerable time, assisting the Mate in the progress of the ship up the river, until a certain point was reached, whereupon he directed the Mate once again.

"Off to the starboard, watch for that point of land, Mr. Tyler! Because on the other side is the entrance to the North West Branch of the Patapsco River. So steer north by northwest...and soon we will be docking at Baltimore City."

"Aye, aye, Sir!" The Mate shouted out in answer, shivering notably, as he followed the order.

It was not long before the somewhat flat, featureless coastline drew closer, as the ship plowed through ever increasing chunks of broken ice. At this point a brisk, bitter wind had sprung up, ushering in sudden heavy snow flurries, which attempted to cover the ship's decks with blowing snow flakes that made visibility more difficult.

Captain Phillips. Who was still on deck directing the ship's crew, pulled his coat collar up around his neck and tried to avoid touching the rail, that was coated with ice and hung with tiny icicles, as he attempted to make his way back over the snow slicked deck, so as to order the Mate at the wheel once more. "These can be dangerous waters in winter, Mr. Tyler!" He shouted above the wind. "Have the crew take soundings! Now....steady as she goes...it may be necessary to reconnoiter for a possible anchorage if the harbor is iced in!"

"Aye Sir....what if it is iced in? It is hard to see from here," questioned Mr. Tyler, who was straining to see the shoreline, still some distance away.

"It looks from here like a gray beach, Mr. Tyler....and we have a fair wind in our favor, "Phillips shouted back, as he peered intently at the distant shore. "It is indeed an inhospitable sight, this town we have come to...is it not? Yet, it looks as though the harbor is free of ice blockage....there are only chunks floating here and there!"

Phillips continued to stare at the harbor area of the town that lay off the port bow. It was indeed a stark scene, he noted to himself. For there was naught to see, but a white snow covered shore that sloped to the water's edge, with square box-like buildings built right along the shore. But the dock appeared to be clear of solid ice, so the Captain shouted out directions to the Mate again.

"Ah....no need to seek other anchorage! The dock looks clear from here. Aye...soon we can put an end to this cursed voyage.... and none too soon either! Make haste, Mr. Tyler....see to the docking in short order, while I go below and ready the appropriate documents to present when we make shore!" At that moment, an unfamiliar voice shouted at him, over the wind.

"Pardon....mon Captain....I beg a moment of your time!" It was the student priest, whom the people referred to as Father Joubert. He was somewhat out of breath, but continued to beg the Captain's indulgence. He stood there shivering, holding his cloak together across his chest in an effort to ward off the frigid wind. His black, somewhat shabby, attire was dotted with flecks of white from the blowing snow, and the rim of his tattered hat was decorated with a mantle of white that seemed somewhat pleasing, in a ludicrous way, since it matched the gray white flecks on the beard of his unshaven face.

"What are you doing above decks.....by what right do you come upon me in such a manner?" The Captain shouted, in reprimand.

Joubert's tired eyes reflected the deprivation that he had suffered during the voyage. The white area of his eyes was considerably blood shot, and deep dark lines were evident on his face. He was obviously weak from lack of proper food and his deep cough was evidence of a severe congestive ailment. But the expression in his eyes was intense, for his faith was ever with him and had not been shaken by what he had been through. His stare mirrored this deep faith, as he looked intensely into the Captain's eyes, and implored.

"Mon Capitan....I can see that we will soon be landing...and that you will probably be going ashore immediately. I know not if this is where my people below are to be put on shore, but I beg of you to allow me to go ashore with you, and plead for blankets and food for those so in need on this vessel. Even if this is not the appointed destination....perhaps some kindly souls on shore would assist us with provisions for these people, who have suffered much, so they can still go on. Please....I implore you, Sir....they are so in need down there. Many are sick and dying from the cold and short rations. Others need heavier clothing or blankets, so that they can survive. Have you not been down there to see for yourself, Mon Capitan? It is a terrible sight to behold...come, I will show you that I do not lie!"

Edward Phillips was obviously unnerved by the entreaties of this humble man, and he certainly had no intention of going below in that cargo hold to see for himself. He had mental unrest enough to last a lifetime already, so he pondered Joubert's words silently for a minute before he shouted his answer above the wind. "All right.... all right...you may accompany me. I may need you anyway to help make arrangements for help to get these passengers off the ship. For this is where they are destined to be put ashore....and someone will have to see to their needs. Thankfully, that will no longer be my problem....for I will soon be shed of you all!"

———

"Here, young man...drink this...it will make you warm again!" Charles reached out and took the cup of hot rum from the hand of the slightly buxom woman, who had spoken to him. As he did so, her face brightened into a warm smile, and she laid a garment on the boy's outstretched arm, while at the same time offering more words of comfort.

"This belongs to my son. He is about your age. But he has two waistcoats, and you need one badly....the one you are wearing is so worn. Here...try it on."

Charles slipped his arms into the coat, when the woman held it up for him. He then tried to offer his appreciation as best he could, before the woman continued speaking. "Thank you, Madame....you are so kind to help us!"

"Just as I thought....it fits you perfectly. I shall tell Samuel that his coat will be put to good use." As the woman spoke, she peered over Charles' shoulder at the other young man, who sat behind him with the two young women and a baby. Looking from Charles to the others, she extended her warm smiling face in their direction, as she continued speaking in her lively fashion. "Do you young people speak English....can you understand me?"

"Yes, Madame....we can comprehend some," replied Josef. "My name is Josef Theriot....these ladies here with me are Madeleine Bourgeois and Louisa LeBlanc, holding her baby Joseine, who was born during the voyage. And this young man, to whom you so kindly gave the coat, is my younger brother, Charles Theriot."

"Welcome to you all," exclaimed the woman, as she directed her warm smile their way. "My name is Abigal Smith. Jonathon and I came to Baltimore City some years after we were married in Ireland. So, you see we, too, were new in this land. But do not worry, for now you are among friends after the terrible times you must have endured on that ship. My husband told me of your plight, after he went to the ship, shortly after it docked some hours ago. He related that he had never seen such terrible conditions on any ship, than that which prevailed in the cargo hold of that abominable vessel you arrived on! But no matter....you are here now. So, do not fear....we are Catholic, like you, and will help you to get on your feet once more. Then, you can begin to make another life here in this new country."

"Madame," Charles implored, almost before she had finished speaking. "Do you know of a family that may have been brought to this place from Acadie? It is the family of Jean Theriot....our parents and sisters. Have you heard of them? Do they perhaps dwell nearby? Oh yes, were there any other Acadian families, who may have come on ships before us? Madeleine, here, is searching for her family, from whom she was separated?"

Abigal Smith looked shocked at these questions, and this was reflected in her voice, as she answered Charles. "Do you mean there was more than one shipload....are there more displaced people like you? Oh, dear God! Your ship was the first to come here with Acadians. There have been no other....I would have heard about it, if one had docked here. But can such a thing be true....that your families were taken too, but on different ships? Merciful God, how can such a thing happen? Your ship is the first to come here from Acadia, unannounced and unexpected. Why, the Magistrate knew nothing about your coming....he told the Captain that when the papers were presented, shortly after the boat docked. In fact.... Jonathon told us that the Magistrate gave that Captain a piece of his mind, as a result. For he had no facilities or supplies with which to take care of so large a number of people in such dire need. Tell me....were you even told where you were going?"

"No Madame," Charles answered, obviously saddened at the news she had just related to him. "The English took many shiploads of our people from Acadie....and I thought that even though we had been separated...we would still meet again in the new land. Where could they have been taken, Madame? Please ask your husband if he has heard anything about other shiploads of people."

"Of course, my boy....do not fret....I will find out what I can. But do not get your hopes up...for your vessel was the first, from your former country, to dock here." Abigal exclaimed excitedly. "But perhaps there will be more coming. Oh my good Lord..... where will we put them, if this is so? Right now, we are fortunate enough to have the use of Mr. Edward Fotterell's two story house, that we now occupy. But as you can see, it is filled to capacity.... and I fear some will have to be moved to private houses until we can make more arrangements. But we will make do! I will pray to God, to help us through this."

With these words, Mrs. Smith rushed over to where another woman was serving hot soup from a large steaming pot across the room. She made her way carefully, amid the crowd of ragged Acadian men, women and children, who had been taken off the ship.

Charles slumped down on the floor and leaned back against the wall, as he tried to fight back the tears that had welled up, immediately upon hearing Mrs. Smith's words. Madeleine watched him, and was suddenly filled with compassion, so she sat down beside him. Putting her arm around his shoulders, she whispered softly what words of comfort she could muster at the moment. "Do not despair, Charles...perhaps someone else here knows of them. You cannot give up....maybe we will yet hear word of them, and of my Papa and Mama, and Louisa's husband and Papa, too! Here... let us go over and get some hot soup. It will make us all feel better."

Together, the four of them, with Louisa carrying the baby, walked over to the line that had formed at the soup table, as Louisa remarked loudly. "Oh....how wonderful the soup smells! It has been so long since we have had anything hot to eat!"

Just then, one of the ladies, who had been helping with those Acadians too weak to stand, came up to Louisa. She stood there for a moment, wiping her hands on her apron, and smiled at the baby in Louisa's arms, as she remarked.

"My name is Anne Dorsey, and if you wish I will mind the baby while you eat your soup. I heard you say to Abigal that her name was Joseine. It is a lovely name....but most unusual."

Louisa looked directly into the kindly bright eyes of this rather tall, lean woman, who had just spoken to her, and gently handed over the baby, as she spoke. "The child is named after my friends, Madeleine and Josef, who had much to do with her birth....and my very survival on board the ship. Since I know not where my husband and Papa were taken by the English....they, and young Charles here, are the only family I now have."

"Oh, my dear....how terrible for you to have given birth on that horrible ship. But you are fortunate too...because you have friends such as these," the woman exclaimed. "Do not worry about the baby....I will bath the poor little dear and dress it in some fresh, clean clothing that was once used by my own children. It will be done while you eat...so, enjoy your soup, my dear!"

The line moved slowly, but soon a deep bowl each of the steaming soup was being handed to them by a woman, with silver gray hair who was ladling out portions. With a look of compassion, she handed Charles his soup and spoke. "My boy....Abigal told me about your family. My name is Martha Carroll, and I consulted my husband, William, who is now up on the second floor assisting your Mr. Joubert with those, who are ill. William is usually kept informed of happenings down at the docks, and he would certainly know, if anyone would, about others from Acadia, who were brought here by ship. But alas....it is true....there have been no other ships, from that land, carrying your people. Perhaps, they were landed elsewhere...and we may yet learn of them. So, pray, my dear..... pray."

The three young people found a place to sit and enjoy their soup portions, but they were silent for a while, having decided it was too painful to speak about the matter. Since the kind lady had related the disappointing news, it was Charles, who was the first to speak. "It is like she said.....They were probably landed somewhere else. So, we must all get settled here for the winter...and maybe come spring, there will be word of them."

Josef smiled broadly, as he reached over and hugged his younger brother, speaking exuberantly and loudly a he did. "Charles....you are indeed fast becoming a man. It is as good a plan as any, for you are right! First, we must get on our feet....then we can search for Mama and Papa and the girls. Besides, Madeleine and I cannot even be married until there is more to offer. We have not even a roof over our heads that is ours, as yet!"

"Josef," Madeleine exclaimed, frowning at him. "You know that does not matter to me. Perhaps our Father Joubert could marry us soon....after the bans of marriage are proclaimed in church...but then he is not as yet ordained, and there is no church in this new place."

"You see...it is true, Madeleine!" Josef admonished her. "It is not right....we cannot be married until I have accumulated something in this new land."

Just then Abigal Smith approached the three young people, who were deep in serious discussion. At her side was a stocky man with a stern, but kindly expression on his bearded face. She lost no time in introducing him. "My dears....this is my husband, Jonathon. I have told him all about you....and suggested that we take you in, until you are able to make your own way."

The man grinned at them, as he stood awkwardly at his wife's side. He had a mature face that showed many lines, which had resulted obviously from years of hard work. But his blue eyes displayed a pleasant twinkle, and served to soften somewhat the gruffness of his voice.

"We are by no means wealthy...but our house keeps us snug and warm through the winter. We have a son, still at home, who is the age of this boy here, and they could share a bed. Abigal says that she will fix up the loft room for the two young ladies and the baby....and there is a small room attached to the barn, where my indentured man sleeps. This young man can share that with him. Now, I will have you know on the onset, that this gesture is not strictly a charitable one, for you will certainly be expected to earn your keep. I will be needing help in the tobacco barn and the smokehouse. And come spring the fields must be plowed and sowed....and we will be adding to the apple orchard.....and....."

"Enough....enough, Jonathon!" Abigal interrupted. "You will wear us all out, just listening to you. The chores will come soon enough....but first these young people must regain their health. All right....the matter is settled...is it not?"

Josef, Madeleine, Charles and Louisa looked in surprise from one to the other, as perplexed and appreciative expressions were evidenced on their faces. They obviously had comprehended the words just spoken to them by the kindly couple addressing them. But it was Josef, who was the first to collect his thoughts and attempt to answer. "Madame....Monsieur....we are overwhelmed at your kindness. It is difficult to find words of proper meaning at this moment...so tormented have we all been in recent months with the cruelty of our fate....."

As Josef struggled to collect his thoughts in order to express his gratitude, it was Madeleine, who interrupted excitedly and summed it up in just a few words. "Madame...Monsieur...what Josef is trying to say is that we accept your offer....and we will work hard to pay you back for your kind gesture. Besides, Josef has told me that he must make something of himself in this new land, before we can marry. So, this will be a beginning for all of us. Thank you...Madame and Monsieur. We thank God for you!"

Abigal and Jonathon were obviously moved by the words of these young people before them, as they accepted the offer extended to them. Brushing a tear from her eye and nodding in agreement, Abigal reached her arms out to the girls and hugged them to her, as Jonathon's extended hand was grasped eagerly by Josef and then Charles, both. Then, they all suddenly laughed out loud, somewhat carried away with the spontaneity of the moment.

"My...my...this is a happy group, I must say!" Anne Dorsey proclaimed, as she walked up amid the laughter. "Here, my dear....I have brought back your little one, all bathed and dressed in clean clothes. She is a dear wee babe...you are most fortunate. Here.... take her, she wants her Mama to feed her now."

Louisa reached out and took the child from the woman, as the laughter subsided somewhat. But her smile remained, especially upon viewing the baby, all attired in dainty clothes and wrapped in a warm fleecy blanket. At that moment, her delight seemed to know no bounds, when she saw the child so prettily attired. All at once, her voice was filled with emotion once again, as she tried to speak—choking back tears of joy.

"Oh Madame....how beautiful! Joseine never looked so lovely....this is the first clothes she has ever had! How can we thank all of you for being so kind to us? Because of you, perhaps this little one will have a chance for some kind of future....I will never stop praying to the Lord, to have Him bless you all for your goodness. God bless you all!"

CHAPTER - 11

TO HAVE AND TO HOLD

Madeleine stood there looking at herself in Mrs. Smith's looking glass. As her hands ran over the new homespun cloth folds of her skirt, she inhaled deeply and noted with satisfaction how her slim figure filled out the white blouse, above the cinched in bodice, that she wore.

"How pretty you look, Madeleine," exclaimed Louisa, who was helping her to dress in the new attire. "Here is your bonnet....put it on, so we can see how it looks. Careful now...do not disturb your coiffure!"

How strange it is, thought Madeleine to herself, to realize that three long years had passed since that cold winter day, when the Smiths' had taken them in after that terrible voyage from Acadie. As she stood there, admiring her new clothes, she continued to dwell on the many things that had happened since then. She smiled with satisfaction, as she recalled how hard they had all worked to pay the Smiths' back for their generosity.

The crop had been good this year, and the tobacco barn was filled to capacity, after harvest time. Also, because of the efforts of Josef, Charles and Adam Gibson–the indentured man–Monsieur Smith would soon have an apple orchard double the size of his original one. Yes, and if the new trees proved to be anything like the full grown bearing trees, which had produced so bountifully this year, Madame

Abigal will have her hands full with cooking and drying apples from now on. Ah yes, Madeleine decided to herself, God had indeed been good to them all. But this was to be the very best day of all. For it was her wedding day, and soon she would be Josef's wife.

"It is such a beautiful fall day, is it not?" Questioned Louisa, as she adjusted the white bonnet cap on Madeleine's head. "But make haste, for Father and everyone awaits at the chapel in Monsieur Fotterall's house."

Louisa realized that she had interrupted her friend's thoughts somewhat. But it was just as well, because they both knew they had spent too long, dressing for the wedding. Madeleine hastily tried to relate this, as she answered. "Thank you, my friend....I am much too slow this morning. It is just that I want to look so pretty for Josef. He has worked so hard toward this day. And I am so fortunate to be marrying such a good man...am I not, Louisa?"

"Oh yes, my dear...you are indeed fortunate," Louisa hastened to agree. "To think that he—in spite of the work he has done for the Smiths' still found the time to build that two room cabin of logs and mortar over on Charles Street, where you two will reside. Of course, Charles and Adam helped when they could. But Josef worked as if possessed by the Almighty, to get it finished so you two could be married. He is indeed a good man, Madeleine....now hurry...we must go, so the ceremony can begin."

The late morning wedding Mass, that the priest performed for them, would always be memorable for the couple. The celebratory gathering at the Smith house afterwards was attended by many of their friends and acquaintances, who were with them on the voyage that brought them all to this new land. This was in addition to so many of their new friends, whom they had come to know in Baltimore City, since then.

As for Josef, the entire event passed as if in a dream. For as he enjoyed the celebration reception, there had been several minutes when he was lost in thought. In such moments, he couldn't help but recall the chain of events that had led to this special day. But festivities were over, and he was now standing before the new cabin, that he had built for them both. And here she was, his new bride, standing there with him. She glanced shyly at him, as she took the first step to enter the door. Oh, how he had longed for this day, when his beloved would finally be his wife. The years of waiting had been almost unbearable for him. But he simply had to be a man of some worth, before he could marry. Otherwise, he would have no self respect ever again.

How different it would have been, he thought, had they been allowed to marry in Acadie. For he would have had so much more to offer her there, that is if the English had allowed him to retain his section of the rich diked farm land along the Minas Basin, that was to be part of his heritage. But it was not to be, and he had finally accepted this. Because God had apparently deemed otherwise, resulting in their being brought to this new land—for what purpose, he knew not.

It was as if a cloud had momentarily marred his expression, as he dwelled on these things. But as he looked over at the face of his beloved, there with him at the door to their humble cabin, his face brightened. Then, he displayed a broad grin that was beamed in her direction, to show her the elation he felt then. At that point, he wanted nothing, but to become lost in the interminable depths of Madeleine's warm, brown eyes.

As Josef held the door open for her, his bride walked inside into the dim room. Although, the afternoon sun had not as yet set, the cabin was dark, because there was only one window and it was shuttered. "Wait...I will light some candles," Josef exclaimed, as he hurried over and reached for the tapers that lay on the shelf above the fireplace. Upon stooping down to light the candles from the glowing coals of the cooking fire, that had been lit hours before, he further explained apologetically.

"Someday, we will have panes of glass for the windows and we will not always have to secure the shutters. But until then, we just have to make do."

"Oh Josef.....there is no need for apologies," admonished Madeleine, as she stood there, looking around curiously in the dim light of her new home.

The main cabin room was small, but ample, she noted. Besides the stone fireplace that was against the far wall, there was a rough board table, on which two deep wooden bowls had been set. There were shelves along the wall and pegs for holding clothing. On one peg, Josef's rough work shirt already hung. A bunch of dried tobacco was hanging on a peg near the fireplace, and a basket of apples had been placed near the hearth. A half-log bench stood near the table and one black iron kettle, filled with hot water, hung simmering over the glowing coals in the fireplace.

She continued to look around the room with interest, for Josef had not allowed her to see the cabin until after the wedding. And now she was viewing it for the first time. When her eyes had become fully accustomed to the dim light within, she looked into the other room and observed the homemade, rough hewn, four poster bed, that had been placed against one wall. At that moment, she felt a fleeting twinge of embarrassment, but she hoped that Josef would not notice.

Apparently, he had not taken note of her uneasiness, upon seeing the bed. For he was standing there silently and somewhat awkwardly near the hearth, waiting for his bride to finish looking around the two rooms. But he was fast to note when her eyes had finally settled on the bed against the wall, whereupon he rushed over to it, nervously blurting out words, as he did so.

"Look....my dear one....Madame Abigal made a fine mattress of feathers as their wedding gift for us. See....she even covered it with Mama's patchwork quilt that you had cleaned and repaired after we brought it from Acadie. You know....few couples have such a fine mattress for their bed, when they are only just starting out."

All of a sudden, Josef's face flushed with a pink twinge of embarrassment, upon pointing out the bed so obviously to his new wife. And he immediately changed the subject, bounding as he did so across the room to the fireplace, and to the pot that hung steaming over the coals. Nervously, he looked away from her and reached up on the mantel board for the two gourd cups, which he had previously put there, extending his voiced invitation to her as he did so.

"Madame Abigal gave me a portion of her tea leaves....and the water is hot. Perhaps you would like a cup of tea before going to bed." Josef blushed again at his mention of the bed, and hastened to speak out nervously once more. "Or....perhaps you would rather have a cup of cider that you, Louisa and Madame made from the orchard apples?"

She could not contain her amusement, as she smiled to herself upon noting Josef's nervous actions. But she suddenly realized how ridiculous all of this uneasiness between them was. After all, they had been through so much together already—even before being married. It then occurred to her, that perhaps she should make some gesture that would put him at ease. So, with this in mind, she slowly walked over to where he stood, nervously awaiting her answer to his offer of tea or cider. She stood close to him, placed both of her hands up on his shoulders, and looked deeply into those dark eyes of his that now suddenly seemed to be filled with so much uncertainty. Slowly, she slid her hands around his neck and pulled him close to her, all the while marveling silently to herself how such a fine man, so strong as Josef, could be so in command in very difficult situations. Yet, he could become so uncertain and nervous, when dealing with a new bride. At that moment, so many thoughts ran through her mind. Had the circumstances been different, she would have asked her Mama for answers, had they been married back in Acadie, as originally planned. But now, she would simply have to find the answers to these many strange things as best she could.

Lost in thought for the moment, while holding him to her tightly, Madeleine rested her head against his shoulder. Then all at once she felt his arms encircle her waist and suddenly grasp her body to his with a force that literally took her breath away. "Josef.... not so tight....or surely I will break! Be gentle...my dear one... go slowly, for I am afraid!"

"Poor little Madeleine," Josef murmured soothingly, loosening his grasp on her somewhat. "I am so sorry...but it is difficult for me to take my time. I have waited for you and dreamed of how it would be with you, for such a long time. Forgive me, if I am over anxious....but I am."

They continued to stand there, holding each other. And for Madeleine, it was an experience like no other she had ever had. For strange feelings were beginning to take hold deep within the very depths of her being. She could sense his ever growing excitement too, for now he was kissing her cheeks, her forehead, her chin, her neck with a fervent intensity. But when he slipped one of the sleeves of her blouse ever so slightly over her shoulders, the thrill she felt was really intense. As he continued to plant a series of tiny kisses there, it made her giggle with delight.

It was then, that he put a hand to her chin and tilted her face up to his and kissed her full on the mouth—at first gentle and somewhat unsure, but then with an increasing force. Her lips quivered at this loving encounter and the excitement she felt made her tremble in his arms.

A moment more and Josef took both of her hands in his and led her over to the bed, where they sat down together on the edge of the soft feather mattress. They sat there a few moments more. Then, looking longingly into each other's eyes, they both began to laugh together, all at once from the delight they both felt at that moment. But as soon as it had begun, their nervous laughter ceased almost at once, and his arms drew her to him. And at that point, they fell together, as the feather bed caressed their bodies as they lay down upon it. Then, time seemed to lose all meaning for them both.

Later, Madeleine lay there staring up into the darkness of the room, listening to the deep easy breathing of Josef, who lay sleeping beside her. As she pulled the patchwork quilt up to her neck to ward off some of the chill of the early morning hours of this new Fall day, she recalled the earlier events of her wedding night. How grand it was to have Josef's love, she thought. For to be possessed by him was a wonderful thing, even though somewhat overwhelming.

She smiled sheepishly to herself, lying there in the dark of her marriage bed, as she remembered how forceful and manly this new husband had been. And how he had thrilled her so, only a few hours before. He had wanted her so much, and his passion had been such as to take her breath away. But she did recall some moments of unpleasantness too, for it had been somewhat painful, when he entered her. However, she had not spoken of it to him as she did not want him to know. Besides she was convinced that it would surely pass. But if only she could have asked her Mama about these things, it would have been such a comfort. Well, she decided silently, she would simply have to deal with all of these new experiences as best she could.

Just then, Josef stirred restlessly in his sleep, changing the position of his body to face the shadowy form of his wife, who was lying next to him. As he blinked his eyes groggily in an effort to awaken, he immediately noted that the room was still quite dark. But he sensed that his bride next to him was awake. So, he whispered softly in her ear.

"My dear....you know that today you must think about going to stay on the ship, that is anchored in the harbor, because of the Indian raids not far from here. I know you do not want to go...but Madame Abigal, Louisa and the baby are going too, along with the other women and children. It is only until it is safe again, after the Indian uprising is put down!"

"No, Josef." Replied Madeleine emphatically. Her body stiffened as she spoke. "I will stay here in our new home with you.....we should not be separated now! Just because the Indians from the western hills have been raiding the settlements, they will surely not come into Baltimore City. We have been through too much together already, to be separated now!"

Josef was silent for a few moments, as he pondered his wife's words. For he fully realized how stubborn Madeleine could be when she was set on something. Also, he knew only too well how difficult it would be to get her to change her mind. But he reasoned to himself, that it was to be for her own safety, as well as his peace of mind, to have her stay on the ship until the Indian problem could be put to rest. However, the question in his mind remained as to how, indeed, could he get her to go of her own free will? He knew of no other way but to forcibly carry her on board, and this he certainly did not want to do. However, all of his pondering seemed to be to no avail, for when she spoke again her mood had changed, and she no longer sounded obstinate. Indeed, her voice had become soft and gentle, and this new husband sensed deep down what the outcome of this—their first confrontation—would be.

"Josef...my dear one," Madeleine whispered closely into his ear, in a notably different tone than her previous statement of defiance. "How can you send me away...especially now that we have known each other in the marriage bed? Here....touch me...hold me.... tightly...lay your head on my breast. Will you not miss all of this, if I am away from you on that ship...and you are alone here in our cabin? Please...my dear...do not send me away from you!"

With these softly murmured words, she hugged him closely and kissed him provocatively on the ear, as she stroked his head softly with her hand. At that moment, Josef realized all to well, that no power on earth could make him send her away from him now. So, troubled as his conscience was, he inwardly relented from his stand and—with an audible moan of capitulation—he roughly pulled her warm body close to his.

––––––––

The springtime of the year must be beautiful everywhere, thought Louisa, as she walked briskly along Charles Street, on her way to Madeleine and Josef's cabin. Remembrances of springtime back home in Acadie were still very sharp for her. But as she marveled at the beauty of the spring season in this year of 1763, around Baltimore City, it was difficult to decide whether the budding trees and the colorful wild flowers bloomed more profusely here in this new land, or back home. However, no matter what, of one thing she was sure. It made little difference where spring made an appearance, since it always resulted in an awakening for everything and everyone.

Adam Gibson, the Smiths' former indentured servant, walked along the street with her, and he too appeared happy to be alive. But then, she knew this was partially due to something else. For Louisa had known for some time, that Adam was enamored of her. Why, only last year he had proposed marriage and said that Joseine needed a father and he wanted to take care of them both. Of course, it was out of the question, and Louisa remembered telling him so. After all, she was still married to Batiste LeBlanc, and one day he would find them and come to know the daughter, whom he had never seen.

Louisa continued to dwell on these things, as she walked along holding onto Joseine's hand. My, how her little girl had grown, thought she. Indeed, it was difficult to realize that Josiene was now eight years old. And she had to admit, Joseine had been a constant reminder of Batiste, during all those years. There was just no denying it. For the child had those same penetrating eyes and that wide grin, which was so like her Papa. So, Louisa thanked God everyday for her daughter. This was not only because of the joy she brought her Mama, but because she helped to keep the memory of Batiste alive. For someday they would all be together again. Of this, Louisa was convinced. So, remarriage was out of the question, even though Adam's gesture had been grand, and she had told him so. But she did want to remain a good friend of this quiet, considerate man.

But for Adam Gibson, it had been a difficult time, being so close to this pert, young woman, whom he had come to love. Indeed, he pondered as he walked beside her, she had been the main reason that he had remained in the service of the Smiths'. After all, his indentured time had been up a few years before, and he was free to leave at any time. He had served six years that was agreed upon, and had received his due of a suit of clothes, three barrels of corn, and enough tools to tend 50 acres of land, that he could have headrights to. But he simply could not bring himself to leave. Instead, he agreed to stay on indefinitely, working for the Smiths' as a hired hand. It was just that he wanted to stay as close as possible to Louisa. For his future lay in the small, but competent hands of this little woman, who walked beside him this day.

The late afternoon sun felt warm on their faces, as they neared the cabin of their friends. Louisa remembered when Josef and Madeleine had moved into this dwelling after they were married. She also recalled how much land had still remained on Charles Street then, but that had been almost five years ago, and the area had grown considerably. In fact, so many of the Acadian people had built houses in the area of Charles Street, that the section had become known as French Town. Ah yes, her memory was filled with all manner of things that had happened since the time when that awful ship brought them to this land.

As they approached the Theriot cabin, the figure of a little girl of about four years of age, came bounding out of the door, running in their direction, all the while giggling as she ran.

"Oh...it is little Rosarie! Look....Joseine, she runs to meet us!" Louisa exclaimed, holding out her arms to the child. "Next to you, my dear, this little child of Josef and Madeleine is dearest to me.... look how big she has grown!"

"Come in....come in," Madeleine called to them from the doorway. "It is so good that you are here....Charles and his friends are inside!"

Adam, Joseine and Louisa, carrying little Rosarie, entered the door to the cabin, wherein Madeleine, Josef and Charles, with two of his young friends, waited. Upon seeing them, Charles grinned happily in their direction, and grasped Adam's hand in greeting, as he introduced his friends to them.

"This is Felix Blanchard and Augustave Chaisson, my friends whom I have come to know. It is so strange…they too came to this land after the time we arrived….but their ship was sent over the bay to the eastern shore. There, both Felix and Augustave were taken in by a planter on the Wye River in Talbot County. We only just met recently when they came to seek work at the iron works at Whetstone Point. They are from Boudro Point back in Acadie. But were picked up by the English and taken to the ship while at the settlement of Melanson on the Gaspereau River. They, too, were separated from their families and want to go back to find them."

"Charles….what are you speaking of?" Josef questioned in surprise. "What makes you think that Mama, Papa and the girls…. or the people of these young men have been taken back to Acadie? It is more likely they were taken to someplace else!"

"Josef….we have tried all these years to learn word of them!" Charles exclaimed. "It has been of no use…so maybe they were never taken….maybe they were relocated in Acadie!"

"Monsieur Josef….it is as Charles says," Augustave interrupted. "We have had no good fortune in finding our family either….and we have seen many others, who were seeking their people in recent years. But we personally have known of only one, who has succeeded here in Maryland. It was back a few years ago, that we learned of such a thing from an Acadian man, who came to the eastern shore in search of his family. He told us that he, along with another man, had received permission from the authorities in Philadelphia and New York, where they had been taken, back when we all were, to travel to Maryland in search of their families, from whom they had been separated when the ships left Acadie."

"Yes," Felix agreed. "This man had heard God favored a friend of his, for he had discovered his wife and children at Annapolis. But so far the man, who was also seeking, had not had such good fortune. So, he was still searching....when he took his leave of us on the Wye River shore."

"It is true," Josef agreed. "We too have met others, who were searching all of these many years. But how can you think, that going back to Acadie is the answer? Besides...how could any of us get back there....we have not enough money for passage....and it is just too far away!"

"There is a way, Josef!" Charles replied anxiously. "Word has come that a ship carrying some people of Acadie has run aground south of here on the coast!"

"It is true," agreed Felix. "The story we heard is that they, too, came to this country at the time we did, but far south of here in the colony of South Carolina. Poor things....unlike the good people, who received us here in Maryland....they were put to work and indentured by the authorities of that colony in the fields of cotton and indigo....but together, they managed over the years to acquire enough to purchase two very old ships."

"Yes...but the ships were too old," added Augustave. "For those ships went aground off of the Virginia colony, far south of here..... and no one there would help them. Instead...the people on shore robbed them of their goods and made them put to sea again in those old ships. But they managed to proceed off the coast, until they ran aground again...only this time off this colony."

"Josef....it is true!" Charles exclaimed. "Only yesterday a party from their ship was in Baltimore City, to ask help to repair their vessel....and we have decided to go and help them. Then, when the ship is repaired, we can get passage to Acadie, for that is where they are bound."

"Charles....all of this sounds like the answer you have been seeking," Josef said quietly. "I know, my brother, how sad you have been since we were put here...away from our family and home. But if these ships are as old as you say....then it is unlikely that they will be seaworthy enough for the long voyage to Acadie. No....I think that this is not the best thing to do!"

"Oh, Josef.....it may be the only chance for us," Charles remarked. "Felix and Augustave and I have agreed that this is what we want to do. Even if the ships prove not seaworthy and go aground again....we can continue back to Acadie overland. Others have left to attempt this...and surely they must have made it! I have spoken to some of them before they departed on such a journey....they had it all mapped out. They planned to travel northward along the coast of the New England colonies, up through the wilderness forests of Maine, then along the west shore of the Bay of Fundy....and they would cross at the Isthmus of Shediac and go on to Chignecto and finally make it to Grand Pre and home!"

"Charles....are you mad? You have not the supplies or arms for such a perilous journey!" Josef admonished his brother. For now he was becoming angry at the brashness of these three young men before him. "I know you are a man of 20 years now, Charles....and should be able to make up your own mind. But think what such a journey could involve. Surely, you cannot expect us to go with you....we must think of the women and little girls. They could not endure such a trip! Also, have you thought of the hardships for you? What of the Indians along the way...and the lack of supplies for such a long journey? Even if you make it by some grace of God.... there will be nothing for you there. Do you not remember the fires before our ship left? The English burned everything....nothing is left to go back to...we own nothing in that land anymore! Think what you are doing, my brother. There must be a better way!"

"There is!" Adam suddenly exclaimed. "We have heard about the treaty that was signed earlier this year....it means the Indians in the hills to the west are not at war anymore! Surely, you have heard that many of your people here in the Baltimore City area

are speaking of traveling to the western land and down to French
Louisiana, far to the south of this country. We all know that most
of them did not attempt to go before....but now with the Indian
threat lessened, the mountains could be crossed with some safety!"

"But what is there?" Questioned Charles, frowning with
annoyance. "Why should we go to a land we know nothing about?"

"Charles, your Mama and Papa may be there...it is said that
many of your people from Acadie have traveled there," explained
Adam. "Besides....it is a country of your people. The language is
French...they are of your Catholic religion...and it is said that
settlers can get rich land there."

"No....I want to go back to Acadie....and will never rest until
I do....even if I die trying to get there. It will be worth it ....for
there is no rest for me anyhow!" Charles proclaimed loudly, getting
to his feet and gesticulating emphatically.

"It is as Charles has said," Felix agreed. "We have decided to go
and help with the ship and ask for passage...then we will take our
chances."

"Well...we cannot stop Charles from going with you. But I beg
of you three to consider what you are attempting," Josef implored,
grasping his brother's arm as he said so. "Adam's plan seems the
better of the two. At least, we will be among our countrymen if we
get to Louisiana. With your way...there would be nothing for us...
the English have already taken everything in Acadie....and I cannot
risk going back to nothing!"

"Even though I am not French, Josef," Adam said. "I feel as
though you and the ladies are my family. So, I want to go with you no
matter what you choose. But it looks like French Louisiana would be
the best venture to undertake. I have learned that a number of your
Acadian people in Fredericktown, north of here, have petitioned the
authorities to allow them to embark on the journey to the French
settlements on the River Mississippi. Why only yesterday, I spoke
with one of their number, who was in Baltimore City on business

with Mr. Smith. And he explained the route they planned to follow overland. They plan to cross the Potomac River at Shenandoah Falls at Mr. Harper's Ferry. From there, they plan to follow the Appalachian Trail along the east side of the great mountains. If we decided to join this group, I can learn of the details. But we must make haste, for they are planning to leave soon. What do you want to do, Josef? What about you, Madeleine…and you Louisa…what do you think about this?"

Louisa was the first to answer his question. "I shall go wherever Madeleine and Josef decide…for without them, neither Joseine nor I would still be alive."

Madeleine was quiet for a moment, and she chose her words carefully, while looking imploringly into Charles' eyes. "It is difficult to bear a separation….for you Charles have become like my own brother. But I believe Josef and Adam have the better plan….and I do wish you and your friends would reconsider and come with us. There is so little left of our family….it is hard to bear losing you too!"

Charles hastily looked away from her, but not before she saw the obvious pain that filled his eyes. Finally, Josef broke the uneasy silence that had resulted after Madeleine's words, and spoke of his decision. "It looks as though we have decided to try for French Louisiana….maybe there we will find some of our lost family!"

Choking back the obvious emotion he felt at that moment, Charles once again spoke up with conviction. "Then there is nothing left to be said….but our goodbyes. Tomorrow, we three will leave for the ship that is aground south of here, on the bank of the Bay of Chesapeake. God willing….in time we will be back home in Acadie. There is just no other way for us!"

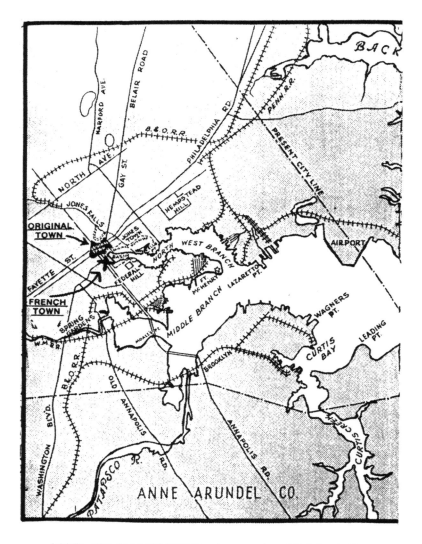

MAP OF BALTIMORE shows the "Original Town" (black area on left), and the site of "French Town" (the cross depicts that area).

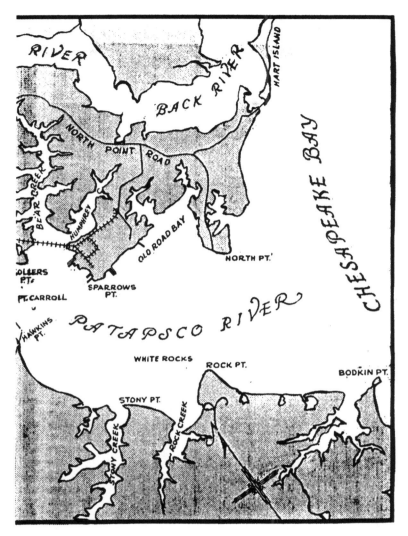

"FRENCH TOWN" was an area of Baltimore, along the Basin of the Northwest Branch of the Patapsco River. This is the site where many Acadian exiles settled after 1755.

CHAPTER - 12

THE JOURNEY CONTINUES WEST

The tall trees of the lush forest, that lined the dirt road out of Fredericktown served to shade them from the brilliant May sun, as they made their way slowly west.

Madeleine could not stop thinking about all of the goodbyes they had said in recent days. Indeed, saying goodbye to so many people, whom they had come to love, was one of the most difficult things that any of them ever had to do. It was especially so, considering they would probably never meet again. Bad enough, thought she, saying goodbye to Charles–stubborn young man that he is–but he wanted to go back to Acadie, and nothing any of them could say would deter him from that goal.

She sighed deeply, recalling Charles' determination with regret as she walked along the dusty road at the side of the oxen drawn wagon. Adam was at the reins, with Louisa, Joseine and Rosarie riding with him in the wagon, along with all their worldly goods. But Madeleine chose to walk for awhile, and since the lumbering oxen pulled the wagon so slowly, she was able to keep up the pace. Besides, the ride on the wagon over this dusty road was certainly not smooth, so walking seemed like a good idea for now.

Their wagon was the last one in this group, which were now lumbering on in a westerly direction out of Fredericktown. It was as Adam had said, she remembered, their decision to join this group of Acadians destined for French Louisiana, had come almost too late. For the group had been planning for some time to set out in the spring, and when they learned of the treaty between France and England, that had been signed in February of this year of 1763, they were more anxious than ever to be on their way. For they all knew, that after such a treaty, it would be easier to cross the great mountains to the west, since the Indians would no longer be such a menace. Before the treaty, a safe crossing of those mountains would have been almost impossible, what with all those Indians on the war path. Considering their impatience to get started on their way, it seemed to Madeleine that it had been very good of these families to delay the start of their journey, in order to allow the Theriot group, from over in Baltimore City, time enough to make ready for the trip. Yes, she must remember to give thanks in her prayers for their consideration.

Suddenly, in the midst of her thoughts, Madeleine was jolted when she stumbled on a loose stone that lay in her path on the road. As a result, she almost fell down. But she caught herself in time to keep from falling. However, her near fall did not go completely unnoticed, for Josef, who was walking at the head of the ox team, heard her cry out slightly and looked back to call to her. "Madeleine....are you all right? Would you rather ride in the wagon?"

"No, Josef," she shouted back at him, as she dusted her skirt off and brought one hand hastily up to adjust her bonnet, that was now somewhat askew. "Do not worry, I will walk awhile more."

Yes, the walking felt good to her, and it gave her an opportunity to be alone with her thoughts, and there was much to think about, too. But for now, her mind wandered as she caught sight of a bright yellow and black butterfly, which fluttered around her head for a moment. It was as if, it was inquiring about her presence on the road on this fine day. Then in seconds, the lovely creature flew on it's way, and she looked after it longingly, wanting to bid it stay for a while more. Ah yes, she thought, it could be likened to the wanderings of people, for they too sometimes flutter around in one's life, only to go away after a time, never to be seen again.

Dwelling as she was on such partings, thoughts of Madame Smith all at once came to light within her mind. She recalled Madame's emotional reaction, when they related to her and Monsieur Jonathon their plans to leave. As these remembrances became more vivid, Madeleine swallowed hard and stifled a tear that had only just welled up an instant before. Yes, how could she ever forget? Madame had reacted to the news as if they were her own children, going away from her. However, it did seem true, for they had all become like family to each other. So, as a result of such deep feelings by all, saying goodbye was virtually impossible without the accompanying presence of many tears and much emotion. Oh, how the Smiths' had begged them not to go, she remembered. But in the end this kindly couple understood why it had to be. However, realizing these things did not make parting any easier, and leaving these wonderful people, who had been their salvation in this new land, was almost more than Madeleine could stand.

All at once, a surge of tears came into her eyes and spilled over onto her cheeks, as she continued to remember. Making no effort to stifle the tears, Madeleine sobbed openly as she walked along this road, which was leading them further and further away from the Smiths', and the place that had become home to them, during the last six years. Oh, how wonderful it felt, to let the tears flow and release the pent-up sorrow that she had been keeping locked up inside. It was good to be all alone, in order to cry privately for the loss of the Smiths' and for the loss of dear Charles, also. Madeleine believed that this feeling of sadness was her own personal thing, and she needed desperately to get it out of her system. Such things, she reasoned to herself, should be put behind. Then, the mind can better cope with what is to come. She realized only too well that they would all need their wits about them, if they were to survive the rigors of this long journey, on which they have undertaken. True, the good Lord had been good to them in recent years, but Madeleine believed deeply, that they must help themselves and each other on this trip, and not expect God to intervene on their behalf in every endeavor. Indeed, thought she, God knows what lies ahead for us, and He will expect us to be ready for whatever is to come.

Just then, the sound of galloping hoofs was heard, coming toward this rear wagon, alongside of which she walked. With a hand up to shade her eyes, she soon recognized the approaching rider on a horse, as Mathew Mould, the guide. He had been hired to take this group of wagons and people through the valley, east of the great mountains. Accompanied by a cloud of dust, he reined his horse up short, alongside of Josef, who was walking ahead with the team that pulled their wagon.

"Aye...mate....keep that team movin' steadily....don't want to fall behind now, do ye?" Matthew Mould shouted down at Josef, in his lisping voice sneering in Josef's direction all the while.

From where Madeleine walked, further back, she could almost feel Josef's neck stiffen and sense his teeth gritting together, upon hearing Mould's bossy manner. She had observed, ever since they joined this group to travel west, that Mould was not a very likeable man; this was obvious to everyone. But Madeleine decided that this was probably due to his unfortunate life.

She recalled how fascinated she and Louisa had been upon learning about this man's past. He told them about the years before, when he had been a seaman. The story goes that he had gotten into some kind of trouble while his ship was in port, and as a result was jailed. After that, he had to work out his indentured 14 years sentence on the ore banks at Whetstone Point. Following that, he made his way as a free woodcutter and by collecting bounties on the bears and wolves he killed. He later worked as a driver, transporting wagons of supplies to the out-lying settlements in the foothills—even

THE JOURNEY CONTINUES WEST

during the times of unrest with the Indians, in recent years. As a result, he had come to be considered quite knowledgeable about the Indian ways and the dangers, which lurk along the mountainous trail. So, the group in Fredericktown hired him to see them safely along.

Well, he would just have to be tolerated, Madeleine thought to herself. But Mould certainly made all of the women feel uneasy whenever he was in their presence. She shuddered slightly just thinking about the way he looked each woman up and down with those lusty eyes of his. Of course, if he knows the trail and the Indians, like they say he does, and would get them to the appointed place previously decided upon between the men, then all the women would just have to put up with the rakish manner of this unnerving and undisciplined man.

Of course, the poor man is to be pitied, she reasoned, so in need of Christian understanding and compassion is he. It was little enough for all of them to accept him, she decided emphatically, considering the life he has had. Dwelling on this for a moment, she recalled how he had told them about himself, back in Fredericktown. He even bragged about it in the process. She had noticed the letter "H" that was branded on his arm. When they inquired of this, he boldly related to them that once he was caught stealing hogs, and that was the penalty inflicted for that crime. However, he had been in trouble with the King's law more times than this, and Madeleine cringed inwardly upon recalling how he had bragged when relating how the authorities had ordered his tongue to be bored through, years before for swearing against the King. She decided that this would account for his lisp, whenever he spoke. But nothing deterred the man, it seemed, for it was common knowledge among the Acadians on this trip that Mould had probably been in the pillory for numerous minor offenses, more times than he could remember.

Pondering these things, she marveled at the wretched life Matthew Mould had led, as she watched him turn his horse back toward the lead wagon and gallop off in that direction. For the sun was fast sinking in the west and soon they would be stopping for the night. At that time, she felt sure, Mould would be ordering everyone about, as was his custom. And this was to be so, for it was just as the sun set, that Mould began shouting orders to everyone, in preparation for the overnight camp. They had arrived at the junction of two rivers, and that night they camped outside of the settlement of Shenandoah Falls at Mr. Harper's Ferry. It was then at this encampment, that the Acadian travelers were directed to plan on crossing the river the next day. As they soon learned, it was the junction of the Potomac and Shenandoah Rivers.

They were told that this was the only place to cross for many miles, because of the ferry that was maintained there. It seems that in 1761, an Englishman from Philadelphia, named Robert Harper, had obtained the right to establish and maintain the only ferry in that area. As a result, many travelers going west made use of his facility. It was to be the same for this group. So, with the dawning of the following day, the Acadian travelers stood on the high shore, viewing the point of junction where the two great rivers met.

The site where the two rivers met was a beautifully spectacular one. Indeed, the overall forested view was equally awesome. It was at that point, where the swift waters of the Shenandoah River rushed to join the Potomac, with it's own fast current. Thus, both rivers ultimately blended together to hurry on it's unencumbered way to the Bay of Chesapeake, many miles to the east. Indeed, this scene of such spectacular beauty and force would surely not soon be forgotten by any of these travelers.

On that morning, when they were to cross, the current was swift. However, the rivers were not flooding as these often did at certain times of year. So, Mould assured them that their families, wagons and stock could be safely ferried across, if they would pay heed to using proper precautions. So, in spite of the Acadians' misgivings upon seeing the swiftness of the current at this river junction, they agreed to try for the western shore. Mould maintained that had they arrived a month before, it might not have been possible to cross safely. Others in that settlement related to the Acadians about the bad flood years—particularly in 1748 and 1753—when the waters went on a dreadful rampage and drove the early settlers in that region to much higher ground. They did hasten to assure the Acadians that this year, by comparison, had been uneventfully calm. Thus, they crossed on the rickety ferry—one wagon at a time—with no great loss. That is, with the exception of Monsieur Babin's cow, which was carried away down river in the swirling water.

On the far shore, they spent the rest of the day and part of the early evening hours drying out and getting wagons, contents, stock and people time to recover from the ferrying experience across the tumultuous river. Then, they rested for the night. However, their anxiety level was high, wondering what the next day was to bring. Because with the rising sun of the coming day, Mould had informed them that their wagons would then be following the trail along the Appalachians in a more southerly direction, and not many days would pass thereafter before they would enter the great valley of the Shenandoah. This route, Mould told them, is the one they were to follow southwest into the Virginia country.

It was as he had said. For some days thereafter, they followed a trail that wound along—more or less—parallel to the great blue mountain ridge that was ever with them on the horizon to their right. However, even though the sight of the great mountains on the horizon was notable, it was not overwhelmingly so for these travelers, especially after they had journeyed for days along the greater length of the grand Shenandoah Valley. For indeed, just as others had been, these Acadians were also awed by the grandeur of the softly rolling surface of the landscape there. So, they would not soon forget the impressiveness of this land. But however rich that this valley appeared to be, it was not where they were bound. No kindred of theirs dwelled there, so they hurried on toward their ever nearing encounter with the great mountain ridge to the west.

———

The Indians called the mountains to the west Unaha, so Matthew Mould had told them. Madeleine remembered his words well, when they had gathered around the camp fire the night before. He was advising them to leave the valley trails of Virginia and travel more westerly toward the great smokie ridge on the Carolina horizon.

"Aye...there she be...the great Ararat mountain!" Mould shouted, pointing toward a high peak to the south of where they camped. "It is our guide....just as it is too for the Indians. But she is called Jomeokee by them....and a mighty guide she be, too!"

For the Acadians, it was apparent that this high peak to the south of their present position must serve as some kind of beacon for travelers. Obviously, it marked the place along the route where they should go due west toward the appointed mountain pass.

This was indeed the case, for from that day on, their travels took a notably more due west direction, toward the great blue ridge. This was a ridge, which became more awesome in size with each day that brought the travelers closer, into the mountain foothills of the Carolina country.

Steadily, the oxen pulled the wagons along the edge of the Yadkin River, toward the Watauga country to the west, where they hoped to reach the conjunction of the north and south forks of the Holston River, which was well into the great mountains. But first, they would have to travel the tall mountain paths, that were dark and foreboding, and little used except by Indians and the beasts of the great forest, which covered this primitive wilderness.

So, their wagons traveled on over the higher foothills of the mountains, where the trail sometimes narrowed to little more than a path that seemed more conducive to travelers on foot, rather than animal drawn wagons. But they persevered, lightening the loaded wagons from time to time, by having everyone walk, as well as carry some of the contents of the wagons. This was so that the oxen could better struggle up the steeper inclines. It was at these times, which were becoming more frequent in number that they all realized how far from civilization they had come. When a particularly steep incline had to be traversed, these traveler's thoughts dwelled on the value of their worldly goods, which they carried with them. For here, in this primitive place, where they were left to their own devices, the value of the few muskets, powder and shot that they carried, as well as the bags of salt, seed, traps, cross-cut saws and grubbing tools suddenly became valued above any monetary consideration, that they might previously have had, back in the lower valley of the Shenandoah.

Climbing steadily toward the blue line of mountain ridge, that still lay before them, the travelers kept close watch on their stock, for fear of losing the two cows and the small number of pigs, that they had brought with them. For the vast forest was becoming denser and darker, as they penetrated into the depths of the mountains.

After some days spent with each day's trail apparently reaching higher toward the sky, in this awesome mountain range, they soon found themselves entering an eerie realm that was particularly damp and misty. They soon discovered that they were walking through clouds on the higher range, and as they endeavored to keep to the path along the rocky river bed of the stream that cut through the deep peaks of the dark forest, they finally reached a gap where the stream bed cut through a high pass. There, as they emerged from the shadowy eerie mistiness of the clouds that capped many of the peaks, they suddenly felt the sunshine warmly upon them. At that point, they gasped in disbelief, when all at once they viewed the spectacular panoramic sight that stretched out before them. From this place, on one of these higher peaks, they could see far off into the distance, where the mountains and valleys were laid out before them, seeming to run on and on to a distant horizon, which was spotted in places with the whiteness of clouds that hovered over some of the land mass below. They camped that night in this dark, seemingly impenetrable forest, where naught but Indians and beasts roamed, and they warmed themselves well from the chill of this foreign place at their campsite fires—fires made with rifle flint and powder.

Every night, their cows, horses and oxen were hobbled to graze under the high shadowy canopy of the tall forest trees. The pigs were contained, where these could root around the camp for roots and acorns, well into the evening. But night in these eerie mountains was filled with a darkness the likes of which none of these Acadians had ever seen. Indeed the night was filled with a blackness in this place, that was unlike anything, which evening time had ever brought to them down in the lowlands.

The eeriness of these mountains, the intense darkness of the night, the realization of being so completely alone in a place that seemed so foreign to them, made all of them cling together more than ever. Thus, a closeness resulted among these Acadians, that had not before been as evident down along the coastal plain, from whence they had come.

Madeleine clung closely to Josef in the night, as they reclined in the wagon, with Rosarie asleep beside them, for those dark foreboding mountains frightened her so much. It seemed to her, that these mountains were all knowing, nurturing secrets as old as the world itself, and she wanted to put this frightening place far behind them as soon as possible.

There were noises in this eerie, dark place—long sharp, quivering screams of creatures of a type unknown to them. Sometimes, there were choruses of cries in the darkness that covered these mountains in the night—screams, shrill calls, high pitched wails and low growling moans of a sort never before heard by them. So, they kept the fire blazing each night for fear that the beasts, which made these noises, would wander into their campsite while they slept.

One night, the screeches were so foreboding, the horses bolted from their tether, the cows cowered together in the shadows and the pigs wandered off and had to be tracked the next morning. Even the dog, they had gotten from the settler in the valley of the Shenandoah, crawled under a wagon with it's tail tucked underneath it's body, quivering with terror and whimpering all the while. This night passed too slowly for everyone, and the first light of day couldn't dawn fast enough for this party of frightened people.

With the coming of morning, everything seemed better, even though the towering trees continued to block out most of the sunshine, with thick branches that seemed to reach to the sky. It appeared to Madeleine, that they were perpetually traveling in dark shade, with the exception of occasional spaces on hillsides and in high valleys that looked as though devastatingly singed by a great fire which must have raged unabated in recent times. Often, along the way through these mountains, it was necessary to cross rushing streams of water that threatened to carry off some of the animals. But Madeleine was glad to come across the streams, for at least here the constant dark canopy of trees became parted for a bit—enough to let the sun's rays find them there on the banks of those streams that ran with clear, icy water.

Each time they left a high mountain valley and set out to cross another ridge, after their usual meal of dried apples, cornbread and the cold water of a stream, along with what milk they could get from their travel weary cows, the trail seemed interminable. Indeed, it seemed without end, winding as it did through the vastness of these mountains. Sometimes, the sound of water falling from a high place could be heard off in the distance, but only once did they see such a water fall.

They marveled at the size of the spectacular trees, that they be held in these mountains. For the trunks of these foliaged sentinels appeared awesome in thickness, and indescribable in towering height. This was an undisturbed realm, where bears, eagles, wolves, snakes and all manner of God's creatures dwelled. Once, they came across the large tracks left by one of these beasts, on the side of the trail. Louisa set her foot down into the track, and it took three lengths of her foot size to match the long indentation. Thoughts of such a tremendous beast caused them to burn the camp fire even brighter each night, after that encounter. But they had been warned by some settlers, who dwelled back in the lowlands, about the great bears that inhabit these mountains. Many were the tales told about such creatures, with thick brown fur, that stood twice the height of a tall man. Such tales had already become legend, tales about these huge beasts with muscular bodies of unbridled strength—strength that could maul and kill with the fierceness and agility of their great paws from which steel-like claws protruded. Many were the personal accounts of low landers about these great bears that could take a man's scalp off with one swipe of a giant paw, and crush the ribs and entrails of anyone unlucky enough to get caught in one of those smothering bear hugs. As a result of these warnings, the travelers intended to avoid any such confrontation with such awesome beasts, for they knew that it would probably take several musket shots to bring down such a bear. Consequently, this realization made them all feel very uneasy.

On the perimeter of their next camp site, Louisa kept recalling those terrible bear stories, as she picked her way carefully through the underbrush beneath the towering tree canopy, that was ever with them in this primeval forest. The thick carpet of leaves beneath their feet rustled audibly with each step she and Adam took, as they went about the chore of picking up twigs and small fallen limbs to be used in their camp fire.

Even though they were only a yard of so from the place of encampment, where the wagons had pulled together for the night, Louisa walked close to Adam, stooping now and then, as she gathered small pieces of wood. It was late afternoon and the shadows were lengthening considerably, so that the usual dull shade within the thick forest was fast taking on the semi-blackness of early evening.

Suddenly, there was a rustling sound, to the left of them, coming from only a few feet away. Instantly, Louisa screamed and bolted toward Adam in panic. Her arms went out with a rush and grasped him roughly around the neck, almost choking him in her terror. She buried her head against the homespun cloth of his shirt, trembling with sheer panic all the while. For the stories of the great beasts, and the tracks they had come across days before, constantly filled her mind.

Adam Gibson also had shown some alarm upon hearing the rustling sound not far from them, and he immediately tensed with fearful anticipation. But he soon relaxed, as soon as he saw a young doe bolt from behind the closest tree trunk. "Fear not, Louisa," Adam reassured her, as she still clung to him. "It is only a deer...see it goes there...running off. Look!"

But Louisa would not look. Instead, her arms tightened around his neck, and her shoulders quivered with terror as Adam heard her muffled sobs. He held her quietly for a moment softly stroking her dark hair, all the while uttering words of comfort for her ears alone. "Oh, my little one....do not fear! I will protect you....here sit down on the soft leaves for a time....you are trembling so that I fear you will fall down."

She did as he said, for Louisa suddenly felt completely exhausted from the nervous frenzy she had just worked herself into a moment before. Then, she tried to express her feelings to him. "I am so afraid in this forest, Adam....if only we could put these mountains behind us...it is such a fearsome place."

"I know....my dear," Adam agreed. "But we are now on the western slopes...did not Mould say we would soon be out of here?" He put his arms around her and they sat there together, silently for a few moments in the semi-darkness of the forest. Then all at once his arm tensed and he grasped her to him abruptly, and began frantically kissing her on the cheeks and forehead, on her neck and then full on the mouth. She responded to his wild rush of passion, clinging to him and moaning each time he kissed her. The thick layer of leaves on the forest floor received their bodies with a soft rustling sound, as Adam eased Louisa to a reclining position. And they continued to cling together in a wildly passionate embrace.

In the midst of their embrace, Louisa suddenly stiffened, as though being awakened abruptly from a dream, and she endeavored to push him from her, exclaiming all the while excitedly. "No....no, Adam...we must not! I am married to another....and some day he will find me again. Please, Adam listen to me."

"My dearest...your husband is never coming to you again....he is no more...will you ever realize this?" Adam murmured into her ear. But so excited was he because of her nearness and the passionate encounter they were sharing, talking became almost impossible for him. So, he continued to kiss her and clasp her to him, with a force that she could not deny.

With one arm, he held her close to him, as he continued to ply her neck with little kisses. His other hand caressed her back, her shoulders, and then made way into her bodice. Louisa lay back on the bed of leaves, and suddenly this shadowy place, that some moments before seemed to her to be so fearful, now had miraculously become a magical realm of enchantment and love. And it was because of Adam, who continued to kiss and caress her. It was so good to be held and loved again, she thought, for it had been so long since she had lain with her husband. But then, maybe Adam is right, she thought. Perhaps Batiste would never come back to her again, and she would have denied herself all of these years needlessly. Besides, Adam was such a dear and he did arouse deep feelings within her that she had begun to think no longer existed. Just then, she gasped as she managed to murmur. "Adam....my

Adam....how dear you are. I do not have the strength to deny you anymore."

It was at this moment of near surrender, when Louisa's eyes that had been misted over with the passion she had been feeling, widened now in terror. For now, over Adam's shoulder, she beheld three figures emerge from the shadows. Suddenly, she became alert and her body stiffened at the sight of what she beheld, only a few feet from where they were laying on the ground.

"Louisa...what is wrong...why do you push me away?" Adam implored. But upon seeing the look of terror in her eyes, he turned with a jerk to observe the sight that held her so petrified.

Three Indians stood there, staring curiously down at them on the ground. The Indians were clad in deer skins and were obviously young braves, probably out on a hunting party. Adam's eyes immediately darted to the bow and arrows and the musket they carried, as he hurriedly got to his feet, pulling Louisa up at the same time. They brushed themselves off and Louisa tied her bonnet back on and smoothed down her apron and skirt. All the while, she was striving to recall the manner in which her Papa had greeted their Micmac friends back in Acadie. Perhaps, she thought, these Indians might comprehend that they meant no harm. So, she made sign to Adam to be still, for she knew that he had never dealt with Indians before. But before she could speak, one of them stepped forward and addressed them in fractured speech. "English dogs!"

"No," Louisa hastily answered back, noting their obvious distaste for the English, and their apparent comprehension of the French language. "We are French....not English...we are friends!"

The expression on the faces of the Indians softened ever so slightly, upon hearing her words. So, Louisa concluded to herself from this, that they probably had lived or fought amiably alongside of the French, possibly in recent times. Immediately she recalled how Josef had told them about his Micmac brother, back in Acadie. Yes, she hastily decided. Josef would know how to talk to such as these. So, she made sign for them to follow. Then took Adam's hand, turned slowly and began to walk cautiously back in the direction of the campsite, continuing to make sign for the Indians to accompany them. Thus, in this manner, Louisa and Adam made their way back to where the wagons were. They were followed closely by the three Indians in their soft moccasins that made little sound, except for the rustling of the thick bed of dried leaves that covered the forest floor.

————

CHAPTER - 13

NORTHWARD TOWARD ACADIE

Charles shivered in the biting sea coast air, as he forced one foot in front of the other, along the rocky ground. For the penetrating fog, accompanied by the piercing dampness, had chilled him to the bone.

As the three young men trudged on, it seemed difficult for them to realize that it was really summer along this coastline of New England. Because they were accompanied from the start of their journey by the usual presence of gray horizons of fog, that would—almost daily—drift in from far out at sea. As it moved in over the coast, it shrouded everything in a clammy atmosphere of dreariness. But then, whenever their path near the sea would take them over a sheltered area, sometimes bright sunshine would abruptly stream down on them from a clear blue sky. This remained for a short time, lessening the dampness they had felt from the fog's chill.

Such conditions had been part of life for the three young men during several weeks, now. For during their travels near the coast, over the rugged, rocky hills, inlets and low-lying shores of the New England coastline, time seemed to have no meaning. Because it felt more like months, rather than weeks, to these struggling young men, who pushed on—ever northward.

Ever since the old ship, that they had embarked on from the Bay of Chesapeake with the hard pressed group of Carolina Acadians had put to sea, there had been no end to problems. The old vessel was certainly not seaworthy to begin with. But in spite of this, they had all worked together to repair it as best they could, in order to put to sea again and keep it afloat, sailing ever northward toward Acadie. However, it took the combined efforts of all on board, to keep it from floundering on numerous occasions. But it finally it did go aground again, on a long narrow sand spit, off the coast of what they figured to be the Colony of Massachusetts.

Luckily for those on board, the vessel had gone aground off of a deserted stretch of beach. So, they were not observed. These Acadians believed—and with good reason—that the English in that colony would certainly not have looked favorably on them, had the authorities learned of the ship's plight. After the unfortunate encounters with English authorities in the Carolinas and the Virginia coast, where this group had been so ill treated, they certainly wanted to avoid anymore confrontation with his Majesty's representatives. Therefore, the Acadians on board were prepared to wait for a higher tide, in order to float the old vessel free again.

However, the three restless young men—Charles, Felix and Augustave—had become impatient with the multiple problems of the old sea weary vessel. Therefore, they elected to leave the ship and take their chances on shore.

As a result, ever since that day when they had gone ashore on that lonely Massachusetts Colony beach, they had been trudging northward. They followed the coastline as best they could. But they were always careful to avoid being seen by any settlements—both English and Indian. For they had only one musket between them, and would be no match for any armed adversaries.

After a seemingly interminable time of walking northward, they figured their coastal trail to be finally traversing the far northern

English Colony of Maine. And they were awed by that sector's thick evergreen forests, rimming the coastline.

Days before, they had exhausted the small supply of dried apples and dried fish that they had carried with them. Now, they were trying to live off the land, as best they could. Because of this, the rigors of the rough coastal trail and the haphazard diet, that they were now forced to rely on, was taking a great toll in the vigor and energy of the three men.

During the journey on foot, it had often been necessary for them to cross numerous rivers and inlets that emptied into the sea. Usually, they would cut a few saplings, bind these together, load on their meager belongings, and float the small makeshift raft in the shallows of the shore. Of course, numerous times, they would become caught up by the swift current in the center of a stream. This often resulted in their being deposited much further downstream than was their intent. However, they persevered, pushing northward toward the direction of their beloved Acadie.

But the further on they progressed, the weaker did their health become. So, upon finding themselves once again on the south shore of another great river that emptied into the sea, they had not the strength to attempt the crossing that day. Instead, they made camp at dusk, as well as they could, for the night was fast approaching. They pushed some leaves, twigs and small branches together and lit a fire with flint and powder, hoping to at least warm their chilled bodies. There was nothing to eat, and they had not the energy to search for anything. Resigning themselves to another hungry night, the three men reclined next to the fire and covered themselves with their thin blankets, in hope of getting some rest. Tomorrow, they had decided to look for berries and maybe try to catch a fish in the shallows of the large river that flowed just a few feet from their campfire. But for now, they would sleep—albeit an exhausted, fitful repose, for these young men were suffering exceedingly from exhaustion.

Because of this, the early morning light of day came much too soon for these three, who felt almost completely drained of all energy. As a result of their condition, when the first rays of sunshine pierced the atmosphere, from the eastern horizon, they had little drive to get up. So, it had been necessary for each of them to literally force their bodies out of their reclining position, where they lay near what had been their fire, but was now only a heap of dark gray ashes. Felix was the first to stagger to his feet, stride over and kneel at the near river bank, to splash cold water on his face. But then, Felix, who was the stronger of the three, with a stockier build, seemed to have fared better than Charles or Augustave on this journey. Even though he was not particularly tall by usual standards, he had become hardened and muscular from years of log cutting and such. So, it was not surprising for him to be up and ready for the trail, earlier than the other two.

After he stretched his strong arms outward and yawned audibly, Felix announced his intentions to Charles and Augustave, who were still sitting there on the ground, rubbing their eyes and contemplating getting to their feet.

"My belly pains me so from hunger...we must have something to eat or we will never travel much this day! Perhaps there are berries in that underbrush over there. I will go and search for some."

With these words, Felix proceeded to walk into the forest that surrounded them, and was soon out of sight, hidden by thick underbrush and towering evergreens.

"Be cautious....Felix," Charles shouted after him, as his eyes darted to the loaded musket that lay next to him. "Here....Felix, you had best take the weapon with you!"

No sooner had Charles uttered these words when a zinging sound flashed near his head and an arrow pierced the trunk of the tree nearest to him, with a thud! Thus shocked out of his partial grogginess, Charles lunged for the musket and at the same time shouted a warning. "Make haste....Augustave....Indians! Hide yourself behind a tree."

Just as the two plunged behind tree trunks, four more arrows came zinging toward them, each piercing the trunks of trees just to the side of Charles and Augustave. A moment more, and Charles aimed and fired the musket point blank into the dark shadowy stand of trees, from whence the arrows had come. After the loud noise sound from the weapon being discharged, there was a scream of pain that was heard. This was followed by a rustle of underbrush, which sounded as if their adversaries were apparently beating a hasty retreat. Then all at once, the sounds were heard no more. And there was silence. Not even the sounds of birds and small animals in the brush could be heard.

Charles and Augustave waited there, crouched behind a large tree trunk, for a few minutes, while they readied the musket and listened alertly for the next volley of arrows to come—perhaps from another quarter. But none pierced the still air with that ominous sound. After a time, the two cautiously made their way over to the area from whence the arrows had come.

"There is no one here...Charles!" Augustave whispered, as he stood there, looking toward his companion, who had his finger on the musket trigger—ready to fire at an instant notice.

"It would seem so...but look...what is that over there on the ground?" Charles exclaimed, as the two of them hurried over.

Augustave gasped in surprise, as he stared down at the figure which lay at his feet. "It is an Indian, Charles...you shot an Indian! Is he dead?"

Charles dropped to his knees and cautiously put his hand to the chest of the man, who lay there, all the while staring at that painted face in fear. He could feel no heart beat under the deerskin shirt the Indian wore. It was then, that he noticed the wound in the side of the Indian's head. But before he could speak of it, all at once, the two were startled with fright, as shouts and taunts were suddenly heard, from a distance off.

"What is that?" Exclaimed Augustave, as he turned toward the river bank from whence the voices came. "Oh God....Charles, look there...Indians in a canoe....and they have Felix with them! What can we do?"

Immediately, Charles ran to the river bank, lifted the musket and fired at the canoe. But the shot fell short, as the figures in the canoe were now out of range. As he stood there feeling helpless and frustrated, his words came haltingly, as he struggled for some course of action. "We will go after them....but we cannot cross the river until we first build a raft...and that will take time! Come.... let us get started. We must save Felix from those savages!"

Pushing their weakened bodies in order to accomplish this task, the two frantic young men took up meager tools and began hacking at some of the small saplings that were growing near their campsite. So excited and so filled with foreboding for Felix had they become, that they paid little heed to anything except getting the saplings felled so that they might follow across the river in pursuit of the Indians, who had taken their friend. In fact, in his haste to attempt to cut down the small trees necessary for the raft, Charles had carelessly dropped the musket at the river bank, some feet away from where they were chopping at the saplings.

"Will we be in time, Charles?" Augustave cried out loud, breathlessly, just as he succeeded in felling one of the saplings. "The Indians have such a start on us...and there is no telling what they will do with Felix!"

Before Charles could speak, they were startled when another voice answered that question. "Stupid boys....you will never help anyone when you pay so little heed to your own weapon!"

In an instant, Charles and Augustave spun around in the direction of the voice. They were then faced with a buckskin clad, bearded man, who stood just a few feet from them. He was holding their musket, pointed at them. Frantically, the two friends darted alarmed glances at each other, then hurriedly stared back at this strange man in their midst. Charles dropped the hatchet he had been using to chop at a tree, and managed to speak first. But his words were halting and uncertain. "Monsieur....we have done no harm...we are only poor Acadians, passing through this land. We have nothing of much value...if it is your intent to rob us!"

"You have nothing I want...but it is good to hear you are French, so now we can talk. Here, take your weapon," the stranger directed, as he held the musket out toward the two men. "Naturally, I prefer that you keep the musket unloaded while we talk. Now....tell me how come you to be here, two such as you, who so obviously do not belong here in this wilderness?"

The stranger listened patiently as the two blurted out their story. Throughout the long explanation, the stranger's rough, weathered face showed little emotion, except for an occasional sneer that marred his expression. This was each time that either Charles or Augustine made mention of the English authorities.

"And this is our story...this is what has happened to us." Charles commented, finishing up his part of the explanation.

"But you forgot to mention about the one Indian who did not get away, Charles!" Augustave added, as he pointed in the direction of the thicket where they had previously discovered the mortally wounded Indian. "Look over there....he lies over there!"

Upon hearing this, the stranger immediately hastened over in that direction, taking long strides in his moccasin feet, that made little sound. When reaching the spot where the Indian still lay, the man suddenly reacted emotionally. He spit on the ground and let go with a vocal barrage of obscenities as to his opinion of that tribe. "Mohawk dog....Mohawks...the curse of the forest!"

"What do you mean?" Charles questioned urgently, interrupting his vocal barrage.

"It means that this is an animal...a savage Mohawk....an enemy! That is what it meant." The stranger shouted out excitedly at Charles.

"But Monsieur, back in Acadie many of the Indians were our friends...can this not be so here in this land too?" Augustave implored anxiously.

The stranger looked at them in annoyance, as he attempted to explain. "Yes...some Indians are as our brothers, here too. But not the Mohawks! You see here in me, before you, a blood brother of the Hurons. They are friends of the French. The Mohawks are not our friends. And this one lying here is a Mohawk....and to be stepped on as an insect!"

"How come you know of these things, Monsieur?" Charles questioned the man anxiously.

"Me....I am know as Etienne. I am what they call a coureur de bois. All these many years my home has been in the Huron villages....where I have even taken a Huron woman for wife. So, I know these many things," the man announced with obvious pride. "Over there on the bank you can see my canoe, which is filled with many pelts...it will be even more full when I finish trading along these river banks. My canoe was on the river beyond that bend, only a small distance from here, when I heard your musket shot. I have voyaged down from the Atobique country, far to the north of here, trading along the way to this great bay you see here off in the distance."

"Bay....of what do you speak?" Augustave questioned. "Are we not still in the wilderness of the Colony of Maine?"

"No, my boys!" Etienne answered. "That vast water out there is Bay Francoise."

"That...that would mean our beloved Acadie lies on the far shore, which we cannot see. Does it not? Is this so?" Cried out Charles excitedly, as he peered intently off in the direction toward the horizon, where the vast water met the sky.

"Yes...it is as you say," agreed Etienne. "But this is only if you had a boat. For without one, it is a long walk around Beaubassin and Cobequid to your land. But enough of this...we must make haste to set out after those cursed Mohawks, who have taken your friend. Come....we will cross this great river in my canoe....hurry!"

———

THE OTHER SIDE OF
THE MOUNTAINS

Josef noted to himself how much easier the trail had become, since their wagons had at last left those high awesome mountains behind them. However, he could not stop thinking about the three Indians, whom they had encountered while camped on the high western slopes.

How like his Micmac brother had those Indians been, he thought, recalling in detail the recent encounter on the trail. But they were—from their own account—members of the Cherokee tribe, whose lands ranged throughout the vast mountains, the high valley areas and the hill country to the east, in this wilderness land.

Remembering the events that transpired when they had made camp with them, Josef recalled well the story the Indians told of betrayal by the English forces. This was during the recent fighting, when many of their warriors had been killed. And their women, children and old people had fallen prey to starvation and white man's diseases. Their story of betrayal had sounded like an extremely familiar one to the Acadians. So they, in turn, related the tale of their betrayal by the English, as the reason why their group was here, trying to cross these mountains. Indeed, they had all exchanged many stories, during the time the three Indians had sat with them at their campsite each night, sharing the meager food cooked by the Acadian women. Afterwards, the men—Acadian and Indian—had smoked the pipe and spoke of many more things.

Yes, the encounter had been good, Josef decided. For the three mountain Indians had remained with their wagons for some days, all the while guiding the Acadian party down the western slopes of the great ridge. And, before taking leave of the group, the Indians directed them to the best route to the Watauga River country, to the west. They advised, this would then lead them to the Holston waters. And from there, it would be onward to the stream of the great river of the Cherokees, or the Tanase River as they called it. White men pioneers referred to it as the Tennessee River.

Josef continued to reminisce, as he held the reins of the oxen, which doggedly pulled the wagon along the rocky shore of a river that flowed to the right of them. According to the directions of their Cherokee friends, who had taken their leave of them some days before, the Acadians figured this stream to be the Holston River, which they were now following.

As he pondered all of these many things, suddenly the wagon directly in front of Josef's pulled up and halted abruptly! But so dense was the foliage of the thick trees on the side of the narrow trail, he was unable to ascertain the reason for stopping. That is until Adam, who had been walking ahead ran back and shouted for them all to hear. "Settlement ahead....we have been directed to halt here!"

Settlement? It turned out to be little more than a wide clearing along the shore. But they soon found out—perhaps even more than they wanted to know—about this small primitive settlement on the bank of this river. For it appeared to be somewhat of a trading post, run by a half breed man, by the name of Leder, who was exceedingly talkative. The settlement consisted—from what they could see—of two log buildings in the midst of a small Indian encampment. Alongside of this were several wagons that housed another group of newly arrived Acadian families, who as it turned out were also bound for French Louisiana.

But small as it was, the clearing around the log buildings teemed with movement as the few Indians and the Acadian family members went about their activities. Children ran about along the river bank, laughing while they played. Small babies, too young to walk, were crying as they sat on the ground near their mothers, who were busily in the process of preparing the evening meal.

Upon entering the larger of the two log buildings, it was like entering another world for the Acadian families, who had been so long on the trail. It appeared as a place set apart from the wilderness. This place contained all manner of items from the civilized world, as well as the mountain realm. As they ventured through the rough door, that was hung with leather hinges, and which probably was greased with animal fat to prevent squeaking, those in the Acadian party were met with the musty smell of wood smoke, intermingled with tobacco and all manner of other odors that emanated from the varied stores within the large room.

They stood apart—each one for some moments—slightly in awe of the supplies that were displayed in that building. For there was ground meal in a large container on a table, over which were hung hunks of dried meat from hooks on the ceiling timbers. In one corner was a barrel of nails and a few hoes, wedges and spades. Above those were hanging hatchets, saws, bridles and traps. Over in another corner were stacks of deer skins and what looked to them like beaver skins, too. And there were also grindstones and whetstones for sharpening knives. In boxes on one end of the counter were colorful beads, as well as thimbles, needles, fish hooks, a few bolts of linen and even a bottle of black ink for writing. Barrels lined up against one wall contained salt, corn and various garden seeds. On a far wall, there hung a few muskets and a flintlock, alongside of numerous types of knives and small tools.

Leder, the man in charge, was attired in the same type deer skin clothes and moccasins that appeared to the travelers during their journey, to be the usual attire for backwoods men and Indians, alike. So, Leder's attire did not seem to be unusual. But it was his manner of speech that sounded strange, as he attempted to answer their questions animatedly, in a jumbled mixture of English, French and Cherokee dialect, which was difficult to comprehend.

However, as best they could make out from his story, it became apparent that he had been born to an Indian woman in the high valley country of the Great Smoky ridge. But far to the north of where they now were. He went on to explain how his Papa, an Englishman named Samuel Leder, had crossed into the Shenandoah, back around 1716, while a member in a party of explorers from Williamsburg. In his tortured English, French & Cherokee, he retold the story that his Papa passed on to him many years before.

As Leder related, most in the party of English explorers, who had come into the great valley of the Shenandoah, had returned after this endeavor. But his Papa and a handful of men had remained in the valley, to make further explorations into the wilderness. His story unfolded, and it became a long one. For Leder continued to relate how these men had subsequently joined a roving band of friendly Indians and eventually made their home with them, never to return east again. Since his Papa's death some years before, Leder proudly announced that throughout his boyhood he had remained with his Mama's Indian people, most of whom had eventually settled in the area where they now found him. But he had done much commerce with white people on both sides of the mountains, during his wandering years when he came to manhood. So, he seemed to have acquired considerable knowledge of both cultures

Leder was a medium man of stocky build, whose face was deeply bronzed, probably due to his heritage, and so much of his lifetime having been spent in the sun. His Indian bearing was pronounced and at a distance, he appeared as if one of them. But on closer observation, it could be noted that he had not the high cheek bones of his Mama's people. Also, there were his eyes, which were of a decidedly clear blue color. As he spoke, it became increasingly more obvious that Leder was proud of his small trading settlement, where—as the Acadians had seen—certain basic items could be obtained. But when Matthew Mould ventured to inquire as to Leder's right to trade in that area. Mould went on to inform him of the English King's decree, that any settlement west of the great mountains was forbidden.

Upon hearing Mould's words, the Indian nature in Leder surfaced suddenly and dangerously.

"Tomahawk right say it is so!" Leder shouted in his tortured English, as he walked to the door, pointing as he did over in the direction of a large tree at the edge of the clearing. His blue eyes glared with anger all the while, as his other hand tightly clutched the handle of the Indian hatchet he carried in his belt. "See ..tomahawk mark make this place belong...me! King law....no law here.... only our law true!"

Thus having shouted his piece in anger, Leder abruptly pulled the stone blade hatchet from his belt, leaned back in an effort to take hasty aim, and then let the tool fly toward the trunk of the large tree, which he had previously pointed out to Mould at the beginning of his tirade.

The tomahawk sliced through the air and found it's mark, becoming duly imbedded in the tree trunk, only an inch or two above another large mark, which appeared to have been previously gorged out of the bark perhaps months, or even years before. So, the meaning of Leder's reference to tomahawk rights was made definitely clear to all within earshot of the clearing. As a result, no one in the group present that day ever again ventured to question

Leder's right, or dispute his claim to that particular place. For Leder had definitely made his point.

The first hint of fall was becoming apparent. The leaves of the trees were starting to take on the amber, gold and rustic hues of the season, converting the foliage of the thick forest, that surrounded the Acadian encampment, into a blaze of vivid color. Still, they had remained at Leder's settlement, for a very good reason. But the time had not been wasted, during the interim. For they had been anything but idle, since arriving there. On the contrary, the Acadian families had ventured into a previously unknown realm—unknown, that is, as far as they were concerned. For their journey was about to take a different course.

During those first days at the settlement, they had become persuaded by those in the other Acadian party, that had preceded them, as well as by the advice of Leder and some of the Indian leaders, who were camped at the settlement, that river travel would offer them all a better chance to get to French Louisiana. So, in exchange for their oxen and wagons, Leder provided them with the supplies and instructions necessary, to build the flatboats that were necessary for this voyage. Of course, Leder stood to gain by this exchange, since his trading settlement was the only source of supplies for these families, in that section of the vast wilderness, west of the great mountains. No doubt about it, their lengthy stay was proving to be quite profitable for Leder's business. Because already the Acadians had camped in his clearing for more than a month, and as a result had done considerable commerce in trade.

During that time, however, construction progress on the flatboats, the Acadians were constructing, was very evident along the river bank. For already, the number of tall poplar trees necessary had been felled and cut to size, with the ends hewn out square.

Adam and Josef were working, from sun up to sunset on their flatboat, in order to keep pace with the progress of the other such boats, being built on that river bank. But they were not alone in their labor, for they had joined together with the Broussard family, which included Amond and his wife Octavia, along with their two half grown boys and baby daughter. Also, Claude Arceneaux, with his wife Seraphine and their three small children would be sharing the same boat that they were all helping to build.

Everyone in the Acadian families—from young children to the oldest parent—helped in some way to get the flatboats ready by late fall. This was the time, they had been told, when the boats must be ready to be launched on the first flood tide.

But long before, the auger holes had been bored on the poplars and the resulting two sections, to be used for gunwales, had been split straight and true, they were advised as to the strength these vessels must have. The instructions were, that the gunwales where to be thicker at the bottom than at the top, after which the floor planks were to be fitted into the grooves in what would become the bottom of the gunwales.

All of the flatboats were constructed bottom side up, along the river bank. And when that phase of the work was completed, each vessel was skidded into the stream of water. Then, the boats floating bottom side up were guided out to a deeper spot in the river, where both ends of each vessel were secured with lines lying across the stream. Rocks were than piled on the up-stream side of the vessel, until the weight of the rocks and the current of the river would cause the boat to turn over. This, they had finally accomplished, and with little mishap.

Presently, they were in the process of erecting stanchions—white oak frames with hickory pins driven in solid and sawed off even. Soon, the seams of the cabin shed on the raft would be ready for caulking with hemp. After this, they had only to rig the stern with a long sweep oar, and the bow with two long oars. Then, they would be ready to load their meager possessions and supplies onto the craft for the next leg of their journey—this journey that sometimes seemed to the Acadians to be without end.

But just as the time seemed interminably long for most of the Acadians, who were anxious to embark on the river voyage, in Louisa's case each day was as glorious as the one before. This was all because Adam was making it so, for her.

Memories of that unforgettable passionate encounter on the high mountainside between the two were precious to Louisa. Of course, Adam's amorous advances toward her had been interrupted by those three Indians. And afterwards, they had never since then had a chance to be together alone again. But still Louisa had recalled over and over again the deep feelings that had been awakened within her. It was as though, for her, another door to a new life had opened.

Adam had made her feel alive again, with an intensity that Louisa believed had been lost to her. For she had not felt such, since that forced separation from her husband Batiste, back in Acadie so long ago. Yes, much had happened since then, she thought. Always before, she had believed that someday she and Batiste and their little girl would be together again. But with the passing of each year, her convictions were becoming considerably weakened. Now, with the presence of an adoring man like Adam in her midst, dare she hope for more? As weeks and months passed, Louisa pondered these things to herself. Would God forgive her for such thoughts? If only she knew for sure about her husband. Was he dead and lost to her forever, as almost everyone close to her believed? If not, Louisa wondered, how would she ever be allowed a life of her own? And how she wanted to live, not merely exist, especially now that she had found so much to live for.

Adam had spoken of his intentions to take Louisa for his wife, and to care for Joseine as his family, only once since that memorable encounter in the mountains. And then, only briefly. But she knew the depths of his caring, for his eyes displayed this love each time he looked at her, even in passing during the day, as they went about their chores. Indeed, how could Louisa not know? After all, Adam had expressed his intentions only two days before, in the company of Josef and Madeleine at the campfire, during the evening meal.

Oh, how pleased Madeleine and Josef had been, she recalled. They all decided then and there to see to the matter of their marriage after they reached Louisiana. For the church had to be consulted in respect to such a marital matter—especially where the demise of a former spouse was in question. It was true, that deep down, Louisa grieved for Batiste. Because she had loved him dearly. But if he were really gone from this world, she would still have to go on, she reasoned to herself. Then too, there was Joseine to be considered. The child needed a Papa to provide for her, and Louisa wished not to impose on the generosity of Josef and Madeleine indefinitely. So, she simply must make a decision, at least by the time they reached Louisiana.

So, with each passing day, these matters continued to worry Louisa. But more and more she suspected, when the time came, what her ultimate answer to Adam's proposal would be. But for the present, Louisa felt that life was good to her, with each day providing the thrill of Adam's nearness in her world, and that was enough.....for now!

———

CHAPTER - 15

HARSHNESS IN THE WILD

Etienne held out slivers of raw fish and motioned for them to partake. But Charles and Augustave exchanged glances that failed to hide the revulsion they felt at that moment.

"Fish is good....bon appetite!" Etienne remarked, imploring them to take the portions of fish he was extending in their direction. "You must eat....the fish will nourish your bodies. Eat, my boys! I know it is not cooked....but you well know we cannot risk a fire, so close are we on the heels of those Mohawk dogs, who took your friend. But if you choose not to eat, neither of you will be strong enough to rescue your friend when the time comes. Here.... Etienne speared this good fish just for us....eat!"

The two young men looked sheepishly at Etienne, all the while absorbing the words of this man of the forest, from whom they had accepted help. Then together, as if by silent agreement, both of them reached for the raw fish slivers, being offered them. At the same time, Charles managed an apology of sorts.

"Forgive our stupidity, Etienne....you are right, we must eat or we will not have strength enough to even follow the trail."

Augustave agreed, as he started to eat the fish. "It was just that we had hoped for some cooked food to help warm our bodies, against the chill of this night of waiting."

"My boys....I too would prefer it cooked. But the Mohawk dogs would be on us, for the smoke of our fire would guide them here." Etienne said, while chewing vigorously on the fish meat as he spoke. "With a fire....I, Etienne, would prepare this meal in the manner of my Indian brothers, and your bodies would be stronger for it. We would first grind some corn between two stones....and fetch some water from the river with which to fill the pot. Then we would throw in a bird or two, that we downed with an arrow or a musket ball....add a few whole fish, caught in the shallows, and boil it all together for a soup, that you would not soon forget."

The two young men again sneaked a glance between them that clearly showed the disgust they felt as they listened to Etienne's vivid culinary description.

But this man of the woods paid them no mind. He merely continued eating, and speaking softly of other concoctions that he had apparently learned about from the Indians, with whom he had dwelled most of his life.

"We must eat well and rest some this night, for with the sun's first light, the trail awaits. Pity, that moonlight overtook us before we could rescue your companion....for we can do nothing in the darkness against these Mohawks, who have the eyes of owls at night!" Etienne remarked, as he finished up the last of the fish.

"Will they harm Felix this night...do you think?" Augustave ventured to ask, almost regretting his question, now that it was voiced. But once out, both he and Charles stared beseechingly at their knowledgeable wilderness companion, and awaited his answer.

Etienne considered the question and the urgent expressions on the faces of the two young men, who sat there with him in the moonlight of their campsite. But he did not answer at once. Instead, this man of the forest looked away from them, apparently hesitating to look into their eyes. Rather, he chose to direct his full attention to polishing off the fish bones that remained. In doing so, he sucked audibly on each fish bone, before discarding it on the ground. Then he spoke.

"Many years have passed since I joined my Huron brothers in their villages....and there have been many stories to tell. I have seen bad things happen at the hands of the Indian enemies....even the holy men were sometimes not spared this wrath. As for your friend, who is now in the camp of those Mohawk dogs...he is in danger every moment. But it is not for me to say what they will do. I can only relate what I know they have done many times before.... And because you have taken the life of one of their warriors, your friend may be made to pay dearly for that!"

"But Etienne.....why do we sit here, wasting time? Let us be gone after them!" Charles exclaimed, getting to his feet in alarm. But he was then motioned to sit back down, by their new companion. "My boy....it is no use...we can do nothing in the dark! At first light, I will pick up their trail again....and then we will do what we can. But we are but three. By now, that small Mohawk party may have joined others of their tribe, and we are no match for them!"

"Will they kill him...Etienne?" Augustave ventured boldly to ask, as Charles reluctantly sat down, dejectedly near them.

"That would be merciful, my boys!" Etienne replied haltingly, as he continued to explain. "You both must be prepared for what might be. I tell you this for your own sake. For even some holy men, who meant them no harm, were sorely treated in their camps. Do you not know of their methods to prolong death? I will tell you, so you will know. Sometimes, they pull out the fingernails of their prisoners to begin with. Then they beat their bodies with clubs to a bloody pulp. After this, if the victim is still conscious, he is forced to run their gauntlet, which few ever survive. But sometimes, before all of this, they set the young braves on them to pull out the hair and beards of their victims and allow the small Indian children to place red hot coals and ashes on the bodies of their bound prisoners. Sometimes, when a war party became short of food....they sliced flesh from their prisoners, to add to their cooking pot, or even to roast over the fire."

There was no sound from the two young men, upon hearing this dire news. So shocked were they, about the torture related to them, their eyes expressed the terror they felt. Their mouths had gone slack with awe and disbelief, as they both stammered, endeavoring as they were to express their shocked emotion. But Etienne spoke first, before their words could become coherent.

"I tell you this....it may not be so for your friend. Sometimes, the Mohawks use prisoners for slaves and even trade them to other tribes. In such cases, your companion could be spared—not well treated—but his life would be spared. He might still have a chance... if he is strong and can keep his wits about him!"

Almost before Etienne's last words had been uttered, there was suddenly heard a muted moan, followed by numerous piercing screams, that echoed through the forest from some distance away.

"Oh God...it is Felix....it must be!" Charles cried out, jumping to his feet in alarm.

"Stay quiet!" Etienne cautioned in a whisper, as he grasped Charles' arm, to keep him from bounding into the forest. "We must keep our heads!"

"We have to help him....please Etienne...let us try!" Augustave beseeched this man, in whom they had put their trust, just as another series of terrifying screams emanated from the dark depths of the forest.

"It will be light soon enough," Etienne implored of them. "Then....we will find their campsite. Until then, my boys.....we can do nothing!"

———

It was just as Etienne had said. They could do nothing for the moment. But the sporadic screams continued for what seemed to them like an eternity. But in reality, it was more like thirty minutes. Afterwards, silence prevailed. And with the silence came a sort of respite for Charles and Augustave. Because by now, they had both worked themselves into such an emotional state, from having to listen to those excruciating screams, fully realizing all the while that they were powerless to do anything about it. So, because the two were quite exhausted, when silence finally prevailed, they nodded off into a temporary nervous slumber, while they sat there in the dark, with their backs resting against tree trunks.

It was an uneasy slumber at best though, and when Charles opened his eyes, he realized that the sun's rays had begun to light up the small area where they sat. Roughly shaking Augustave, who still slumbered next to him, Charles looked around for Etienne, who was nowhere to be found. And he exclaimed in alarm to his companion. "Augustave...he is not here....Etienne has gone!"

The two of them sprang to their feet, almost at the same time. Charles picked up the musket that had lain beside him, and without a word the two hurried into the forest, in the direction from whence those terrifying screams had come the night before. But before they had gotten very far, Etienne suddenly appeared, emerging all at once from the shadowy depths of the thick trees. Then he made sign for them to halt, whereupon he was bombarded with questions from the two perplexed and frightened young men.

"What happened....where did you go, Etienne....have you seen the Mohawk camp...is Felix still alive?"

"Yes...yes...the camp is but a short distance from here. But the Mohawk dogs have gone." Etienne answered, avoiding their imploring stares, as he did so."

"What of Felix....have you found him?" Charles exclaimed, grasping Etienne's arm in alarm."To which Etienne answered.

"Yes....I have found him. But you must not see....come let us be gone from this place!"

"No....no....we must find him!" Charles shouted, as he and Augustave ran together, past Etienne, into the thick forest. Disregarding any caution, the two young men crashed, for some distance, through the thick underbrush, beneath the ever present canopy of trees. They then emerged into a slight clearing, rimmed by the sheer rock wall of a small ridge. There, the two abruptly stopped, out of breath from their exertion, and cautiously looked around.

It was as Etienne had said, the remains of what must have been the Mohawk camp on the previous night, were still evident. But there was no sign of Felix anywhere.

Charles walked over and kicked at the still smoldering camp fire, stooping to examine the site more closely. But then, his attention was suddenly distracted by Augustave's emotional shout, which came from behind a thicket near the clearing. "Ahh....Charles.... Oh God...come quick!"

Charles sprang up like a shot and bolted in the direction of the emotional shout from his friend, who was now staring as if transfixed. Indeed, Augustave's attention was fixed on a spot beyond the thicket, from which he could not bring himself to look away.

The reason for this became clear, when Charles approached. There, on a spindly birch post, which had obviously been thrust into the ground for the purpose at hand, was the decapitated head of what was apparently left of their companion—Felix. The ashen head, that they were suddenly confronted with, had been slashed numerous times along the cheeks. It had been scalped and there were only sockets left where once Felix's dark brown eyes had been—only the morning before.

Augustave suddenly went limp and fell to the ground, covering his face as he did so. He sat there on the forest floor, sobbing and moaning uncontrollably. Charles stood there dumbfounded in disbelief for some moments. Then, he too slumped into a sitting position on the ground, continuing to stare as if in a trance, completely oblivious to his surroundings.

The forest was quiet, except for the chirping of a lone bird on a branch high above them. A squirrel scurried up a tree trunk, it's bushy tail jerking from side to side, as it went.

Etienne stood there quietly, looking down at the two young men on the ground before him. Then he spoke, choosing his words carefully as he did so. "Come...boys....you must go from this place. You cannot help your friend now....he is no more. But you still have far to go. Come.. I will guide you on your way to your land of Acadie. Do you not still wish to go back to your homeland?"

The mention of Acadie seemed to penetrate Charles' shocked mentality. And slowly as a result, he began to regain his composure somewhat. "Acadie...yes...must get back there," he murmured, as he struggled to his feet.

Deliberately, Charles avoided looking over in the direction of that terrible thing on the post—all that now remained of what had been their friend. Both young men would probably agree, that the sight of this atrocity perpetrated on their friend, would plague them until the day they would die. He groped his way over to where Augustave still lay on the ground, sobbing.

"Come, my friend....we must be on our way!" Charles implored, as he gently assisted his friend to his feet. Etienne will put us on the right trail. We must go back home to Acadie....we have come too far to stop now!"

———

CHAPTER - 16

WESTWARD ON THE RIVER

So far, they had only lost one boat. It was when the Pitre vessel went aground on a rocky shore, sometime ago after they embarked on this river journey in late November. Luckily, those on board managed to make it to shore safely. But most of their possessions were lost when the craft broke up from the impact, and sank in the swift cold water. This happened near the mouth of the French Broad River.

The flatboat, that carried the Theriot group, as well as the Broussard and Arceneaux families, had been directly behind the Pitre boat when it went aground. Then, it was only by swift maneuvering, that they were spared the same fate. However, the four men managed to direct their flatboat away from shore, in order to avoid such a collision. However, so busy had they been, struggling to save their own vessel, they could not put ashore further downstream on a more hospitable stretch of river bank. Thus, they were unable to make it to shore, in order to pick up the survivors of the demolished vessel.

Madeleine would not soon forget that scene. For as she looked back to see those cold and wet children, who had been pulled out of the river water near that rocky shore, she observed a memorable scene. Celina Verret, who was drenched herself from head to foot and carrying her crying baby on one hip, could be seen on the bank, running about making sure all of the children remained well away from the edge of the rushing river. But from her increasingly distant vantage point, as their flatboat continued to move down steam and away from the site, it appeared to Madeleine that Charles Guidry and Paul Breaux had managed to pull everyone safely onto the shore. It was there, that they all huddled together, shivering from the cold winter air.

However, so swift was the river at that point, that none of the other flatboats behind them were able to make a landing downstream, either, in order to attempt a rescue. So, it looked like no vessel would be able to rescue the survivors. Because each of the boats directly behind the one, from which Madeleine had observed the drama, were unable to beach at a likely spot. That is, until the very last vessel made it's appearance. As this last craft approached the scene of the mishap, those on board had apparently time enough to observe from a distance what had happened. This alerted them, to plan their rescue maneuver. Thus, they were able to aim their vessel toward a more likely shore, some yards further downstream, from where the survivors shivered on the river bank.

So as it happened, this last flatboat, which carried the Dupre and Robichaux families, managed to take the survivors from shore onto their flatboat. But these added passengers caused this vessel to become dangerously overloaded as a result. However, they all managed until later at a downstream campsite, where the extra families were divided up and taken onto three other flatboats, to continue the journey.

Of course, from the start of this river voyage, there had been times when one or the other of the vessels had gone aground. But always before, they had managed to push off and once again maneuver back into the mainstream of the rushing river current.

Even though the winter rains had come early this year, the Acadian families had been ready in time. Because they had already completed and loaded the vessels, in preparation to be off on the first flood tide of the season. Finally, for the anxious Acadians, it came time to embark—all twelve flatboats that had been built on the Holston River shore. At that time, they took their final leave of Leder, who—as a final gesture—offered them the valuable services of a guide for the dangerous river journey ahead.

Leder personally praised the Indian guide, explaining to them all that he was of the Cherokee nation and was called Hogogechee. He was named, as they soon learned, after a great river, on the shore of which his mother had given birth to him, and from it's waters had nourished him throughout his childhood. Hokgogechee was fondly recommended by Leder, for the Indian was reputed to have twice before traveled down the Tennessee, past the Chickmauga, past the curve of the Mocassin Bend, past Crow villages and the place of the Creek's crossing. Also, he had even gone through the lake of many shoals, then north from the Occachappe to the great Ohio waters.

In his blunt manner, Leder had made it clear to all of the Acadians, that without Hogogechee to guide them, they would never live to see French Louisiana. Of course, after convincing them of this, Leder extracted another of his fees, from what was left of the group's few resources, in payment for the services of the Indian guide. But then, it was agreed, that such a guide was necessary. So, they set out, together, with Hogogechee traveling with the Babineau and Dugas families, in the lead boat.

Once the boats were out into the middle of the stream, very little effort was necessary to navigate the vessels. For the current seemed to capture each craft in a manner much akin to what happens when a fallen leaf is bourn on riverlets of rain drops, that come pouring forth down a slope of ground.

The bank on both sides of the river was thick with trees. And the tree limbs, bearing what was left of remaining fall leaves oftentimes were bent over and touching the swift water along the shore. So thick was the forest on both sides, that little could be viewed through the dark mass, so as to observe the untouched wilderness, which abounded everywhere around them.

Occasionally, small parties of Indians were seen on the shores and whether they were friendly or not, only Hogogehee knew. But usually, the vessels were propelled so swiftly by the current, that few encounters were to be expected—providing that the vessels were maneuvered well off of the river banks.

Sometimes at night, when they would tie up together to camp, usually on an island in the river for safety, their Indian guide would tell them of the many tribes of people, who dwelled to the east and southeast of where they now were. Often, he would also speak of the Chickasaw people to the west, and the Creek and Choctaw tribes to the south. He also told them of a British fort, that had once stood on the banks of the Little Tennessee. It had been called Fort Loudoun. But it was now in ruins, having been put to the torch, about two years before by his Cherokee people.

But once their flatboats passed the mouth of the Chickamauga stream, Hogogechee had warned them to be on watch for Indians in that area. For when they approached the high mountain that could be viewed from some distance away, and which he referred to as the great high rock, that comes to a point, his expression was grave. He once again warned them all to be particularly on guard for Indian attack, since it would likely come from the place of the Chatanuga village on the south shore.

Sure enough, it was not long after Hogogechee's last warning when trouble began. It was just as he predicted. As the flotilla of flatboats passed the Shallow Ford curve in the river, where the high rock that comes to a point could be seen in the distance, looming above the tree tops, that a large group of Indians suddenly appeared on the shore.

The Indians on that river bank called out to them, some even going so far as to wade out into the shallow water along the rocky shore, in order to better hail to the boats, as each craft came into view. Their manner appeared friendly and the Indians smiled as they held up items that they wished to trade. They gesticulated with sign language and much arm waving, endeavoring all the while to call attention to themselves.

This seemed not to be the manner of hostile Indians, thought Josef. Others on the boats agreed, and for a few minutes they were tempted to put into shore in order to better see what the Indians had to trade. However, all of those on the vessel—as they had agreed—continued to heed Hogogechee's previous advice. So, they all followed the lead boat, which steered well clear of that shore, from whence the Indians called out to them.

As it turned out, it was a very wise course of action. Because when the Indians on shore realized that their cajoling was obviously to no avail, since the boats were moving away and steering well clear of their shore, their manner abruptly changed to hostility.

When this change of manner was observed, an order to take cover was heard, being shouted from boat to boat. For the Indians could now be seen taking out previously concealed weapons, and taking aim at the boats with bows and arrows. Some of them had boarded canoes and were swiftly paddling in pursuit of the Acadian boats that were swiftly moving away from that site by the strong current.

As a volley of arrows descended on the last boat in the group, those on board hurried to take cover behind the cabin shed, using the parcels of supplies that were lashed onto the deck, for protection. Luckily, the Indians had waited just a bit too long in their canoe pursuit of the boats. Because once past the dangerous shore, all of the flatboats became caught up in a strong current, that swiftly wafted them away into the swirling waters of the turbulent river channel. However, the canoes continued to follow, with some of the Indians paddling with a vengeance, while others in the canoes let fly continuous deadly arrows. But a series of shots from a couple of the flintlocks on the last boat apparently discouraged those in the canoes. For they soon gave up the chase.

————

After the abortive Indian attack from the Chatanuga village, the journey continued. But it then became the dangers of the river and the days of bitter winter cold, that now plagued the families exceedingly. In spite of this, the tenacious flotilla continued to move down the Tennessee River, toward their still distant destination. While it was true that threats, from occasional Indian parties sighted on shore, proved to be a problem that had to be dealt with, from time to time, it was the weather that had now become more of a factor for concern. The bitter icy winds of February and March caused much suffering for those on board. Some had already succumbed to ailments attributable to the lack of medication, inadequate warm clothing. And then, there was insufficient shelter on board, to provide protection from the snow and ice that prevailed on the flatboats of this small flotilla in this winter wilderness.

The children, particularly, were constantly coughing and many of them ran high fevers as a result of deep congestive maladies. In fact, so many had become ill, that the cabin sheds on the flatboats were filled with the most seriously ill—many of them were children. But then, the adults did not fare much better, as many of them had become quite ill themselves. Of course, usually, they pushed their bodies to go on, in spite of many times running fever in the process.

Madeleine and Louisa had slight coughs, as did their daughters. But they were all holding their own. Fortunately, Josef remained well, in spite of the seemingly endless cold days, that he spent manning the rear oar of the flatboat. However, Adam had developed a deep hacking cough, ever since he had been swept overboard into the icy water, by a low hanging branch of a willow tree, when the flatboat was inadvertently maneuvered too close to shore. This had happened only days before they came upon the junction of the great Ohio River.

At that point, the flotilla attempted to steer for an island they had spotted at the mouth of the Tennessee River, where it entered the Ohio, in order to tie up for the night. But they were hard put to accomplish this feat, as it was difficult to go against the tremendous current of the Ohio River. They soon realized that the channel was on the Ohio's far north bank and the current tended to carry crafts toward that side of the river. There, the water appeared deep and the current was extremely rapid, making for difficult maneuvering to avoid being pulled onto that shore.

As a result, those manning the oars that day had to exert even more extreme physical effort than usual in order to keep the boats from being pulled onto the far shore. So, every man pushed himself to the limits of his endurance, and in some cases past that limit.

Thus, when at last they succeeded in getting the flatboats tied up onto the small island in the channel at the junction of the Ohio and the Tennessee rivers, daylight was gone and a strong bitter cold northwest wind began pelting them all with blowing snow. It was then, that Josef called out loudly in alarm, over the whistling of the strong wind that had sprung up. He was calling out to Louisa, who was within the cabin shed, helping to tend the sick Broussard and Arceneaux children. "Come quickly, Louisa! Adam has collapsed!"

Louisa heard his shout above the din of the blowing tempest outside of the cabin door. Instantly, she handed the crying Arceneaux baby, whom she had been holding, to Madeleine. Hurriedly, she pulled her weathered cloak tightly across her chest, and went to Josef's aid.

The darkness and the blowing snow, which had suddenly increased across the flatboat deck, made it difficult for Louisa to see in order to make her way over to where Josef was kneeling. She soon saw, that he was kneeling to help Adam into a sitting position. She reached out to help Josef, and bent over to touch Adam's face. She then cried, above the wind. "Josef....he is burning up....Adam has a terrible fever! Quick....let us get him into the cabin, out of this wind!"

With the help of Amand, they carried Adam into the crowded, noisy cabin, and laid him on a blanket along one wall. Louisa hurriedly covered him with another quilt, and she brushed the snowflakes from his eyebrows and beard. She rubbed his face soothingly with both hands, murmuring all the while to no one in particular. "Dear Adam...you are so feverish. Why did you not tell me how sick you were? Foolish man...now you have gone and made yourself worse."

As she murmured and comforted him, the driving snow and frigid wind went unabated all through that night. It was a miserable night indeed for those on the flatboats—especially so for those, who tended their sick through the dark night, and for those huddled together within the cabin sheds, trying to keep as warm as possible.

In this way, they survived that terrible winter night at the junction of the two great rivers. At that site, they were forced to spend two more days tied to that island, because of the winter storm, that had yet to wear itself out. But it was just as well, considering that most of the men were either too exhausted, too sick or too cold at that point in time, to push off into the unknown icy waters of the great Ohio River.

———

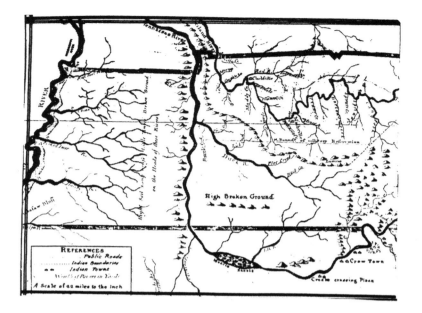

EARLY TENNESSEE MAP, showing Tennessee
River route, taken by many travelers, to the Ohio
River, and then to the Mississippi River. The
Holston, French Broad, Chickamauga and Chatanuga
Rivers are also prominently pictured.

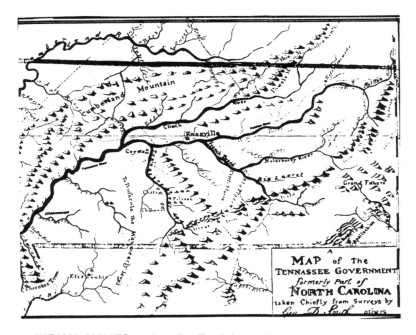

INDIAN NAMES and earlier English spelling of rivers
and places are prominent features on this map.

CHAPTER - 17

COLD HOMECOMING

They slowly made their way, following the coastline wherever it was possible. The forest had more and more begun to take on the look of the fall season. The trees—with the exception of the evergreens—had become covered with the gold, bronze and crimson leaves of the season.

The call of the sea birds could be heard along the coastline, as each one soared out above the beach. Some of them came to rest now and then on the sand. The terns and plovers stood there on long legs, preening with their long beaks. High above, silhouetted against the blue sky, the wild geese were flying. They flew up there, as this species did every year at this time, journeying on toward a winter home, the destination of which the birds always seem to know. It was a mysterious, instinctive sense of direction—the origin of which still escaped all human reasoning.

But the two somewhat haggard looking young men, paid little heed to their surroundings, so intent were they on pushing ever northward along the coastline. However, the southward bound creatures of the sky, and the signs of the Fall season all around them, did serve to remind them of one important fact of life. Winter was fast approaching and their journey was still not at an end.

As he mentally forced his body to put one foot in front of the other, Charles Theriot was thinking of many things. Indeed, memorable thoughts filled his mind. He knew how much he and Augustave owed to that man—Etienne—who had helped them when they were so in need. And this was a man, whom they would no doubt never see again in this world. They were so thankful, that he had promised to bury the remains of their friend Felix, and also to say a few last words over the grave. Because neither Charles nor Augustave could have done it, without breaking down completely.

Etienne apparently knew this, when he made the promise, and set them on their way in the direction of the Isthmus of Shediac. He had even given them some dried meat and two deer skins, from which they could fashion capes to wear when the cold winter winds would begin to blow. But now, as they walked on, it had been quite a while since they last took their leave of Etienne. If the directions he had given them were correct, Charles reasoned that they should reach the Petitcodiac River before the end of the day. Once there, they hoped to meet up with some of their countrymen. So, they both took comfort from this thought, as they hurried on.

As the end of day neared, it was as they had hoped. The Petitcodiac River bank was finally reached, and on it's shores they encountered a handful of Acadian families, who had built shelters along the river. The two young men observed that these families had very little in the way of supplies, and only one weapon between them. But nevertheless, the families offered to share their meager meals with the two new arrivals, urging them to stay on and winter with them on the shore.

But these new arrivals soon learned from Albert Comeaux and Paul Clement, who appeared to be spokesmen for the group. They had all escaped from the Shepody settlement at the time of the expulsion. Then, after much wandering, they finally built cabins on this shore, where they hoped to begin anew. In turn, Charles and Augustave related their tale, and their intent to get back to Grand

Pre. To which, Paul Clement related to them some news, that they did not want to hear.

"Everything is different now....our old homes are no more. It is no use going back!"

Charles listened intently, but discouragingly, to this news. After which, he answered. "No, Monsieur....we must go back! We cannot rest until we return home." At the same time, he extended an invitation for any of the group to join them on the journey over the Isthmus of Shediac.

In answer to this, only one agreed to accompany them. It was Albert Comeaux, who was now a widower, having lost both his wife and new baby the previous month, during childbirth. He said that he had nothing to keep him at Petitcodiac now. So, he agreed to accompany them on the journey.

So, the next day, the three set off over the Isthmus, with the cold winds of early winter ripping at them. They arrived at Beausejour, only to discover that little remained of French habitation at that place. Even the name no longer was the same, for Beaubassin had been re-named Amherst. And all the farm lands were now occupied by English people.

Everywhere they went, it was the same. There was little left to show, that less than ten years before this land had belonged to French farmers. Now, the English people were there, and many of the names of places, previously known to these Acadians, had been changed to English names.

Cobequid was now known as Truro. Piziquid had become Windsor. So, for these three travelers, it was like a nightmare—only worse, because it was true!

Everywhere they traveled, English speaking people stared at the three ragged, bearded men in awe. The three bedraggled young men were offered little in the way of shelter and assistance by these strange new people, who only wanted them to be on their way as quickly as possible. Because these English farmers had no desire to be reminded of those people, who once dwelled there.

Doggedly, the three struggled on whenever they could, on those days when the winter weather would allow travel. At last, they crossed the Gasepereau River and approached Grand Pre, with a sense of foreboding. There was no conversation between the three, as they struggled to walk the last few miles to Grand Pre. It was as if Charles was afraid to speak of it, because perhaps he felt that in some small way the energy he exerted in speaking might serve to deplete the strength needed to reach his home. But it was more than likely, that the anticipation that had welled up inside of him simply made speech impossible for him, so filled with a sensation of dread was he.

Upon arrival at this place, for which they had struggled so long, it appeared their foreboding had been well founded. Indeed, the long journey could not have had a less gratifying destination, for they soon found out that the Grand Pre, they had known, was no more. It was now called Horton, and all that Charles had remembered was gone. All the farm houses, every barn and building, even the church of St. Charles, that he had remembered so well, were all gone— burned to the ground years ago. Only the dikes remained the same, along with the endless expanses of rich farm land that generations of his people had reclaimed from the sea, was still there. There were new structures, though. But only English farmers were on the land that had been stolen from the Acadians. Everywhere the three men went, they were met with the same hostile reception that had been theirs at the previous places through which they had traveled in that land.

Augustave and Albert implored Charles to move on, for they heard every place around was the same, even at Boudro Point and River Canard.

"Maybe Annapolis Royal will be different, Charles…let us go there!" They had urged him.

But Charles insisted on finding the farm of his family once more. However, this was not easy, considering that all of the landmarks had changed and the farm house was probably no more. Besides, the landscape was completely covered with the white snow of winter. This caused everything to blend together in a somewhat confusing landscape. But nothing would dissuade him. So, Augustave and Albert followed after Charles, as he hurried along the road that had once led to the home of his family.

"There they are!" Charles exclaimed, as he stopped suddenly on the snow covered road, after they had gone a couple of miles. He was pointing anxiously at a tall stand of willow trees, which now stood bare, at this wintertime of year, exclaiming all the while. "The trees are still there as before....down this way is where the house was....hurry we are almost there!"

Upon hearing his shouted words, Augustave and Albert stared at each other with concern, each displaying the fear they both felt at Charles' recent unrealistic behavior. Then, they ran after him, through the freshly fallen snow that covered a field, which had once been the Theriot property. They caught up with him, as he stood dejectedly in the middle of the field, staring at what once had been the house he was seeking. But now it was only a ruins, made white with a covering of fresh snow.

"That was it....that was where I lived, my friends!" Charles muttered softly, more to himself than to his two friends.

"Come, Charles.....let us go....there is nothing left...you can see!" Augustave tried to persuade him, as he placed his hand softly on Charles' shoulder.

"But look...Augustave....look Albert....there is another cabin! Maybe Papa came back and built another house. Let us go and see!" Charles exclaimed all at once, as he bounded off in the direction of a small building a few yards away.

Smoke was coming from the chimney of the building, as they approached. And the three young men also noted a small barn near the house. Before they could stop him, Charles had dashed up to the door of the cabin and was rapping urgently on it, with all of his might.

"Yes....what is it? Who is there?" A voice from within asked in English.

"Mama....Papa...it is I, Charles," the despondent young man shouted back in French. "I have come home.....let me in!"

The door abruptly opened to reveal a somewhat stocky man with dark hair and a light complexion, who appeared startled upon seeing the three bedraggled men before him. Behind him was a plain looking woman, who stood there wiping her hands on an apron, that was tied around her waist, questioning all the while in English.

"Who is it, Samuel? Who knocks at our door?"

"What do you want here?" The man demanded of the three, who stood shivering in the winter wind on the doorstep.

"Mama....Papa....where are they?" Charles implored of the man in French, as Augustave hurriedly stepped in front of Charles, and in his broken English tried to speak to the man, who had come to the door.

"My friend, Charles Theriot, whom you see here, used to live on this land with his family. Do you know of his Papa, perhaps? Jean Theriot, who owned much of this land?"

"No more French here...this land belongs to me—Samuel Stiles! We have been here for four years. We were brought over here from New England to take over this land, me and my brother, Nathan. He farms land some miles from here. You will get no pity here. You knew not how to hold on to your land, so it is no concern of mine!" The man shouted angrily, as he began to shut the door in their faces. "Be gone from here.....you French have no claim on this land anymore!"

———

A bitter wind had sprung up and the sky showed signs of more snow on the way, when they arrived, after having covered those many miles to Annapolis Royal. Of course, it had been difficult for Augustave and Albert to keep Charles going, so despondent had he become after that encounter with the New England farmer, who now occupied his Papa's land. It was as though Charles refused to believe such a thing had come to be, so intense had he been in recent years, about getting back to Grand Pre. Indeed, this dream had become an all consuming passion for him. Because he believed so intensely that if he could just make it back home, everything would be alright again. He so wanted his Mama and Papa to be there, as he remembered them. Then, all would be well in his world once more. As he found out, it was not as he remembered, and would never be again. But this realization was apparently too much for him to accept.

After that encounter, Charles just appeared to give up, allowing his companions to lead him anywhere. Thus, when they finally trudged into the Annapolis Valley and reached Annapolis Royal, Charles continued to be docile and uncaring.

Of course, their arrival in that town brought no joy for Augustave and Albert either, for they were met with similar conditions, as they had encountered in the other places in Acadie. The only difference here was that the name of the settlement still remained the same, just as they had known it before. But the English inhabitants there were pretty much the same—displaying great irritation toward them, upon their arrival. They too, offered the three exhausted, cold, hungry wandering young men little to nothing in the way of hospitality. At that point, Augustave, Albert and Charles could no longer go on. But then, there was no place left for them to go anyway, for Annapolis Royal had been their last hope.

However, they found shelter with a handful of their people, who were subsisting in makeshift huts in the forests outside of the town. As the three new arrivals soon learned, these few Acadians had either escaped, or had been left behind at the time of the expulsion. In the beginning, they had been taken in by their Micmac Indian friends. They had lived as best they could there in the forest, until they were able to gather together with others of their people and travel to Annapolis Royal, in hopes of finding some place left for them to start anew. But so far, their hopes had been dashed, and there they remained with no place left to go—merely living in horrific poverty.

Like Charles, most of these Acadians had lost all faith and were merely existing from one day to the next. More times than not, they would all pass the long winter evenings recounting tales of how they came to be there. For they had come from various places, like the Salmon River, Cobequid, Miramichi and Shepoudie. So, there were many stories to tell.

Since coming, once more, to live with his own Acadian people, Charles appeared to regain some of his old personality. He even began to hope again. But the months passed, during which time their numbers grew. For other Acadian families had arrived, bedraggled, exhausted and seeking their old homeland. In fact, so many were arriving, that apparently something had to be done about relocating these people, who were sorely in need of some manner of sustenance.

Amazingly, help came from an unlikely source. It was from the English officers of the local garrison. They arranged for the Acadian families to receive grants of land along the shores of Saint Mary's Bay, not many miles to the east of Annapolis Royal. In December of 1767, these grants were formerly made a reality.

———

They had trudged along the miles, following the company of English soldiers, who had been ordered to escort them overland to the coast of Saint Mary's Bay. This was a motley group of Acadian men, women and children, who had endured so much, during the past twelve years. Now, they were at last being offered a home, albeit along an inhospitable, previously unsettled, coastline.

Upon arriving on that harsh coast, they looked at this new land and they could see that it was obviously not rich, like the diked farms they had known. Obviously, this new soil would never be. For in some places, high wooded cliffs looked out over the blue waters of the bay, making the coastline totally unsuited for diking. Charles stood there, somewhat apart from the others, looking out over the wide expanse of water. Then, he glanced down on the ground on which he was standing. He kicked his toe against the cold, frozen ground, noting the color of the soil, wondering silently to himself about the kind of crop it could sustain.

Shivering a bit from the sharp December wind, that was gusting in from over the bay, he turned to look over at his companions, with whom he had made the long trek. Then, his gaze took in the area where a few soldiers were now in the process of building a fire, some distance away from where he stood. At that moment, he marveled at the irony of it all.

It had been English authority that had sent them away. Now, it was by English authority, that they were being allowed to stay.

But it mattered not, he supposed, for the important thing is here and now, and that they were once again standing on their own land, back in their native Acadie. Yes, they were back home in that beloved place, where they all wanted to be in the first place.

CHAPTER - 18

DESTINATION REALIZED

Suddenly, there it was! They could see it now, just as the boats rounded the final bend of the Ohio River. "It must be the Mississippi River! Madeleine...Louisa...come and see," Josef shouted from this vantage point, standing as he was at the rear oar of the flatboat. But only Madeleine emerged from the cabin, holding the hands of Joseine and Rosarie, both of whom anxiously ran to the edge of the deck, to get a better view of what was ahead.

"Look...Madeleine," Josef exclaimed. "The lead boat has already entered it's waters. See how swiftly the current of the great river carries off the vessel? With such current to take us south, we will not be long from Louisiana! Where is Louisa?"

Madeleine had taken her place alongside of Josef at the rear of the boat. She was straining to see the sight he was pointing out for her. Upon hearing his question, Madeleine looked down, and with tears in her eyes attempted to answer her husband's question. "It's no use, Josef....Louisa will only sit there in the cabin staring off at nothing. She will take no interest in anything......and I know not what to do for her!"

As she spoke, vivid thoughts of what had transpired for them in recent weeks were being recalled for Madeleine. These thoughts brought back everything in a flood of mental pictures. Such recollections particularly encompassed the things that took place, after they had endured the winter storm on the island, where the Tennessee and Ohio Rivers met. She remembered well, how blue the sky became after that storm, and how the bright sunshine had warmed them so, only three days after that tempest. But even though the snow was still on the ground and the temperature was quite chilly, the wind was no more and there was some warmth, to rejuvenate some of those on deck. Of course, for others, who lay so seriously ill within the cabin shed, more was needed to help them—more than they had at their disposal on these boats.

Adam was one of this number, who had remained seriously ill, with no change for the better being evident for days. Louisa tended to him steadily, during those days, and they had all prayed for him, and for Amand's young son Pierre, who also had lain quite ill for many days. There were more sick people on the other boats, too. So, it was decided to set out as soon as the weather permitted for the French fort, that Hogogechee said was on the north shore of the Ohio, only a short distance from where they were at that junction of the Tennessee. They all hoped that there would be a doctor at the fort, who could help those down with sickness.

It was as Hogogechee had said. For a stronghold, called Fort Massiac, was soon reached on the north shore, the same place where the Indian remembered it had been, when last he had made a similar journey on these waters. Upon reaching that site, they found the French fort to have been strongly constructed of logs, with substantial block buildings within. The sight of it was to the Acadians in this strange wilderness, as an oasis would be for those traveling in the desert. Hogogechee said it was a French stronghold, and the Acadians were hopeful. For here was a fort of their own people, who would certainly give aid to their own kind.

However, disappointment was destined to be their lot. Because upon arrival at the Fort, they soon discovered only one officer and a force of just fifteen enlisted men. They were in the process of preparing to depart soon for Fort de Chartres. As a result, there was no doctor there.

The officer in charge had welcomed them, though, and extended what hospitality that he could for the hard pressed travelers. But he could do nothing for those, who lay ill, except to share a few provisions with those on board. He had explained to them as best he could, that after the previous year's treaty of 1763, French lands east of the upper Mississippi River had been forfeited to England. So, the fort was being evacuated, and they would have to depart Fort Massiac before much longer. Also, he hastened to inform them, that their destination down river—Louisiana—was now under Spanish rule.

Upon hearing this, the Acadians became alarmed. But he hastened to further inform them that many, like themselves from Acadia, were being welcomed down there by the Spanish, who apparently valued their farming ability and industrious nature. In fact, the officer had urged these Acadians to continue on their way, directing them to stop along the eastern shore, some miles above New Orleans in the St. James region, for he had word that many Acadian people were being welcomed there.

So, once again, in a few days, the tenacious flotilla of flatboats put out into the river current. They were somewhat refreshed and much better informed as a result of the kind help of the officer and his company of enlisted men at the fort. However, regrettably there was still no medical help for those on board, who lay ill.

But once underway, Louisa continued to tend Adam, putting cold compresses on his forehead and keeping his tormented body that was often racked with fits of shivering, as warm as possible. She soothed him all the while, whenever he cried out uncontrollably. Then, it happened. From the depths of unconsciousness, as his high fever raged on unabated, the very night after they had departed from the fort. Louisa was lying next to Adam, as she had done for some nights now, ever since he had taken ill. All at once, she jolted awake from her somewhat nervous sleep state. The cabin shed was quiet, except for the sounds of slumber from the people in their group, who had crowded into the cabin for a night of warmth and rest.

She immediately sat up and looked down at Adam. His body appeared quiet in the semi-darkness of the cabin. How grand, Louisa thought instantly to herself. He had stopped shivering. Now, maybe his body will rest better. Then, as she had done countless times before, Louisa reached over and lay her hand on his head. But her hand trembled, as she felt the coldness of his forehead.

"Oh no!" Louisa exclaimed, loud enough to disturb the silence of the cabin. Whereupon, she hurriedly placed both of her hands on his face, and began to rub his forehead, his cheeks, his neck and his chest vigorously. "My Adam is so cold.....I must warm him!"

Madeleine, who was laying next to her, was jolted awake by Louisa's words. She squinted in the dim light, in an effort to see what was happening. Rubbing her eyes, Madeleine looked over to the prostrate form of Adam, and to Louisa, who was rubbing her hands up and down along the sides of his body, murmuring to him all the while unintelligently.

"Louisa....what is it?" Madeleine implored of her.

"Adam is so cold, Madeleine....I must warm him," Louisa replied in an assured manner, as she continue to massage his arms and chest.

Madeleine immediately reached over and felt Adam's forehead. She was shocked at the sensation she felt as a result of the touch, for it was as though she had touched ice. After that moment, memories of that night were as a nightmare for her. It was the same for everyone else on the boat, as well. For it was apparent that Adam had died quietly in the night. Only Louisa refused to believe it, and she continued to implore over and over again to them all.

"I will warm him....let me try...he will be alright again, you will see...let me try!"

Again and again, she begged of them all, apparently not wanting to accept the truth. Even after the men had taken his body on shore the next day, held a service and then buried Adam's remains on the river bank, still Louisa refused to believe. She continued to convince herself that he was really gone from her. She had even refused to attend the service on the river bank. Instead, she continued to sit near the pallet, upon which he had lain those many days. It seemed that this depressed woman could do nothing but continue to murmur to herself, all the while waiting for them to bring Adam back to her.

———

Days passed, after they entered the strong current of the Mississippi River. At that point, the bulky flatboats were immediately caught up in the swift southward flow of that great waterway. From the beginning, the Acadians were somewhat in awe of this wide, ever twisting, turning expanse of brown water. Even Hogogechee was wide eyed with wonder, when relating to them about the meaning of the river's name. He said in Ojibway it meant "big river".

But the people on the rustically fashioned flatboats felt that their vessels had already proven seaworthy for river travel. So, they were prepared to take what was to come on this strange vast waterway. Thus, the small flotilla continued to move on, but now in a southerly direction.

The heavily wooded shores, along both sides of the great river, were lined much of the time with large cypress trees. And there was also an abundance on both shores of willow trees, the lower trunks of which were usually underwater along the muddy shore. Caught up in the strong current, the vessels were often captured temporarily in small rapids and sometimes made to whirl around in treacherous whirlpools, then to swiftly experience sliding sharply around the bends and curves of the river.

Sandbars were encountered where one or two of the boats ran aground. But usually these were soon extricated by the rushing current. However, they had to be on the lookout for snags and large fallen trees, which floated concealed with only branches protruding above the water line. Sometimes, to avoid particularly treacherous currents and whirlpools in midstream, the Acadians would maneuver their boats close to the river bank, and move the crafts along in the high water there, by pulling on the bushes at the shoreline, until they would get past the stretch of river that they wished to avoid.

Occasionally, they encountered canoes with Indians. But they were careful to keep the boats far out in midstream at such times, so as to be availed of the swift current, which could sprint them away in case those in the canoes gave chase.

But mostly, the days turned into weeks, with the strong current and the hazards in midstream of the curving, twisting river to fill their every waking moment. However, as they moved slowly southward, putting the Chickasaw Bluffs behind them, the flotilla went past endless flat wooded shores, where the water over flowed the banks on both sides of the river. For spring was with them now, and the river's tide had swelled considerably. But it appeared not to matter how high the water level was for the areas of the high bluffs, which emerged further down river from the flooded flat banks. For these elevated cliffs were much too high to be affected by the highest rise of the great river's waters.

As the flotilla moved further southward—sometimes along shores where grew giant oak trees, which appeared to be draped with strange gray hangings of what looked like moss, the clear air and bright sunshine served as a tonic to the Acadians. Because of this, many of them remained on deck in order to absorb the warmer temperatures, during the daylight hours. This proved to be an elixir, especially so, after the cold they had endured for such a long time.

"Feel how warm it is....and look children, over there at the budding trees along the shore," Madeleine exclaimed, pausing for a moment from braiding Rosarie's long hair, to point over the water toward a group of trees growing along the bank. "It is springtime, my dears.....and it comes earlier in this land than it did in Acadie. Do you not agree, Louisa?"

Madeleine looked over at Louisa, who was also sitting on the deck, braiding Joseine's hair. Ever since Adam's death, Louisa had not been the same. But she did manage to come out on the deck into the sunshine now and then. And this was a big improvement for her, considering that for days she even refused to come out of the cabin at all.

"It is as you say, Madeleine," Louisa replied softly, sighing in resignation as she did. "Yes...the sunshine does feel good."

"Oh, Louisa....it is so good to have my dear friend back again," Madeleine hurriedly remarked, momentarily encouraged by Louisa's brief positive statement about the sunshine. For so despondent had she become, it was rare that she even spoke.

Louisa looked up upon hearing Madeleine's exclamation and slowly remarked. "Your friend is not back with you, Madeleine. The Louisa you knew will never be back again! There is only what you see here before you...a pitiful woman, with no future."

For a few moments, Madeleine pondered her friend's depressing words. But did not answer, for she realized only too well that Louisa's deep seated despair could not be alleviated by her. Nor could it be by anyone else on the boat, for that matter. Indeed, during recent weeks everyone had tried to reach her—each in his or her own way. But all had failed to succeed. So, Madeleine decided to herself, to let the matter rest for now. Surely Louisa would again be encouraged once they reached the Acadian settlement, on the banks of St. James that they had heard about. Since being informed about that place, they had come a long way toward that destination—getting closer and closer each day.

In fact, if the Indians of the Houma tribe, that Hogogechee had spoken with on the shore only the day before, could be believed, the place they were seeking could well be just around the next bend in the river.

In a matter of minutes, after these thoughts had filled her mind, a shout was heard from Amand, who stood at the oar in the front of the boat. "There....look there! It must be the settlement of St. James....see the lead boat steers toward that shore. We must have arrived at last...we are here!"

Upon hearing this welcomed news, every man, woman and child on all of the boats—with the possible exception of Louisa—began to cheer, all straining their eyes in the direction of the river bank. Because there in the distance could be seen a few small dwellings, scattered about along that shore of the Mississippi River.

Swiftly, the men maneuvered each of the flatboats onto the muddy river bank, jumped out and hurriedly tied the ropes around trees, which grew at the shoreline. They then helped the women and children off of the boats and onto the shore. Together, they all started to walk toward the buildings, located a few yards away. But before they had taken more than a dozen strides, a handful of men, who had been working in a nearby field, hurried over to meet them.

Following behind them, from the dwellings further away, came women and some children, all hurrying to the shore. "Bonjour Monsieurs!" Pierre Guidry, who was up ahead, shouted to the approaching men from the fields. "We have come all the way from Acadie....is this the place of St. James, of which we were told?"

"Welcome....welcome," was the shouted reply from the men, in French, as with outstretched arms all began running toward the Acadians from the boats. "We, too, came here from Acadie!"

The scene, that followed, can best be likened to that which transpires when beloved family members are once again reunited with their kin. For indeed, the feelings displayed during that emotional encounter were manifested by means of hugging, hand shaking, tears and laughter, all intermingled into a melee of delight.

"Bravo, mon amie....you made it!" Shouted one of the men, above the noises of greetings. "This is the settlement of Monsieur Frederick at St. James..... I am called Jacques Bouillon!"

The joyous sounds of welcome continued to fill the air, and much shaking of hands and embracing was prevalent, as each man introduced himself and his wife, and those, who had children even introduced each of them, as their youngsters came running over from their play or chores. It was apparent, that all wanted to join this joyous gathering on the river bank. Notable among those in this group, who welcomed the newly arrived people, were Charles Mire, Alexandre Michel, Antoine Gaudin, Jean Olivier, Felix Mouton, Etienne Roussel and several others–along with their families.

There followed much lively discussion and they all began comparing places of origin back in Acadie. As a result, certain of the new arrivals discovered friends and acquaintances among these settlers on this river, who were from some of the same areas, such as Cobequid, Guthro, Piziquid, Boudro Point, River Canard, Gaspereau River, Grand Pre and Melanson.

Through it all, Louisa had stood alone, somewhat off from the group, observing the joyous gathering. But not taking part. Her gaze took in the entire noisy crowd of people, and she only smiled and nodded politely when one or the other of them came over to say a few words of welcome to her. Other than that, she took no part in this happy occasion. She did continue to watch the others, all of whom seemed to be thoroughly engaged in animated conversation and spontaneous laughter. It was then, that she noticed another person, who also stood apart on the other side of the group. She continued to stare over at this man, as he began to walk in her direction. There seemed to be something vaguely familiar about him. Then, she heard him shout above the melee in their midst. "Louisa....can it be true....is it really you?"

She was startled for a moment at the mention of her name, coming from someone at this strange, new settlement, which was so far away from Acadie. But then, she suddenly recognized him, as he approached her. All at once, he began to run toward her, smiling broadly and laughing uncontrollably with delight.

"Oh God....it is he!" Louisa exclaimed, as she began to run toward him. "Merciful God, you have sent him back to me.... Batiste.....Batiste...it is really you!"

All at once, they came together in an emotional hug, so joyous that it succeeded in directing the attention of the others, to where they were, apart from where the rest were being welcomed. Madeleine looked over at them, grabbed Josef's arm, and together they ran over to where the couple was.

"Louisa....Louisa, my dear one....I cannot believe it is true... so many years have passed!" Batiste LeBlanc shouted loudly, as he hugged his wife to him again and again, all the while trying to explain his plight to her. "The English finally let us out of that cursed Halifax prison, and me and your Papa hurried back home to find all of you. But we were too late. Later, I was separated from your Papa...and sent to the Colony of Georgia on one of those cursed ships. It was hard there....but as soon as I could manage, I got away and came here to Louisiana. I prayed to God, that I would find you here, as so many of our people are locating to this new land. I have been waiting here, and meeting every boat, in hopes that you would be on one of these. And....finally...you are here! Oh...my dear...I cannot believe that you are finally with me again!"

"Batiste...we thought you were dead....I had given up all hope!" Louisa cried joyously, as she held on to him, seemingly afraid to turn loose. Then, a sudden thought struck her and she pulled away from him, turned and called out. "Joseine....come here. Come here and meet your Papa!" She turned back to him, and explained. "It is your daughter, Batiste, whom you have never seen. She was born on the ship that the English took me on to the Colony of Maryland—nine years ago."Turning towards the approaching child, who was running their way, she added. "Welcome your Papa, my dear child.....he is with us again!"

The small girl ran to her mother, upon being called. Then, she stood there timidly, staring wide-eyed up at this man, whom her Mama had just introduced as her Papa. She extended her small hand out to him in greeting. Whereupon Batiste, who was staring at Joseine in emotional awe and bewilderment—and with no little amount of disbelief—abruptly swooped her up and hugged her to him with delight. Then, with a sudden surge of tears marring his vision, he shouted for everyone to hear. "Everyone....this is my own little daughter.....that her Papa is introducing."

With this, Batiste broke down and his tears and laughter became intermingled together in his unabashed joy, as he gathered both Louisa and Joseine to him. He continued to hug them to him tightly, with great emotion, as if he couldn't believe they were finally with him.

Madeleine wiped a tear from her eye, as she stood there with Josef and Rosarie, observing the wonderful reunion taking place before them. Josef, too, was obviously touched. Because he looked down at the ground in an effort to hide his eyes, that had become filled with tears at the sight they had just beheld. Then, Josef picked up Rosarie, took Madeleine's arm and the three of them walked toward the river bank. They strolled some distance from the large group that was still rejoicing at the reunion of Louisa, Batiste and Joseine. It was a bright spring day and the warm sunshine beamed down on them, as they stood there on the shore of the great Mississippi River.

All at once, Josef, in an uncontrollable impulse, stooped down and picked up a handful of loose soil. Then, he took Madeleine's hand and placed the dark gray soil in her palm. Closing his hand over her's, squeezing it tightly as he did so, Josef's eyes misted over with emotion, as he spoke.

"Madeleine, my dear....you are so good and deserve so much more. But I can only offer you this new land....and a new beginning for us. You can believe that I will work hard to make a good life for us here...but it is all I have to give you, my dear. I am sorry it is not more!"

Madeleine looked up into his tear filled eyes, which mirrored the obvious emotion he was feeling, and her heart went out to him. But she hesitated a few seconds before replying. Then, she smiled assuredly up at him, as her words came forth, in a torrent.

"Do you not know, my husband, that I am many times blessed? To have a man such as Josef Theriot for a husband is indeed good fortune enough...and then there is little Rosarie , here, this sweet child of ours. But to also be delivered to such a rich land as this Louisiana appears to be, is almost more than this maid from Acadie can stand. Now...we must get on with this business of living! It is Spring and there are seeds to be sown, if we are to harvest our first crop in this new land, this year. So, let us begin again. Come...by beloved......Louisiana awaits!"

With this, they turned away from the river. Then, arm in arm, walked back toward the joyous group of Acadians, who were still relishing in the realization, that they had finally found a home.

THE END

EPILOGUE

During the expulsion, which continued from 1755 through 1763, Acadians were sent to the Carolinas, Massachusetts, New York, Pennsylvania, Maryland, Georgia, Connecticut, the West Indies, and some were even subsequently sent to France and England. But many escaped being sent away from Acadia, by running away to survive in the wild. However, it has been said that of all the colonies where the Acadians were sent, only Maryland welcomed them with Christian charity and hospitality. This was said to be, because that colony had been settled at that time by numerous English Catholics.

In comparison to many of the other colonies, the displaced Acadians were sometimes made indentured slaves, had their children taken from them, refused entry or had their belongings confiscated. During this period, some 14,000 men, women and children were forcibly sent away in English ships to strange shores. But only a small percentage of them were welcomed upon arrival, as they were in the colony of Maryland. Yes, history reports that only Maryland offered true sanctuary for these people. Thankfully, it was the good fortune of this author's branch of the Theriot family line, to have been sent there.

But strangely enough, in visiting Baltimore, Maryland today, along the area where French Town was reputed to have been, because of the preponderance of Acadian settlers there in the late 1750s, there appears to be no statue, nor any commemorative modern day marker, that this author could discover. Indeed, there appeared to be no evidence of that event, at all. No plaque, to attest as evidence of the countless numbers of Acadians, who were welcomed there in their time of need. Only searches in historical records and volumes point out this charitable fact of life, as it existed then.

Pity, too often do we encounter monuments attesting to man's inhumanity to man. But it is unfortunate, that there is no reminder of such an event, as reported here. Because it should be worth noting the generous, kind gestures of those 1755 circa people of Baltimore City, toward the countless destitute Acadians, who were forced to their shores from Nova Scotia. However, would not such a monument—if it were to become a fact of life—serve as a tremendous source of pride for present day residents of Baltimore, Maryland? Because I dare say, that the vast majority of residents there know nothing of this little know historical event. But such a magnanimous event should be worth noting. After all, no city can ever get enough of that kind of heritage

––––––––

But this author's Theriot ancestors, who were so helped by such charitable people in Baltimore City, were destined to find another home, much further away. That ultimate destination was the place of St. James, which is located just about midway between Baton Rouge and New Orleans, along the shores of the Mississippi River. In later years, German immigrants also found their way to those shores, and subsequently intermingled with many Acadian families there.

––––––––

In the case of those, who returned to Nova Scotia and settled what is today known as the French Coast on St. Mary's Bay, where towns with names like Comeauxville, Saulnierville and Church Point are reminiscent of South Louisiana Cajun names and places, enough cannot be said in regard to their courage, when they returned home in the face of such adversity.

During this author's research visit to the French Coast in 1979, it was my good fortune to be introduced to a very knowledgeable gentleman—Donald Theriault—in the Annapolis Royal area. While visiting with him and wife Barb, and their memorable family, we compared notes and made a remarkable discovery. Because it became apparent, that an ancestor of his Theriault/Theriot line was among those, who found their way back to Acadia, after the expulsion. We subsequently speculated that both his and my family lines came from the same people. Thus, the character of Charles in this book is based on that branch of the family. Since then, this author has referred to my very distant Nova Scotia family members as "Cousin". Some believe in coincidence, but yours truly has come to accept, that there is no such thing as coincidence. In reality, it is only things that are meant to be.

Another point of irony for this author was discovered in the records at the Church of St. Charles museum in Grand Pre. And it was amazing! Believe it or not, this descendant of Acadian Theriots', who were forcibly expelled by the English, discovered by chance a familiar name among the list of English farmers. These were New Englanders, who had been brought into Nova Scotia after the expulsion, in order to take over the Acadian farms. This coincidence was overwhelming, and difficult to believe.

But at that time, my husband, who is a New England native, and I beheld this listing together, we were in awe. For there, on the record was a "Nathaniel Stiles" among the rest! Could it be true, we asked in amazement? Was there really an ancestor of his among those Englishmen, who took over the lands of an expelled French ancestor of mine? Well, it was apparently so. Because here we were, over two hundred years later, together in that land of Acadia where it all happened so very long ago. Provocative, to say the least!

But then, we all well know, stranger things have happened in this world. A case in point is evidenced by the story you have just read.

BON CHANCE....MON AMIE

———

ACADIAN MEMORIAL CHURCH at Grand Pre National Historic Site at Minas Basin--Bay of Fundy region. A statue of Evangeline stands in front of this church in Nova Scotia. The building is a reconstruction of the original church, that was destroyed by the English at the time of the expulsion in 1755. It is the church where Acadian men were held captive by English authority, before they were forcibly boarded onto ships, and sent to destinations unknown to them.

IN 1979 A RUGGED IRON CROSS marked the approximate spot in Grand Pre, Nova Scotia, where the French Acadians were forcibly taken into long boats and rowed out to the English ships for deportation to strange lands. Between 1755 and 1763, it is estimated that some 14,000 men, women and children were expelled. This author took the photo shown here in September of 1979, marking the passage of 224 years, to the month, since the beginning of that tragic expulsion.

"Still stands the forest primeval; but under the shade
of it's branches
dwells another race, with other customs and
Language.

Only along the shores of the mournful and misty
Atlantic
linger a few Acadian peasants, whose fathers
from exile

Wandered back to their native land
to die in it's bosom."

....Henry W. Longfellow

ACKNOWLEDGMENTS

W ith Grateful Appreciation to the following helpful individuals and research sources.

The Donald Theriault family of Annapolis Royal, Nova Scotia– Jack Darrel Wood of Paducah, Kent.–Gertrude Lemmon of Morgan City, La.–Howard Fangue, Jr. of Baltimore, Maryland–James H. Cogswell of Houma, La.–Margaret Elliott of Gautier, Ms.–Zeno Mangum of Gautier, Ms.–Richard Brock of Vancleave, Ms.–"Acadiana Profile" magazine of Lafayette, La.–Parks Canada "Records of First Settlers of Colchester County"–Old Court House Museum of Vicksburg, Ms.–"French Bilingual Dictionary" by Gladys Lipton–"Cabonocey" by Lillian C. Bourgeois–"Expulsion Of the Acadians" by George F. Clarke– "Micmac Indian Medicine" by Laurie Lacey–"History Of the City of Cairo" by M.B. Harrell–Cairo, Illinois Public Library–U.S. Corps of Engineers Historical Division, Leland R. Johnson–Knoxville- Knox County Public Library–Warren County, Vicksburg, Ms. Library–Dept. of Library & Archives, Frankfort, Kent.–"The Cherokees Of The Smoky Mountains" by Horace Kephart–Chattanooga, Hamilton County Bicentennial Library–Illinois Dept. of Conservation Div. of Historic Sites–Murray, Kent. State University–New Orleans Public Library– "History Of the Acadians" by Bona Arensault–"Ft. Massiac Historic Site", Paul E. Fellows–"Colonel Winslow's Journal", Massachusetts Historical Society–"Atlas Of Early American History", Lester Cappon–"The State" Magazine, No. Carolina–"Development Of Early Emigrant Trails In The U.S. East Of The Mississippi River"–Old Charles Town, West Virginia

Library–Genealogical Services of Raleigh, No. Carolina State Library–
Maryland Historical Society, Mary Meyer, Baltimore–St. Louis, Missouri
Historical Society– "Historical Jefferson City" by Millard Kessler–
"Enoch Pratt Free Library, Mr. Bartram & Mr. Parks–Gautier, Ms.
Public Library–"Baltimore On the Chesapeake" by Hamilton Owens–
"West Virginia- A Guide To The Mountain State"–"The French Presence
in Maryland" by Gregory Wood–"The Founding of Baltimore City"–
National Geographic "Shenandoah I Long To Hear You"–"The Changing
Face Of New England" by Betty Flanders Thomson–Washington D.C.
National Archives & Records Service–"Paducah, A Sesquicentennial
History" by E.L. Robertson–"Fort Loudoun, 214 Years Later" by
Donald P. Rapp, Sr.–Grand Pre, Nova Scotia National Historic Park–
"The French Quarter" by Herbert Asbury–"The Land Breakers" by
John Ehle–"Gretchen of Grand Pre" by Lilla Stirling